10 Crack
COMMANDMENTS

10 Crack COMMANDMENTS

BY

ERICA HILTON

10 Crack Commandments. Copyright © 2009 by Melodrama Publishing. All rights reserved. Printed in the United States of America. No part of this book may be used or reproduced in any manner whatsoever without written permission except in the case of brief quotations embodied in critical articles or reviews. For information, address Melodrama Publishing, P.O. Box 522, Bellport, NY 11713.

www.melodramapublishing.com

Library of Congress Control Number: 2008940452
ISBN: 978-1-934157-21-3

First Edition: June 2009
10 9 8 7 6 5 4 3 2 1

Book Interior Design and Layout by candace@candann.com

Words and Music by Khary Kimani Turner, Chris Martin and Christopher Wallace © 1997 EMI APRIL MUSIC INC., WEBLIFE, HERTZRENTATUNE, GIFTED PEARL MUSIC and JUSTIN COMBS PUBLISHING COMPANY, INC.

All Rights Controlled and Administered by EMI APRIL MUSIC INC.
All Rights Reserved International Copyright Secured Used by Permission

1

"Never let no one know how much dough you hold,
'cause you know the cheddar breed jealousy 'specially
if that man fucked up, get your ass stuck up."

–"Ten Crack Commandments," Notorious B.I.G.

1984

W hat's today's mathematics?" Blue Bug asked one of the local kids on the block. Lil Nut watched the exchange between his idol and the young kid.

"Understanding," the kid answered. "And knowledge brings wisdom, and wisdom brings understanding."

Lil Nut stood quietly and listened to their dialogue. He couldn't wait for the opportunity to have his own private conversation with Blue Bug. Blue Bug was a major player in the drug game and had all of Brownsville locked down with this new drug called crack. He was the hood's main supplier and had a flock of young cats who sold for him. At fourteen, Lil Nut wasn't considered built for this game. His height of five feet two made him look twelve at best.

Lil Nut approached the black Mercedes Benz 500SL with gold rims and trim and admired the leather interior. Kurtis Blow's "The Breaks" blared from the Bose speakers. That song was the hood's anthem. It resonated with so many people because everyone had rats and roaches in their cribs, and felt close to the edge. Lil Nut himself believed that if something didn't give soon, he was about to snap.

"What's up, little nigga?" Blue Bug asked Lil Nut as he hopped out of the driver's seat, his gold rope chains swinging wildly.

"I wanna make money," he stated frankly.

"Word?"

"Word is bond!" Lil Nut said and postured. He stiffened his back to appear taller while tilting his head cockily to one side.

"What's today's mathematics?" Blue Bug quizzed the young boy.

"Huh?"

"Motherfucker, if you can huh, you can hear!" Blue Bug barked. "What's today's mathematics?"

Lil Nut wasn't a part of the Five Percent Nation that blanketed the urban areas. In fact, his mother was a Jehovah's Witness and his father was a Baptist. Not to mention, Lil Nut loved eating pork. His daily lunch was a ham and cheese sandwich from the local bodega. Not wanting to miss out on his opportunity to make money, he tried to avoid the question.

"Listen, my man, I want to sell your product and make my own money. I have my own crew—"

"You think you a big man, huh?" Blue Bug interrupted. "You think you tough enough to handle these mean streets?"

"Is that a question?"

"Damn right it's a question, smart-ass motherfucker. You see that fiend over there?" Blue Bug pointed toward a crackhead copping from one of Blue Bug's runners. "If that man is fucked up and needs a hit, you're as good as dead if you're standing in his way. You think you ready for that?"

Lil Nut surveyed the scene and thought about what Blue Bug was really asking him. Lil Nut knew that Blue Bug was challenging his manhood. Was he man enough to handle the streets—the stickup kids, crackheads, and undercover detectives?

With bravado Lil Nut replied, "I'm as ready as I'll ever be."

Again, Blue Bug asked, "What's today's mathematics?"

Lil Nut shook his head. "I don't know today's mathematics. And not for nothing. I'm not a Five Percenter. I don't follow that shit or any religion, if you want to know the truth. I follow me, and my crew follows me. End of story!"

"How old are you?"

"I'll be fifteen soon."

"Listen, lil man, I like you. You got guts. But if you want to work for me, then you gotta be down with the Five Percent Nation. That's how I know you'll be loyal. We have a code that we live by, and when the heat comes around that corner I gotta know that you won't cop out and turn snitch. Right now you're not built to stand on my blocks. If you're serious about working for me, then you'll learn your lessons."

Lil Nut was pissed. He'd been watching Blue Bug since he was thirteen years old. He watched him come up from driving a four-door Corolla to pushing a hot whip. He watched as he pulled out knots of money and wore flashy jewelry. Lil Nut reasoned only the crack game could get him what Blue Bug had. Although his parents provided a roof over his head and clothes on his back, they were still poor by anyone's standard.

Lil Nut stood there and watched as Blue Bug walked into the building. He watched until Blue Bug was out of sight, thinking about how he was gonna murder Blue Bug if he didn't give him what he wanted. And then Lil Nut would *take* the block.

It took Lil Nut three days to put his plan into motion. He knew that his father once kept an illegal Smith & Wesson revolver in the closet for protection, and after their apartment had gotten broken into twice in the past year, that gun was moved under his parents' mattress. Lil Nut learned his lessons, but he took the gun just in case Blue Bug didn't give him what he wanted. As the cold steel rubbed against his flesh, he wondered if he had the balls to pull the trigger. And if he did pull it, then what? All he knew was that Blue Bug better give him some product after he recited his lessons, or else tonight would be Blue Bug's last night. And on that, Lil Nut's word was bond.

It felt like hours passed as Lil Nut waited for Blue Bug and watched the fiends walk up and down the streets, searching the ground for crumbs of the potent crack vials. Most who were already high did their crack jig dance, which consisted of hopping from one foot to the next to music no one heard. Overnight his neighborhood had become like the cult classic movie, *Night of the Living Dead.* These people were zombies.

He watched his third grade teacher, with pockmarks dug deeply into her once flawless skin, searching for a hit. Her silky hair was broken off into a nappy afro. And she looked and smelled as if she hadn't bathed in years. Yet, as he stood there observing the downside of the crack epidemic, the allure of the game was too hard to pass up.

When Blue Bug drove up in his black Mercedes Benz 500SL, his dream was realized. Again, Lil Nut approached the passenger's side of the Benz. Blue Bug rolled down the window.

"What's today's mathematics?" he asked.

"Peace, god. What's today?" Lil Nut asked.

"It's July Second, motherfucker. Been July Second all day!"

"Today is wisdom, god."

"Who is the original black man?"

"The original black man is the Asiatic black man—the Maker, the owner, the crème of the earth, god of the universe."

"How many Supreme Mathematics do we live by?"

"There are a hundred and twenty Supreme Mathematics, also

called degrees."

Blue Bug was impressed that Lil Nut had actually learned the Supreme Mathematics. And he had done so in such a small amount of time. Although he was leery about having such a young soldier on his team, Lil Nut's drive and determination reminded Blue Bug of himself when he was that age. Truthfully, at eighteen, Blue Bug wasn't that much older than Lil Nut.

"OK, you're in. Meet me here tomorrow morning at seven o'clock to start banging."

"I'll be here at six!"

"Motherfucker, I won't be here at six!" Blue Bug shouted. "Learn how to follow directions."

"OK, I hear you. Seven. But why can't you serve me now? I'm ready now."

"Because now I'm going to see my earth."

"Who? Lady Bug?"

"You know it. Her wisdom (mother) isn't feeling well, and I gotta take them to Kings County Hospital. But we'll politick more in the morning."

Again Lil Nut watched as Blue Bug walked off into the night. He couldn't understand why he now had a deep resentment for the man he had always regarded as an icon. The pit of his stomach churned as Lil Nut replayed their conversation. It was the way Blue Bug spoke down to him like he was a bitch or something, constantly yelling at him in ways only his parents did. And he hadn't been yelled at like that since he turned thirteen. He was too old for such shenanigans.

Lil Nut kicked rocks on his way back to his crib. When he got inside he realized that something wasn't right. His door was unlocked and he heard his parents arguing. Fear crept into his mind, because out of all the families in his hood, his parents were considered the Huxtables.

Although they didn't make much money with his father working a city job and his mother being a stay-at-home mom, the fact that he had a two-parent household was enough to make most envious.

"I'm telling you that I am not giving it to you!" Lil Nut's mother yelled.

"You will give it to me, because it's my property. I bought it!" his father yelled back.

"You bought it for me, so that makes it mine!"

"Julie, don't make me raise my hand to you, but I will."

"You wouldn't dare!"

"Dad, Mom, what's going on?" Lil Nut asked as his eyes darted from each parent.

"Your father done lost his mind. He wants me to give him my wedding ring because he claims he owes someone some money!"

"Nelson, go in your room," Lil Nut's dad said. "This is grown people's business. I can handle it from here!" Milton demanded.

"Who do you owe money to?" Lil Nut asked.

Ignoring his son, with glassy eyes and a dazed look, Milton reached out and back handed his wife. She fell to the ground. That was the first time in their twenty years of marriage that he had ever put his hands on her. As Julie cowered in the corner, Milton began to rip off her wedding ring.

"Bitch, didn't I tell you to give it to me! Look what you made me—"

The cold barrel of the Smith & Wesson stopped Milton mid-sentence. His already large, dilated pupils expanded to the size of saucers.

"Son, what are you doing with Daddy's gun?" His words were precise and steady.

"Touch Mommy again, and you'll find out!" Lil Nut spat.

Julie stood to unsteady feet and began to reason with her son. "Nelson, your father isn't worth throwing away your life for. You have a bright future ahead of you, and I don't want you to ruin that. Give Mommy the gun," she said and held out her hand in a weak attempt at exerting authority.

Lil Nut stood firm. His broad nose flared, and he almost couldn't contain the rage and power he felt. One part of him wished he had the guts to pull out his pistol on Blue Bug, but the other part of him was glad that he was now able to put an end to the one thing he hated the most—men who beat women. He never would have guessed his father would stoop so low.

"OK, I apologize. I'm cool," Milton sang. "It's all a misunderstanding. I'll get the money some other way." Milton began to back out of the apartment, yet his eyes held firm on Lil Nut's face. "You think you a man now, huh?" his father asked as he made his exit. "Lesson number one for being a man: Never pull out a gun on someone unless you're prepared to use it."

By morning Lil Nut and his mother realized that Milton was smoking crack. He had looted their whole apartment. The television, stereo, and Walkman Lil Nut got for Christmas were all gone. And this time Milton couldn't blame burglars as he'd done in the past. Lil Nut shook his head. How could he have missed the signs?

ဢၯ

Three weeks worth of slinging crack for Blue Bug, and Lil Nut was chilling. He bought a few pairs of Lee jeans, two pairs of Adidas sneakers, and a sweatsuit, and had also given his mother money for groceries. His next move was to save up enough money for a new Walkman, a rope chain, and an Atari. He was glad that it was summertime because he could work twelve-hour shifts, selling from sunup to sundown. Lil Nut hadn't gotten a haircut, barely showered, and wore the same work outfit every day—black jeans and a black T-shirt.

When he emerged from his house on his fifteenth birthday with a fresh haircut, white-on-white attire, and a knot of money in his pocket, everyone recognized the change. His round, expressive eyes gleamed as he strolled a few blocks to meet his crew. He nodded his head as he bopped down the street listening to a boom box blaring UTFO's latest hit, "Roxanne, Roxanne." The rap was just what he needed to complete his day. A local break dancing crew began doing body movements that Lil Nut only wished he could do. He stopped for a moment to watch as a guy spun around on a large cardboard box and then began doing the caterpillar.

When Lil Nut finally made it to Pitkin and Belmont Avenues where his crew—Lite, Lamiek, Fuquan, Butter, and Triny—were all hanging out, they gave each other pound handshakes. Lil Nut had known them all most of his life. He got along best with Fuquan, Butter, and Lite, because they allowed him to exert authority. Lamiek, on the other hand, was always a problem, and Triny wasn't even on Lil Nut's radar. Triny came around in the summers with his Jamaican accent and funny way of dressing, and he began to influence Lil Nut's crew. Before he realized it, Lite and Lamiek were walking around with red, green, and yellow bandanas and eating oxtails and beans and rice. One thing Lil Nut hated most were followers, unless, of course, they were following him.

The crew couldn't believe their eyes when they saw their friend.

"Hey, man, where have you been?" Fuquan asked. "We've missed you."

"I've been on the low-low," Lil Nut replied.

"Well, we're glad that you're back. It's been boring as hell out here without you," Butter said.

Lil Nut noticed that his light-skinned friend had a really dark tan, and he asked him about it. "We've been at Rockaway Beach almost every day getting with the honeys," Butter explained.

Triny stood in his usual stance—feet spread way apart—making awkward hand gestures when he spoke while twisting his lips toward one side. "Mi hafta 'old dem ofa Jah ros clout."

Lil Nut didn't even bother to acknowledge Triny. He didn't have a clue what he'd just said anyway. "Well I'm back, my niggas," Lil Nut said, feeling the love.

"I see ya pop's been spoiling your ass!" Lamiek said.

The mention of his father put Lil Nut in a sour mood instantly. He was embarrassed that his father was so weak that he would fall victim to a drug. His mother put his father out last week, and they had changed all the locks. His mother worried about paying the rent, but Lil Nut reassured her that everything would be fine. He was now the man of the house.

"Nah, my pops ain't have shit to do with this right here. This all me!" Lil Nut boasted.

"Whatchu mean all you? Where you get that type of money from?" Lamiek asked.

"I've spent the better part of the summer working for Blue Bug."

"You mean you selling that shit to your people?" Lamiek asked.

"My people?"

"Yeah. Your people. Our people. Your customers! Don't you know you're committing genocide?" Lamiek twisted up his lips in disgust.

"Don't preach that bullshit with me," Lil Nut spat back. Lamiek was the main reason he hated Five Percenters. They were so phony to him. They all went around preaching lessons and called themselves "schooling" the youth, yet they were the biggest crooks. Lamiek was a notorious stickup kid, smoked blunts, drank forties, and beat on his earth. But at the drop of a dime, he would call on Allah and look down on motherfuckers.

"Motherfucker, what you call what the fuck you be doing, shoving guns in 'our people's' faces? You just jealous that ain't nobody give your sheisty ass a job!"

Within seconds the tension between the two was palpable. In a crew where both Lamiek and Lil Nut wanted to be the chief, and no one wanted to be the Indian, fists were bound to fly. Lamiek took the first swing and connected with Lil Nut's left jaw. Lil Nut rebounded and gave him a two-piece—a left jab to Lamiek's right eye, and an uppercut to the ribs. Lamiek doubled over quickly, but regained his composure and began swinging wildly. He mostly caught air, but a few good punches landed. Lil Nut, who was heavier and stockier than the slim-framed Lamiek, was able to handle himself. He went after Lamiek as if he was a beast with an untamed rage. When Lil Nut looked down at his white-on-white outfit, now stained with blood, he went berserk.

He reached inside the waistband of his sweatpants and pulled out his chrome Smith & Wesson. No longer did he call it his father's gun. The gun made everyone scatter as he flailed it around.

"Yeah, motherfucker! Talk shit now!" Lil Nut yelled.

The only person who stayed was Lite. Lite and Lil Nut went way back, and naturally he assumed his friend wouldn't harm him.

"So you been slinging for real?" Lite asked.

"Yeah, man. I gotta put food on the table. My pops done lost his mind and started sucking that glass dick," Lil Nut said as he grimaced.

"I know. I saw your pops the other day and I couldn't believe that shit. Is that how you got his gun? Did he sell it to you?"

"He ain't sell me shit. I housed him for it. This my shit. I'm the man of the house."

"Yo, if that was me, kid, I woulda started bussing after that motherfucker, Lamiek. That fake-ass god snuffed you!"

Lite was always good to amp up a situation, but Lil Nut was on to him.

"Fuck Lamiek. That nigga harmless. How you sound? You want me to kill my man over some bullshit?"

"Nah, I'm just saying—"

"Saying what, motherfucker? You a Judas-ass nigga? I gotta watch my back around you?"

"Nah, it ain't even like that."

"Then how is it? You be around that motherfucking Lamiek each day smiling in his face, and now you telling me I shoulda filled his ass with lead."

"Nah, you know that motherfucker be deserving to get—"

Lil Nut's patience had run out, and unfortunately, Lite was in the wrong place at the wrong time. Lil Nut's father's words, coupled with the taunting from Lite, forced him to pull out the Smith & Wesson. Only this time he started bucking shots at Lite.

Blah-ow! Blah-ow! Blah-ow! The cannon exploded, and once again, people scattered. Lite only wished he'd been that lucky. He caught one bullet in his ankle. Lil Nut didn't even stay around long enough to see his friend fall. He took off running down the block, back to the safe haven of his home.

ﾛﾆﾞ

Over the next few days Fuquan, Butter, and Triny reported to Lil Nut on Lite's condition. Lite recovered quickly and never told the police who shot him. He simply said he'd gotten hit by a stray bullet, and in that neighborhood his story rang true.

Finally Lil Nut emerged from his home, but he made sure he was fresh to death with his white, red, and blue Fila sweatsuit and white-on-white Adidas sneakers with thick red laces. He'd gone to the shoemaker and had him put silver taps on the bottom of his sneakers so that when he walked he made a tapping noise. He knew he was the freshest kid on the block, and couldn't nobody tell him shit. He also knew he was a little nigga, and that meant motherfuckers would try to play him, so he was on guard.

As the summer flew by, Lil Nut began to stack some serious paper. He saved close to one thousand dollars. He kept all of his money in an empty sneaker box in the bottom of the closet in his room. Each night after he finished selling off his product, he would separate his boss's money from his profit. He would count the money lying on his bed at least eight times before being satisfied that the count was correct. Then he would bundle up the money in hundred-dollar stacks and put a rubber band on them.

He reasoned that he now had enough money to give his mother the rent, which was one hundred fifty dollars, plus buy himself a gold rope chain and an Atari. Wednesdays were his only day off, and he decided that he would go shopping then.

"Whaddup, god?" Lamiek asked Lil Nut as he came outside and sat on a parked car.

"Yo, what I tell you about that nonsense? I'm not a Five Percenter," Lil Nut said.

"But let your boss come 'round and you're reciting your lessons!" Lamiek was pissed at the hypocrisy. He was also angry that he was no longer the top earner of the crew. With Lamiek doing stickups, he used to be the one who came around with a pocketful of money. But lately it seemed that Lil Nut was making the most money, not to mention that he busted off his gun and shot Lite. Lil Nut was now not only known as a little dude who got paper, but also a little dude who wasn't afraid to pop that thing off.

"You're a fraud," Lamiek said.

"And why do you give a fuck?" Lil Nut asked politely.

"I don't," Lamiek responded. "I got my own shit to think about."

"You? Think? Don't make me laugh."

"Go ahead and laugh and I'll put my foot in your ass!"

Nut tossed his eyes up in the air. "Please. You don't even believe that shit."

"Whatever, nigga. Yo, you heard what happened to Butter?"

"Nah, what's up? Where he at?"

"He in juvie. He got busted in Albee Square Mall trying to snatch a rope chain the other day, and they sent him in. This his third offense. That nigga definitely going down for some time."

Nut thought about Butter. They'd been friends for nine years, and he hated to see him locked up. But that was what he got for being on that robbing shit. "You was with him when he got knocked?" Nut asked.

"If I was with his stupid ass he wouldn't have gotten knocked. I know how to do my shit, and it ain't all sloppy. That dumb nigga Fuquan was with him. Luckily Fuquan got away, but when his moms found out about Butter, she sent him to go live in Bed-Stuy with his pops."

"Man, you serious? Fuquan is out?"

"Yeah, man. We lost Butter and Fuquan, and Triny went back to Flatbush. Since you done shot Lite, I guess it's just me and you. For better or worse, motherfucker, till death do us part," Lamiek joked.

"Yo, since you're my bitch, whatchu doing on Wednesday?" Lil Nut asked.

"You tell me."

"A'ight, check it. Come with me down to Canal Street to cop me a gold rope chain."

"Word?"

"Word. You down?"

"Hell yeah, I'm down. And bring your pistol, 'cause I might come home with a rope chain too."

"I feel you," Lil Nut said, but deep inside he wasn't feeling that shit. He hated motherfuckers who took money when it was so easy to *make* money. He didn't know why he hung around with Lamiek other than the amusing stories he told.

"So what size rope chain you gonna cop?" Lamiek asked.

"Depends on what they're talking, but I want a dookie rope at least this fat." Lil Nut spread his index and thumb fingers two inches apart.

Lamiek's eyes grew large from jealousy. "You got money like that?"

"Yeah. Business is good. Each week I've been saving my money and only dipping in it to give my moms a few dollars for bills, but other than that I got enough for my chain and I might buy me an Atari—"

"Let me find out you're rich," Lamiek interrupted. "So this crack game is paying motherfuckers like that?"

"I don't know about other motherfuckers, but this is the most money I've ever seen in my life." Lil Nut jumped off the car and began to get animated. He was extremely happy about his riches. "In fact, I'ma get the new *Donkey Kong* game too!"

"Get the fuck out of here." Lamiek paused, then continued. "You know I'm really proud of you for stepping up and working for yours."

The sincere words shocked Lil Nut, and he really didn't know how to respond. He shrugged his shoulders, hoping the awkward moment would pass.

"Listen, check it," Lamiek said, changing the subject. "Did I tell you about the time I fucked Alicia's mother and her pops walked in on us while she was giving me head?"

"What Alicia?"

"Skinny Alicia with the wide gap."

"Nah, you ain't never tell me that."

"Yeah, man. Shit was serious. Her moms was straight sucking the meat off my dick and her pops burst in all angry and shit, and guess what I said to him?"

"What?"

"Guess!"

"Man, finish the fucking story. What did you say?"

"I said, 'Man, don't you knock?'"

Lil Nut and Lamiek burst into laughter. No doubt it was a lie, but funny as hell, because Lamiek made the most serious face he could muster as he delivered the joke.

"And what did he do? I bet he whipped your ass," Lil Nut said.

"I wish he woulda tried. That nigga went back out the room and knocked!"

"You a fucking lie!"

"True story!"

ဢ

That night Lil Nut worked his usual twelve-hour shift. The fiends came out in droves because it was the first of the month and everybody had gotten their assistance checks. Lil Nut stood on the corner, yawning from fatigue, thinking about his head hitting the pillow. As he went to put his key in his lock, three masked gunmen ran up behind him and shoved a loaded Ruger in his ribs.

"Nigga, run ya pockets!" the husky one said.

Disbelief that he was actually being stuck up delayed Lil Nut's reaction. Noticing his apprehension, the gunman cracked Lil Nut on the back of the head with the gun's barrel. The sudden impact instantly dazed Lil Nut and he stumbled forward.

"Don't make me ask you twice!" The voice was menacing and unrecognizable.

Without further hesitation, Lil Nut dug deep inside his pockets and handed over his the eight hundred dollars he'd brought in that night.

"Open your door!" the same gunman demanded.

Lil Nut tried to face the robbers, but was hit again in his temple with the butt of the gun. His hand immediately went up to shield himself from further blows.

"Why the fuck you want me to open up my door? Ain't nothing in there but my moms!"

"Open up the fucking door or die now and we'll open it anyway!"

Lil Nut knew this was all a part of the drug game. He hated to admit it, but he was scared to death. He hoped that they would just come in, take what they wanted, and leave without taking the lives of him and his mother. The nightly news was filled with stories of all the violence and murders stemming from the crack epidemic. Lil Nut didn't want to be a statistic. And he certainly didn't want to drag his mother into the mix.

He reasoned that if he did open the door, then they would kill him and go in on his mother, and only God knew what they would do to her. Lil Nut surmised that if they were going to try anything sheisty, then it would have to be in the hallway. He would at least try to fight them off in an effort not to involve his mother.

When the gunman went to manhandle Lil Nut again, he turned around swiftly and punched him directly in his jaw. The dazed gunman tackled Lil Nut and they both fell to the floor, scuffling. The gun dropped and one of the other silent assailants picked it up. All three began to kick, punch, and pistol whip Lil Nut without mercy.

"Hold him down!" the leader screamed. The other two sprung into action and retrieved Nut's house keys. Once the door was open, Lil Nut was dragged inside. They had to literally kick his fingers off the door jam and pull him inside by his ankles.

It only took his mother a few moments to wake from her deep

sleep. When she came into the living room to see what the commotion was, she was shocked at the three masked gunmen and the look on her son's face.

"Oh, Lord!" she spewed.

"Shut up, bitch!" the aggravated lead gunman shouted, and hit Julie in the face with the butt of the gun. Her petite body went crashing to the ground, making a loud thud. Lil Nut began resisting again, but was overpowered by the trio.

"Look, I'm not playing with your ass," the lead gunman began. His breathing was erratic from fighting with Lil Nut. "Go and get your stash or I swear to Allah I will put two in your mom's head. Now test me if you want."

Through her cries, Julie pleaded, "Nelson, do as they say. Money isn't worth losing our lives over."

Lil Nut's heart plummeted at his mother's voice. It trembled with fear and he realized he'd put them both in a precarious situation. His young mind couldn't fully process the grave danger they were in. But he decided to listen to his mother and walked two of the gunmen into the back where his bedroom was. He tried to reach in the closet, but was stopped.

"Nigga, tell me where the shit is. You could be reaching in there for a gun. You think I'm stupid?"

"Nah, I don't think you stupid. I think you're dead for robbing my stash!" The bull in Lil Nut wouldn't allow him to fully bow down, even with guns in his face.

"Yo, say the word and let me lullaby this motherfucker!" the lead gunman said. He looked to one of the gunmen who'd remained silent the whole time. Up until this exchange, Lil Nut thought that the one holding the gun was the boss. But he realized now that it was the other tall, slender guy. The guy shook his head no, and Lil Nut was allowed to live.

The robbers walked away with all of Lil Nut's money and the money he owed his boss, but not before the gunman hauled off and punched Lil Nut in the balls.

"Now you got a reason to be called Lil Nut!" He burst into laughter as Lil Nut toppled over and collapsed in agony onto his dirty, tiled floor. "Call the cops and you're dead."

Lil Nut had no intention of calling any cops. He had plans on finding out who the assailants were so he could kill them himself.

He put that promise on his life.

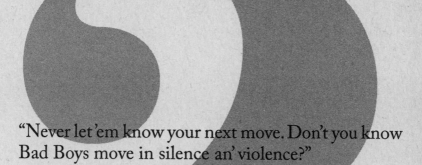

"Never let 'em know your next move. Don't you know
Bad Boys move in silence an' violence?"

-"Ten Crack Commandments," Notorious B.I.G.

1985

A year passed since Lil Nut entered the drug game. Now, at sixteen, he was older and definitely wiser. No longer did he keep his stash in a shoebox in his closet. He had his mother open up a safe deposit box at the Citibank up on Nostrand Avenue, not too far from Kentucky Fried Chicken.

Lil Nut stood in the freezing cold weather, fresh to death in a gray sheepskin from Delancey Street, a new pair of gray Clarks, and a Kangol hat. His longing for the rope chains or Atari games were a thing of the past. Lil Nut reasoned that those things attracted the wrong type of attention. And even though he wasn't a sucker, he didn't want beef with the local stickup kids each and every day. Speaking of stickup kids, Lil Nut had yet to find out who stuck him up and threatened his mother's life. He swore on his own life that he would find out who did it, and no matter who it was—friend or family—they were as good as dead.

Lil Nut had a new cause to believe in now. He couldn't wait until he'd saved up enough money to buy a used Mercedes Benz 500SL. At his young age he didn't realize, or he chose not to realize that Benzes also attracted the wrong type of attention. Blue Bug offered to sell Nut his for eighteen thousand dollars, but Nut didn't want to ride around in what the hood all knew was Blue Bug's ride. He wanted his own ride and his own identity. He now felt that he was too big to be working for a motherfucker who wasn't much older than him.

As Lil Nut stood on the corner of Pitkin and Dumont Avenues eating a piece of chicken from the Chinese restaurant, he smelled the pungent odor before he recognized the voice. "Take off your motherfucking sheepskin before I put two in ya head!"

The pressure Nut felt at his waist was alarming, but he felt confident that this wasn't a threat.

"Do it!"

Lil Nut turned around to face his father. He looked at the man's face and saw his own. Milton was still strung out on crack, which disappointed and embarrassed his son. The two hadn't seen each other since their altercation over a year ago. The usually heavy Milton had almost withered away to nothing. His smooth chocolate skin was scarred with acne, and his beautiful smile had been replaced with corroding teeth and neglected gums. Milton wore a thin trench coat that was tattered and torn with a Champion sweatshirt, sagging jeans, and a pair of oversized penny loafers without any socks. Yet despite his appearance, he still managed to greet his son with a smile.

"Boy, let me feel ya heart beating." Milton laughed and tucked the small pipe back into his coat pocket. That pipe had gotten Milton high on many occasions.

"You know fear don't pump through my veins," Nut said.

"That's 'cause I raised you to be a man and stand up for yourself."

"My mother raised me!" Lil Nut yelled, and then stepped closer to his father. The two men were so close that when Lil Nut spoke, spit flew out of his mouth and landed on Milton's face. "Now get the fuck outta my face before I give you a severe beat-down."

Unaffected by his son's outburst, Milton stood stone still. "I heard what happened last year with you and my wife. You take care of that problem yet?"

Lil Nut realized that even though he ran around terrorizing his own neighborhood, his father was a man and had a heart of steel. Nut also realized now that his father only backed down to him last year out of love, and not out of fear.

"How you hear about that?" Lil Nut asked.

"I hear everything."

"Why the fuck you ain't come around?"

"I'm always around. You just don't see me."

"So you be ghost?"

"Something like that." Milton took his hands out of his pockets and began to blow inside them in an effort to keep warm. "How long before you take care of that situation? Ain't right that a man gotta hear about his wife having a gun thrust in her face and the men responsible still breathing. Now I done gave you long enough to handle that. I did that so that you could feel like a man since you want to play like a man. I'm not gonna give you much longer—"

"How the fuck you sound?" Lil Nut exploded. "You not gonna—"

"Your biggest problem was letting motherfuckers know where you keep your stash. You lucky those niggas didn't R.I.P you and my wife. Now I'm not gonna tell you twice to rock those motherfuckers to sleep!"

Lil Nut couldn't believe his ears. His father was a stone cold crackhead, and he was barking orders to his son.

"You talking like I know who set me up and I'm giving them a pass! If I ever find out who did this shit to me and Ma, I'ma send them to meet their maker!"

His father just stood there staring his son in his eyes, trying to glean whether he was telling the truth. Once he was satisfied, he began walking away. Over his shoulder he yelled, "Keep your ears open. Those stupid motherfuckers will slip up!"

Lil Nut was pissed. His father was talking as if he knew who'd set him up, yet he wasn't telling him. Lil Nut also expected his father to ask him for money, but was surprised that he didn't. He certainly could use money, a hot shower, clean clothes, a hot meal, and a warm bed.

A couple hours later Lil Nut looked down at the telephone number code 500 and the 911 emergency page. It was Lamiek, and Lil Nut couldn't understand what the urgency was. Doing a slow stroll to the corner payphone, he punched in the digits.

"What?" Lil Nut asked.

"Whatchu doin' tonight?"

"Damn, you had me run to the fucking phone to ask a silly-ass question? I thought you were getting pounded on by motherfuckers!"

"Shit. I was standing by this phone for twenty minutes. Your punk ass took forever to call me back."

"Whatever, man. What's the 911 for?"

"My girl is having a house party tonight and she wants me to come through with a few friends. Meet me at eight on Pitkin and Belmont."

"Where's the party?"

"At her crib on Lafayette Avenue. She's not too far from Dekalb."

"OK, but since she's so close to the movies, we should go see *Krush Groove* with The Fat Boys. I've been fiending to see that for a while now. Maybe you can bring ya girl."

"A'ight, I'll ask her."

Lil Nut was excited to go to the house party and then to the movies. Yesterday he went down to Delancey Street and bought a new three-quarter leather jacket. It was almost full-length and cost $220. He was the first in his neighborhood to own one. The coat was burgundy, and he had a pair of burgundy Lee jeans that he would sport with it. He couldn't wait to get some new pussy. He was tired of sleeping with all the girls around his way. He wanted to hook up with someone new, and he was sure with his fresh clothes and knot of money he planned on taking to the party, he'd pull someone sexy.

At home he ate a large plate of baked macaroni and cheese, pork chops, and collard greens his mother had cooked. Now that his father wasn't home, his mother doted upon him night and day. Even though she smiled, Lil Nut could still see the pain in her eyes. She missed her husband. Even though it gave her pleasure to clean her son's room, cook his food, and wash his clothes, her son couldn't hold her at night when she was feeling lonely.

Lil Nut wondered briefly if he should tell his mother that he saw his father. He figured that he should because at least she'd know he was still alive. There were so many crackheads being murdered daily behind the dumb shit they pulled. In the past, Lil Nut never pegged his father to be stupid, but getting caught up in the crack epidemic was the dumbest shit Lil Nut thought a person could do, although their stupidity did provide his riches.

"Ma, I saw Milton today," Lil Nut said.

Julie swung around to face her son. "You mean your father."

Lil Nut shrugged.

"Mind your manners. No matter what, his blood still runs through your veins, and he deserves your respect."

"Do you still love him?"

"Do you?"

"I asked you first."

"If he walked through that door today sober, I'd take him back. That's my man, and I will love him until the day I die. You better only wish you find a wife who will love you the way I love your father."

Lil Nut thought about what his mother said. And he did wish he had a girl who would love him like his mother loved his dad, but it seemed like all the girls in his neighborhood only loved his money. Lil Nut didn't mind sharing his newfound wealth with the ladies. He'd already purchased Gloria Vanderbilt jeans, Gerry G jackets, and leather Nikes for a few girls. But all that was nothing compared to what he'd do when he met his future wife.

Before getting robbed last year, Lil Nut would have taken three hundred dollars with him to the party to front, but now he wasn't that dumb. Instead he took one twenty-dollar bill and wrapped it around eighty one-dollar bills. Now he actually had a knot of money, only it wasn't what people would think it was.

Later that night the cold weather had Lil Nut stressed. He felt like he was too old to be walking. And why the fuck didn't any of his friends have rides? He finally realized that he was a spring-summer type of dude. The tropical weather inspired him, and that was when he made the most money. Now he understood what his father meant when he used to say that the cold weather was for making babies.

"Yo, you ready, man?" Lamiek asked.

"Nigga, I was born ready," Lil Nut responded and tapped his jacket to let Lamiek know he was carrying his pistol. When Lite emerged from the shadows, Lil Nut was pissed. "What the fuck he doing here?"

Lite put up his hands in surrender. "It ain't even like that, man. I don't got no beef with you."

Hearing the plea in his voice, Lil Nut felt exhilarated. Ever since he shot Lite last year and earned a ruthless reputation, secretly he wondered if Lite would seek revenge. He'd watched all the obligatory gangster films that addressed whether it was better to be feared or loved, and Lil Nut decided that he loved being feared.

"We cool then," Lil Nut said.

"Why you got all dressed up to see my girl?" Lamiek asked with a smirk on his face.

Lil Nut had changed clothes three times before settling on his new three-quarter leather jacket, a leather Gucci suit from Dapper Dan's in Harlem, and new burgundy and white suede Puma sneakers with thick white laces. He could see the jealousy and envy in Lamiek's eyes.

"This ain't about your girl. You know I stay fresh."

"Yeah, so I guess the drug game is being better to you than my profession. Maybe I should retire?"

"Maybe you should and come work for me."

Lamiek was disgusted. "Work for you? Nigga, I been running my own enterprise since I was twelve. What the fuck I look like coming to work for you?"

"Shit, you won't be the first motherfucker working for me."

Lil Nut didn't give a fuck about Lamiek's outburst. He knew that he was soft like butter.

"Yo, chill, man," Lite began. "I hope y'all don't blow my high. I got a nickel bag of the best weed from Fulton today. Lil Nut, you should start moving weed."

Lil Nut shook his head. "Ain't enough money in that for me. With weed money I can buy me a hooptie. With crack money I can buy me a Benz. I've been saving up money to buy me my own ride. Soon I should be able to buy me a Benz!"

Lamiek had Benz visions as well, but he didn't have the capital to get one. He knew in order to execute his plan, he'd need backup.

"Listen, how we look walking to this party?" Lamiek asked. "Damn, flag down a cab. I don't want my sneakers to get all scuffed."

Lil Nut looked down at Lamiek's British Walkers and Lite's Travel Fox shoe-boots and shook his head. "Yo, why y'all niggas be buying those bullshit footwear? Y'all not Jamaican. If y'all want something fresh, then y'all should get the new Wallabies."

"Now you think you can tell me how to dress?" Lamiek asked. "This motherfucker here . . ." Lamiek spat and shook his head in disgust.

Lite ran into the street to hail a gypsy cab. Five minutes later a driver stopped. Lamiek ran off the address and then got down to business. "I got a plan that if done properly we can all make a lot of money. Enough to buy us all rides."

"What type of rides?" Lite asked.

"Benzes."

"Get the fuck out of here!" Lil Nut replied.

"I'm telling you"—Lamiek lowered his voice—"that if we rob Blue Bug we could make a fortune."

"Are you crazy?" Lite asked.

"Nah, I ain't crazy. Shit, you scared? He bleed like we bleed."

Lil Nut thought about the proposition, and although he wasn't into taking money, his ill feelings toward Blue Bug resurfaced, and visions of his own robbery crept back up. For all Lil Nut knew, Blue Bug could have set him up. He had to work three weeks without any profit in order to pay back Blue Bug. That was free labor.

"I'm just saying that Blue Bug ain't the average cat to be running up on with a burner," Lite commented.

"If I can get got, then fuck it, he can get got too," Lil Nut spat.

"Don't act like you got heart 'cause you caught wreck off Lite," Lamiek said. "Blue Bug is a different type of motherfucker. He appears to be all polite and nice, but cross that motherfucker and he'll do more than punch your bitch ass in the nuts!" Lamiek replied, trying to embarrass Lil Nut.

Lil Nut didn't respond. He was too busy trying to hide his emotions and steady his breathing. How the fuck would Lamiek know that the gunmen who robbed his stash and pistol whipped him and his mother had punched him in his nuts unless he was one of the three? No doubt, Lite was two out of the three. His father told him that if he listened, he'd find out who set him up. And he had also promised his father once he found out who put his hands on his mother, he would take them off this earth.

"Fuck Blue Bug! I'm telling you he can get got!" Lil Nut stated, keeping his newfound knowledge to himself for now.

"OK, let's meet tomorrow and talk about this. You know I'm down," Lamiek said. He, too, was trying to steady his voice and get his heart to slow its pace. He wondered if Lil Nut had caught his slip about him getting punched in his balls. Lamiek feared what Lil Nut would do to him if he knew that he and Lite had set him up last year. Yeah, Lil Nut shot Lite as target practice, but Lamiek feared that Lil Nut didn't need further practice. If pushed, he would shoot to kill.

When the cab driver pulled onto the block of the party, before the car could come to a complete stop, Lamiek and Lite both opened their doors and dashed out. Lil Nut hesitated for a second, and then followed suit. On the second block, Lil Nut ran out of his new Puma sneaker. He didn't give a fuck whether the driver gave chase or not, he was not losing a pair of forty-dollar sneakers for an eight-dollar cab ride. Besides, if the cab driver got stupid, Lil Nut was prepared to back him down with his gun.

Lil Nut slowed down, turned around, and realized that the cab driver wasn't anywhere in sight. Lil Nut shook his head because the driver had done the right thing. He realized that his life was worth more than eight dollars. After putting his sneaker back on, he adjusted his clothes and stood there for a few minutes to see if Lamiek and Lite would come back looking for him. When they didn't, he walked back around to the party.

Eddie Murphy's "Party All The Time" was blasting from the first-floor apartment. Lil Nut knew if they kept playing music like that, he wasn't going to be staying long. His tap on the door turned into a bang because no one could hear him. That was when he decided to turn the knob on the door and it opened. He walked in to see about thirty people crammed into the small living room, drinking, smoking, kissing, and grinding to the music. Some of the guests looked up to see who'd just entered the apartment, but most didn't. His eyes perused the apartment, looking to see if Lamiek and Lite had somehow gotten there first, but they hadn't. *Those suckers are probably still running,* Lil Nut thought.

A sexy, shapely girl made a beeline directly for Lil Nut. Her smile was welcoming as she extended her hand, "Hi. My name is GG. How did you hear about my party?"

"Oh, my man Lamiek told—"

"Now how can we both have the same man?" GG asked and then giggled. Lil Nut didn't understand her humor, but he smiled anyway. He didn't want to be rude. "Where is my guy anyway?"

"He should be here shortly."

"Good. Do you want me to take your coat?"

Lil Nut didn't have any intention of giving her his coat. That was how motherfuckers got jacked. They piled all the jackets on the bed in a dark room while the unsuspecting sucker got high off weed and liquor, and by the end of the night someone had walked out with his shit. The local thieves would go around the neighborhood, sell the coat, and then come back and give the girl who helped set it up a cut. Lil Nut was far from a dummy. And he'd hate to have to put his hands on a girl, so to avoid all of that, he simply shook his head.

"Yeah, that's probably a good idea that you hold on to it. I would hate to be responsible for such an expensive item. No telling what could go on in here."

GG walked off with a smile, but inwardly she was pissed. She and her brother, Chris, had plans to steal as many coats and sheepskin hats as possible. She knew her brother could have sold Lil Nut's coat for at least ninety dollars, and she would have gotten half. So far they were scheming on two sheepskins and a leather bomber jacket.

GG inched over to Chris, who was surveying the room, and whispered in his ear. His eyes darted toward Lil Nut, who was standing close to the door.

"Who he with?"

"He's with Lamiek."

"What's his name?" her brother asked.

"I didn't ask."

"Why the fuck not?"

"I don't know. I just didn't. What's the big deal?"

"'Cause if he has a name that rings a bell, then I'll know what I'm up against. If he's a sucker, then I can stick him up in the hallway no problem. But if he's known to be trigger happy, then it could get ugly and I might have to pass. I don't want no problems in front of Mommy's door," Chris said.

"OK, I understand. I'll find out more from Lamiek."

"Nah, that greedy motherfucker gonna wanna be down, and I already got to split shit with you. Let me clock this nigga on my own. If he seems soft by the end of the night, then I'm gonna diss him and take his shit."

"Oh, and don't forget to get me Samantha's Gucci bag."

"Samantha? Ain't she your friend?"

"Fuck that bitch. Now that she got that bag she thinks she's flyer than me," GG said.

"Well how you gonna wear that bag in front of her? She's gonna know it's her bag."

"Let me worry about that. All you gotta do is get me her bag!"

GG walked off because she saw Lamiek walk through the door. He and Lite were regulars at her apartment when her mother wasn't home, which was often.

"Hey, baby!" GG said. She wrapped her hands around his neck and gave him a juicy kiss. She could tell that she'd interrupted a heated debate between Lamiek and the guy in the burgundy coat.

"GG, this my man Lil Nut from Pitkin."

"We've already met." GG was now nervous. She had to warn her brother not to try anything stupid with Lil Nut from Pitkin. Chances were that he would be carrying a pistol, and from his reputation he wasn't afraid to use it. She was sure that if he got robbed at her party, he would definitely come back looking for her. And she knew her punk boyfriend wouldn't be able to help her. Although he pulled guns on people almost daily to rob them, he was no killer.

GG's friend Samantha had been eyeing Lil Nut since he'd walked through the door. So had almost every female in the place. Now was her chance to meet him.

"GG, this party is fresh," Samantha said, approaching her friend.

"You know it," GG bragged. "Samantha, you know my man, Lamiek. And these are his friends, Lite and Lil Nut."

Everyone exchanged pleasantries and then Samantha pulled GG to the side to talk.

"What's up with Lil Nut?" she asked.

"I don't know. I just met him. Why? You like him?"

"Well, he is cute."

Samantha wasn't fooling GG. Lil Nut was dark-skinned, and everyone knew that it was all about the light-skinned niggas with the good hair. She knew her friend was only interested in Lil Nut's pockets.

"Ain't nothing cute about that motherfucker, but he seems to have some money," GG said.

"No, for real, he is cute. You're not taking a good look at him. His eyes and his lips . . . and I can only imagine what his body looks like under that coat."

"So go for yours," GG encouraged.

"You think I should ask him to dance?"

"What's that gonna do? If you really want to get to know him, take him in my room and get busy," GG said.

Samantha wasn't down with that. She didn't readily give away her pussy like GG did. She decided that it would be best to ask him to dance, and was happy when he accepted. The DJ put on the smash hit "I Can't Live Without My Radio" by LL Cool J, and the crowd went berserk. They both started off doing the Smurf on the crowded dance floor, and then ended up simply grinding.

As everyone passed joints of weed, Samantha was happy to see that Lil Nut didn't smoke. And neither did she. Although they both drank, they both decided against it that night. For some reason they were both on high alert and wanted to be prepared for anything. Samantha was thinking about her Gucci bag and nameplate earrings that her parents bought her, and Lil Nut was thinking about his coat and reputation. If he allowed himself to get robbed twice, he would never live it down.

After trying to hear each other over the loud music, Lil Nut and Samantha moved their conversation to the hallway.

"What grade are you in?" Lil Nut asked as they sat on the steps of the six-story tenement building.

"I'm a junior at Fashion Industries high school."

"Where's that?"

"I live in Harlem, not too far from the Apollo Theatre, but my school is on Twenty-fourth Street in Manhattan."

"Word? What are you doing in Brooklyn?"

"I used to live in Brooklyn when I was a child, and then my parents moved back to Harlem. My father was born and raised in Harlem. He only moved to Brooklyn because of my mother. They stayed for eight years, and then he couldn't take it any longer."

"It was too rough for him?"

"Nah, not even. Harlem is just as rough if not more ruthless than Brooklyn, but their priorities are different. And my father couldn't understand the Brooklyn mentality."

"And what mentality is that?"

"Well first off he couldn't get down with the Five Percent Nation—"

"Me too!" Lil Nut replied, and then shook his head.

"But you hang with Lamiek."

Lil Nut wanted to reply, but couldn't. His stomach did somersaults because flashbacks of his mother being pistol-whipped flashed into his head. He knew what he had to do.

Samantha continued. "And he was used to men in Harlem making their own money to take care of their families. By the time a man turned eighteen, he was starting a business of some sort. Whether it was a record store, fish fry, or clothing store, they were doing it themselves. In Brooklyn, the common thread was taking money, not making money, and that's not my father's style. He's old school."

As Lil Nut listened he began to admire a man and lifestyle he didn't know. And he also began to take interest in Samantha. Although her friend GG was cuter by any man's standards, Samantha definitely had a head on her shoulders.

"What are your plans when you graduate?" he asked.

"I'm going to nursing school. I want to be an RN just like my mother."

"You know, I don't know not one person who's in the medical profession," Lil Nut replied. He looked off in space and began to think about what he wanted to do with himself. Eighteen was steadily approaching, and from what Samantha had said about her father, Lil Nut should be thinking about opening up a business or something. "You're really impressing me tonight," he said.

She smiled. "I really like you too."

"Do you have a beeper?"

"No. My parents don't like those, but you can call me on my house phone."

"I'ma get you a beeper," Lil Nut promised. "That way when I need you you'll be there for me."

Samantha was excited about how the night was turning out. She had permission to stay the weekend over GG's house, and she hoped that she could see Lil Nut again before she went home on Sunday morning. After they exchanged telephone numbers, he leaned in to kiss her. Samantha thought about how soft his lips were as his mouth slightly parted and his tongue slid inside her mouth. Neither one of them heard the outside door open, but when the cold air enveloped them they both knew they had company. They stopped kissing and looked up to see two stocky men. Each had hoodies on their heads and their hands stuffed deeply into their pockets. Instantly Samantha was afraid.

One guy spoke up first. "Is this where the house party at?"

Lil Nut nodded.

"Yo, you look familiar," the guy said to Nut. "Where I know you from? What's your name?"

Lil Nut grimaced. "Nah, duke, you don't know me."

"You sure? I swear I know you from somewhere."

As the guy spoke, both inched in closer and began to surround the couple. Lil Nut tried to put his hand on his gun, but was unsuccessful.

"Don't move, motherfucker! Run your shit! And you too, bitch!"

Lil Nut and Samantha stood looking at two guns pointed directly at their heads. Lil Nut began to slowly take off his jacket. Inside he was burning. He couldn't believe he was this stupid. He knew he was going to lose his life. He could see it in the eyes of the leader. Although he and Samantha gave them what they wanted, Lil Nut couldn't shake what his gut was trying to tell him. He thought about his mother and how she would take the news of his murder. He thought about his father and how disappointed he'd be in him.

If he could do the night all over, after he jumped out of the car he never would have gone to the party knowing that his two friends had set him up last year. He should have left and waited in the cut, and then bodied both Lamiek and Lite. Why would he still go to the party and still be friends with the wolves? Now it was going to cost him his life.

Lil Nut knew that if he was going to leave this earth before his time, he was going to take someone with him. In one swift movement, he jumped in front of Samantha, reached for his gun, and began busting shots. But the leader was too quick. He squeezed off, and Lil Nut took one slug in the chest. As gunshots rang out in the small hallway, Samantha's screams echoed.

When the smoke cleared, Lil Nut had managed to shoot off six rounds. The leader was grazed in his face, but it wasn't a life threatening wound. The robbers fled the scene.

However, Lil Nut wasn't so lucky. He lay in Samantha's arms with his chest blown open, gasping for air. He couldn't speak and could hardly keep his eyes open.

Samantha pushed him off her and ran inside the apartment to get help. She personally dialed 911 for the ambulance. When she hung up she ran back outside to comfort Lil Nut. His eyes glanced around wildly. Everyone stood around gawking at him, and this infuriated Samantha.

"Get out of his face!" she screamed as she took off her sweater and began to apply pressure to his wound. Noticing the gun, she picked it up and told Lamiek to get rid of it.

"GG, go inside and bring me a soapy rag!" Samantha screamed. "Hurry!"

GG did as she was told, and when she came back, Samantha began to wash the gun powder residue off of Lil Nut's hands. If he lived, she didn't want him to catch a case behind this robbery. All she kept thinking about was that GG's brother Chris was behind it. Samantha knew how trifling he could be, and she knew he saw dollar signs when Lil Nut walked up into the house party.

As the paramedics wheeled Lil Nut out of the building, all Lamiek could think about was how his plan had gone terribly wrong. When he called his cousin Malik from Canarsie, Brooklyn, he gave him specific instructions. Those instructions were to come to the party, follow Lamiek, Lite, and Lil Nut out of the party, and rob all three of them. No one was supposed to get hurt. Definitely not murdered. And with all of them getting robbed, it would take suspicion off of Lamiek. When Lamiek and Lite got separated from Lil Nut, Lamiek quickly called his cousin to let him know the change in plans. There was no way Lamiek could let Lil Nut walk around in that coat when Lamiek didn't have one.

Lamiek knew that if Lil Nut survived—and by the looks of him that was impossible—then Lamiek was a dead man walking. Lil Nut may be a lot of things, but stupid wasn't one of them. Lamiek had pushed the envelope one time too many. And if Lil Nut hadn't caught the slipup in the cab, he surely wouldn't miss this setup.

ॐ

To everyone's amazement, Lil Nut's young age helped him survive the attack. He had to stay in the hospital for three months, and only his mother was allowed to visit him. The police kept a 24-hour security guard posted outside his door just in case the men came back to finish what they'd started.

Lil Nut didn't allow Samantha to visit him, but unbeknownst to everyone, they kept in touch by telephone. Samantha turned out to be an asset. Lil Nut was in the hospital for five weeks before he was strong enough to have a conversation. He had to go through extensive physical therapy, and for months he had a shit bag and also had to urinate in a cup, but his mother was there every step of the way.

When he finally did speak to Samantha, she had a wealth of information for him. She played GG by telling her that Lil Nut told her he was going to kill her once he got better, because he knew she set him up. This plan worked, because GG spilled the beans and told Samantha that she didn't have to worry or look over her shoulders, because it was Lamiek who set up Lil Nut. That was a shock to Samantha, because she always thought it was GG and Chris. Still, she didn't know if this information was true, but she couldn't wait to tell Lil Nut to see what he thought.

GG also said that Lamiek was going to try to get her Gucci bag and earrings back, but Samantha was no dummy. She knew GG was trying to sell her a dream. When GG told Samantha that as soon as Lil Nut got released from the hospital there was a ready-made killer waiting to murder him, Samantha was scared.

GG told her that Lamiek went to this big time drug dealer named Blue Bug and told him of Lil Nut's plan to rob him, and Blue Bug promised to take care of Lil Nut. That way Lamiek wouldn't have to put in the dirty work, and he also felt good knowing that his life wouldn't be in any more danger once Blue Bug killed Lil Nut.

"That's all the information I got. I hope it helps you stay safe," Samantha explained to Lil Nut.

"Well most of it I already knew, but I'm glad that you confirmed it. I know what I got to do. I'll be all right."

Lil Nut couldn't understand how he could fall in love with a girl he'd only kissed once, but he was sure that he did love her. Each day the thought of being with her for the rest of his life gave him the strength to work hard toward his rehabilitation. When his physical therapist told him to do one more round, he did two. He needed to get his strength back. He had a few scores to settle. Three, to be precise.

Finally Lil Nut was released from the hospital, only he didn't head home. He went to stay with his Aunt Mary in Queens, away from the violence. Out of his mother's two sisters, Mary was the one who had her shit together. He was still recuperating, and wasn't ready for the big battle he would face once he showed himself on the streets again.

Samantha took the train and a bus over to his house, and as the days became warmer, their relationship blossomed. He realized he couldn't keep putting Samantha off, pretending like he didn't have the energy or strength to make love. She could tell that he was stronger than ever. In his aunt's basement he bench pressed two hundred pounds. Although he was muscular before the shooting, he had bulked up even more. But Lil Nut was still nervous the first time they made love.

As he lay on his back on the small bench with two hundred pounds gripped in the palm of his large hands, Samantha came over, sat on his groin, and began to grind her pussy on his flaccid penis.

"What are you doing?" Lil Nut asked.

"What does it look like?"

Lil Nut just smiled as his dick began to respond. He put the heavy weight down and motioned for her to lie on the mattress that was on the floor in the corner. Quickly Samantha obliged.

"Take off your pants," he instructed.

Samantha lay back and began to remove her pants and panties as Lil Nut towered over her. He removed his shirt, and she saw the large scar on his chest where the bullet had entered for the first time. That vision was quickly replaced when he took off his sweatpants and boxers and revealed a large, erect penis.

Neither one of them said a word as Lil Nut slowly positioned himself between Samantha's legs. Applying steady pressure, he lowered himself deeper into her tight walls and began to thrust his hips in and out. Soft moans escaped Samantha's mouth as his dick gently brushed up against her G-spot.

Samantha's grip around Lil Nut's waist got tighter as her pleasure increased. Her long fingernails began to dig into his firm, round ass, and he encouraged her by kissing her deeply and passionately. The young couple experienced an orgasm and lay still for long moments, reveling in their shared bliss. When Lil Nut grabbed Samantha and wrapped his strong arms around her waist, she felt loved.

3

"Never trust no-bo-dy. Your moms'll set that ass up, properly gassed up. Hoodie to mask up, shit, for that fast buck she be layin' in the bushes to light that ass up."

—"Ten Crack Commandments," Notorious B.I.G.

1986

"What did I tell you?" Milton asked.

Lil Nut couldn't believe his ears when he stepped outside of his aunt's house and his father was standing there, on the side of his aunt's fence, drinking a forty-ounce of Colt 45 malt liquor and holding a Bible. Lil Nut hated to admit it, but he was glad to see his father, although he wished it were under different circumstances. While in the hospital he'd asked his mother about his pops, but she still hadn't seen him since the night he was kicked out. His mother reasoned that her husband didn't want her to see him in his intoxicated state.

"And what was that again?" Lil Nut asked. He couldn't melt at the sight of his father. He was a man and had to hold his head up.

"I told you that you'd find out who set ya ass up, didn't I?"

Suddenly Lil Nut was furious. Had his father just told him from the jump who'd set him up, he wouldn't have gone to the party with Lamiek and Lite, and he wouldn't have taken a hot slug to the chest.

"What kind of father are you? If you knew who it was, it was your duty to tell me so that I could get at those niggas before they got at me."

Milton shook his head. "It don't go like that. If I tell you what you need to hear instead of teaching you what you need to learn, then you won't survive one day out here in these streets."

"Did you forget that a bullet opened up my whole chest? I almost didn't survive!"

"That was part of the game that you signed up for, and the part that you can't predict. That was part of the game that you're supposed to feel. Animal instincts should have told you that you weren't in the right environment. Don't you know that once you get into the crack game you can no longer think like an average man? Not when there are wolves out there gunning to either take your spot, your life, your cash, or your woman. You gotta think like a beast!"

"I'm trying," Lil Nut whined. He sounded defeated. He sat down on the stoop and hung his head low. He felt like such a failure after being robbed twice, shot, and then whisked away to his aunt's house, hiding from his peers, far away from his neighborhood.

"We need to have a talk. We should have had this talk a while back, but there's no time like the present. You see, everything you need to know is right here." Milton shook the worn Bible that he had in his hand. "There are Ten Commandments for this crack game, and if you follow each one, then you will be one of the very few who are able to get in the crack game and get out without being murdered or incarcerated."

"Pops, that's the Bible."

"I know what this is. Don't you know that this here holds a wealth of knowledge? The Old Testament is what I live by." Milton opened his Bible and began reading Proverbs, Malachi, Daniel, and Psalms.

After Lil Nut listened to his father in great length he was able to see his mistakes, and also deduce that he would have made even more mistakes had his father not taken the time to come to Queens to school him. He asked his father to come inside, but he refused.

"Where are you going to go this late at night?" Lil Nut asked.

"I got something I need to handle. Should have taken care of this a long time ago. . . ."

Again he just walked off, not asking for any money or food. There was a great emptiness inside the pit of Lil Nut's stomach as he watched his father glide down the block. He wanted to run after him and tell him that he was sorry for pulling out a gun—his father's own gun—on him. He wished he could rewind back to the time when he still lived in a two-parent home. He wondered briefly if he should have told his father about how his mother would take him back if he walked through the door sober. Then he realized that his father probably already knew that.

ು಼ಲ಼

The hysterical voice on the other line could have only been one woman. His mother. Lil Nut listened to the barely discernible voice tell him that his father was found murdered in the back of their building from two bullet wounds to the back of his head.

"He was what?"

"They killed my man . . . they killed him!" Julie screamed into the phone.

"Did you just say someone killed my father and left him like trash in the back of our building?"

"He was a good man, once . . ."

"Ma, don't cry. I'm gonna find out who did this. I'm coming back to handle it," Lil Nut said reassuringly. This was the second time he promised a parent he would take care of a situation, and he wasn't gonna let this promise slide.

"No! You stay right where you are!"

"I'm coming home," he stated with conviction.

"What did I say?" Julie demanded. "This was all over you, I'm told. Blue Bug had two of his spots robbed this past week, and everyone said that it was you. I heard that Blue Bug is scared to death that you're planning to kill him, so he wants you dead first. They said that he killed your father to bring you out of hiding."

"Who told you that?"

"You know Leslie from the fifth floor gets all the gossip. She's the one who knocked on my door and told me about your father."

Julie began to sob heavily into the phone. She couldn't believe that someone had snatched away the love of her life. Julie always believed he would eventually come home to her. She prayed each night for God to watch over him while he was on these streets and to bring him back home to her. Now someone had taken away her future.

"They said that he'd just put his name on the waiting list for the rehab center up on Nostrand Avenue," Julie told her son. "He didn't deserve to die like that."

Lil Nut wondered how much of a role his father played in getting himself murdered. When he walked off yesterday he said he had something that needed to get done. There were so many unanswered questions, which Lil Nut knew wouldn't get answered while he was hiding out in Queens. The pain and angst he felt was so palpable that he could have literally killed someone with his bare hands. If they wanted a war, he was prepared to give them one. If they thought he was sweet and wouldn't seek revenge, they were wrong.

ත

Lil Nut made a promise to himself that before his father was given a proper burial, Lamiek, Lite, and Blue Bug would meet his father at the crossroads. He knew he needed to strategize or else he'd be the one meeting his father. What he had on his side was anonymity. As far as the neighborhood knew, he was a ghost. They no longer knew his movements, but he knew theirs. He knew that Blue Bug would be walking with heat and bodyguards whenever he came to see his wisdom. He would be the hardest to catch. Lamiek and Lite wouldn't be that much of a challenge. They were both creatures of habits.

Lil Nut hated to involve Samantha in his plans to assassinate his former friends and boss, but he didn't have any choice. They had gone too far in murdering his father, thus pushing his hand. Even if Lil Nut wanted to chill, he couldn't.

"Listen, I need you to keep your ear to the ground and find out the movements of Lamiek. But you gotta be slick. From what you tell me, GG ain't a stupid broad—"

"She ain't smarter than me," Samantha said defensively.

"Nah, I'm not saying that. I know she ain't book smarter than—"

"She ain't street smarter than me either!"

Lil Nut exhaled. He had to proceed with caution. He didn't want to offend Samantha, but he didn't have time to stroke her ego. His father was just taken away from him for good. There ain't no coming back from the dead.

"Will you just listen and hear me out? Y'all can compare SAT scores later. This is important. My fucking pops is lying stiff-cold in the morgue over these two cowards."

"I'm sorry . . . you're right. This isn't about me, and I want to help you as much as I can."

"OK, bet. Check it. Call GG and see if you can get her to tell you where Lamiek is, or if he's coming over her house tonight. That way I can creep over there and splatter his fucking brains."

"That won't work. As you just stated, GG isn't a dummy, and she'll be hip to my game. If Lamiek told her that he was the reason your father was murdered, and that y'all beef just got heated up, she'll be protective about giving up any info. She's grimy as hell and knows the game from her brother."

"Damn! Then how can I catch him?"

"Well instead of him being the target, why don't you make yourself the target? Why don't you be the bait? I'll help you."

"You'll help me get killed? How that sound?"

Samantha giggled. "Do I even need to say that your remark was stupid? Why would I help you get killed? I love you."

The L word made Lil Nut squeamish. Before they had sex he thought he loved her. Now he realized that he no longer felt that way. And that he never felt that way. It was all superficial. Getting shot and her being there for him had clouded his judgment. She was the only female contact he'd had while hiding out and being on the run from niggas who wanted him dead. Now that he was adjusting back into society, he didn't feel that they had gotten to that part of their relationship yet, and he didn't know how to respond, so he said nothing.

Samantha continued. "What I mean is, I will call GG and tell her that you asked me if could you come over to my house tomorrow while my parents are out of town, and that I was afraid to tell you no. I'll tell her that you said you were coming for some sex, but I don't trust you, and that I think you're really coming to quiz me about getting shot. I'll tell her that if you think I had something to do with setting you up, you'll kill me, and that I'm scared. We both know that she's going to relay that information to Lamiek. Now all you gotta do is be outside and lay low while they're outside trying to lie low on you. When you get the opportunity, then do what you need to do."

Lil Nut had to admit that it was a perfect plan. And gangster. He didn't realize that his book smart girlfriend was actually street smart too.

"I'm really feeling this plan," he said. "OK, ma, put it into motion, and call me back. Remember, be slick about it, and if you think she's on to you in the slightest, let me know."

"I know how to handle GG."

"Cool. Talk to you later. Bye."

In a rushed, nervous voice, Samantha replied, "OK, love you, bye!" And hung up.

Lil Nut couldn't help but laugh to himself. He figured that he'd better start loving Samantha back, especially since she was a good girl and all.

త Q౨

As she promised, Samantha set up everything. She told GG that Lil Nut was to arrive at nine o'clock, so Lil Nut figured that Lamiek and Lite would get there early to wait on him. He wasn't sure if they planned to murder him going into Samantha's, or catch him coming out. He guessed it would all depend on opportunity.

Lil Nut borrowed his aunt's hooptie and made his way uptown to Samantha's residence. He didn't have a clue how Lamiek and Lite would creep up, how many would be in the goon squad, or how much ammunition they would have. All he knew was that he couldn't make any mistakes, nor could they peep that he was there. Before he left he called Samantha.

"I'm sure at some point GG will call me to make sure you're here," Samantha said. "Now if you're supposed to come at nine o'clock, and they don't see you come in the building, they'll probably only wait a little while. If Lamiek asks GG to call me, then I'll say that you're up here and that you came earlier. Do you think that's a good idea? Or should I just say you didn't come yet?"

"Hell, yeah, that's a good idea. You're a pro at this. Remind me never to get on your bad side. If Lamiek gets GG to call you, say like you said, that I'm already there and that I came over early to surprise you. That way they'll only be looking at your front door, and they won't be so on point."

Lil Nut pulled up shortly after five o' clock because he didn't know how early Lamiek would show up. He'd dressed in all black and in layers to prevent the cold from getting to him because he couldn't keep the car running out of fear he'd easily be spotted. He parked on the opposite side of the street, figuring Lamiek would want to be on the same side, not too far from the front door.

As the hours passed, Lil Nut was frozen. He kept running his fingers in and out of his pockets to keep them warm. He desperately wanted to cut on the car to get some heat. As each hour passed, he grew more discouraged that his plan had failed. He felt like a loser. He'd let his mother down last year, and this year he'd let down his father.

Nine o'clock came and went. As eleven o'clock steadily approached, Lil Nut decided to see if he could catch them around their way. Maybe he would get lucky and catch them slipping. First he thought about driving over to GG's, and if Lamiek wasn't there, he'd shoot over to his old neighborhood.

As he wondered whether he should call Samantha to see if GG had called, an old Oldsmobile came creeping down the block. Lil Nut ducked down into the driver's seat and peered through his side view mirrors. The car glided at a slow pace, finally stopping in front of Samantha's apartment building. It was brick cold outside and deserted. Lil Nut shook his head once he saw Lamiek in the driver's seat, Lite as the passenger, and a third person in the back. He prayed to God it was Blue Bug and he'd be able to kill three birds with three stones.

He went over and over in his head how he would do it. He wondered if everyone in the car was strapped. He'd have to be quick as lightning to be able to pull off shooting three armed men without getting hit himself. And on the thought of getting shot again, Lil Nut realized that he didn't have room for error.

Finally, Lamiek parked and cut off his car. As they sat there, Lil Nut sat. Lil Nut didn't know why he was hesitating, but the moment just didn't seem right to him. He kept peering out of his back window, looking back at the carload of men. They were talking, laughing, and even singing. They were too lax. Lil Nut rationalized that they felt he was already inside the apartment. They must have planned to ambush him coming out of the building in the wee hours of the morning.

By four o'clock in the morning, Lil Nut had been there almost twelve hours. He was frozen stiff, and if it wasn't for sheer determination, he would have pulled off and gone home. He flexed his fingers in and out for a few minutes until they warmed up, took one more peek through the back window at the peanut butter and tan colored Oldsmobile, and discreetly slid out of his driver's seat. He crawled down the darkened Harlem street on his hands and knees until he was almost to the corner. Lil Nut tossed his hood over his head and walked across the street. He took another peek and realized that they hadn't spotted him.

In a crouching position, he crept toward the car with his gun aimed and cocked. He could see Lamiek's head resting on the window, asleep, and Lite staring straight ahead. Lil Nut steadied his gun and decided to take aim at Lite first.

Boom! Boom! Lite clutched his chest with both hands and began to scream. Lamiek's eyes popped opened, but Lil Nut was already hitting up the back passenger. *Boom! Boom!* Lamiek opened up the driver's side door and bolted. Lil Nut was on his heels quickly. *Boom! Boom! Boom!* Lamiek fell face-first onto the cold pavement. Lil Nut stood over him and emptied his gun into his head.

"This is for my pops, you faggot!"

A few lights began clicking on inside people's apartments. Lil Nut ran toward his aunt's car, tripping over his sneaker laces and scraping his knee on the pavement. Quickly he hopped back up and tore out of there like he'd just committed a triple homicide. It took him a few minutes to steady his hands from shaking, and for his heart rate to slow down to a normal pace. During the whole ride back to Queens, he continued to look over his shoulder for the police. He hoped and prayed to God that no one had seen him. Then he convinced himself that if he did get caught and had to go to prison, at least those bastards were dead.

As soon as he got inside his aunt's house he called Samantha. He made sure his voice wasn't shaking. He didn't want her to know that he was terrified.

"The police are all over this place!" Samantha's voice had elevated to a high pitch.

"Well what did you think would happen?"

His response must have plucked her nerves, because she replied, "I guess I didn't really think about that!"

"Why are you yelling at me? You helped me do this!"

"I didn't kill anyone!"

"What are you saying? You're gonna snitch me out, because if you do, you're just as much going down with me. If you didn't help me set them up, they'd still be alive!"

When Samantha began to sob heavily on the phone, Lil Nut realized he'd made a mistake involving her. She was already folding under pressure, and the heat hadn't even knocked on her door.

"Did you hear from GG?" he asked.

"No," she whimpered. "I'm sure she doesn't know yet."

"Are you by the window? Tell me what's going on outside."

"What's going on? It's a fucking crime scene!"

Lil Nut had finally had it. That was the last time he was going to allow her to disrespect him.

"Samantha, don't diss me by talking to me like that. One thing I don't do is disrespect women. My moms taught me better. Ya parents should have taught you not to disrespect a man."

"Well I'm sorry you feel that I'm dissing you, but I'm upset!"

Samantha refused to fold, and Lil Nut began to realize that he really didn't know her that well.

"Well I'ma let you go and be upset."

Lil Nut disconnected the line, which only infuriated Samantha more. She called back and the loud ringing threatened to wake up his aunt. He picked up the receiver, hung it back up, and then took it off the hook.

ຕɔຕ

After shooting the backseat passenger, who was not Blue Bug, Lil Nut realized he still had one adversary left. Once he bumped him off, he'd be able to go back to his block in Brooklyn and stop hiding out like a little bitch. Each night he thought about how to get at Blue Bug. He drove around on the low in his unmarked car looking for him, but to no avail. In two days he'd be laying his father to rest, and if he didn't get Blue Bug by then, he wouldn't be able to attend his father's funeral. Not only that, if Blue Bug didn't get Lil Nut soon, then Lil Nut figured his mother's life could be in danger. He told her to stay inside and not to come out until he handled the situation. Word on the street was that Blue Bug planned on kidnapping his mother in order to lure Lil Nut out of hiding.

In a nanosecond the answer came to him as if his father were still lurking around. When Milton told him about the ten crack commandments, he said that anyone was susceptible to setting up a motherfucker, even your moms. Lil Nut had proved that right when he got Samantha to go against the grain and help him set up Lamiek and

Lite. Now he needed another ally.

Lil Nut remembered that his mother had told him that Blue Bug and Lady Bug had broken up, and he'd stopped coming around. Lady Bug's mother had apparently driven a wedge between the couple, because she felt her daughter deserved more than what Blue Bug was giving her. It wasn't a secret in the hood that Blue Bug was a cheap motherfucker. And what Lil Nut had that could work in his favor was a safety deposit box full of money, money that he'd earn back once he was able to go back on his block. His neighborhood was a goldmine with all the crack fiends lurking around. Any smart hustler could make money hand over fist.

Lil Nut made the call, and to his amazement, Lady Bug's mother, Princess, was ready to sit down and make a deal. Lil Nut crept over to Brooklyn in the early hours of the morning. Princess came downstairs to his mother's house because she didn't want her daughter to have any part in their deal.

"Look, Blue Bug gotta get got, and I need your help," Lil Nut said.

Princess was in full gear. She had her head fully wrapped with a silk scarf covering her nose and mouth, and a long wrap covered her from head to toe. The only things showing were her eyes.

"Well my help is going to cost you," she said. "Setting up a man who was almost my son don't come cheap."

"I know that, and I'm already prepared for all that. Name your price."

Princess hated to be a greedy woman, and she always fancied herself smart. She sized up Lil Nut and saw the determination in his eyes. That determination made her feel safer. She knew that if he fucked up and Blue Bug put two and two together, then not only would her life be over, but her daughter's life as well. She'd already heard that Lamiek and Lite were executed in Harlem and the whole neighborhood speculated that they had gotten caught up in a drug deal gone wrong. But Princess knew better. She knew that Lamiek didn't sell no drugs, and after Milton had gotten murdered, she knew it was only a matter of time before those two would end up dead.

"The information that I got will cost you twenty-five thousand."

Lil Nut couldn't believe his ears. He'd gotten Samantha to help him for free. He figured that Princess was accustomed to being spoiled since her daughter dated drug dealers for years, but jeez, twenty-five gees just to know the whereabouts of where a nigga rested his head? Plus, he still had to put in the work. It was absurd.

"You must gonna do the hit too, talking all that dough."

"I see this is a waste of my time," Princess said and began to stand.

"Hold on a moment," Lil Nut said. "Let's be reasonable here. Ma, how much do I got in the stash?" Lil Nut asked his mother, who was listening.

"You only carrying about seventeen thousand, and you can't give her all of it. We got expenses too. Especially now that your father ain't here."

"Well that seventeen thousand ain't gonna do neither one of you any good if Blue Bug murders Lil Nut, now is it?" Princess asked.

Lil Nut exhaled. "All I got is seventeen. Do we got a deal or not?"

Princess smiled like a Cheshire cat until her round eyes became slanted. "Seventeen will do me just fine. You bring me the money and I'll give you the address."

"You get half up front, and the balance upon completion."

"It don't work like that—"

"It will work like that. For all I know I can give you all my dough and you send me on a wild goose chase. And when I get back, you and Lady Bug done packed up never to be seen again."

That thought had actually crossed her mind. As Princess was making this deal she was thinking of a way to outsmart Lil Nut. Not because she cared anything for Blue Bug. He was a vermin to her, but he was in the Five Percent Nation, and that should count for something. Now she realized that the young man standing before her wasn't as stupid or as gullible as she thought he'd be.

"My word is my bond!" Princess said.

As Lil Nut thought about what he said to Princess about cheating him, he realized that if she was capable of stiffing him for his seventeen thousand, then she'd be capable of stiffing him for eighty-five hundred. He was sure that that was more money than she'd ever seen at one time in her whole life. He decided to up the ante.

"You know what, I don't trust you," he said. "In fact, the only person I trust is my moms. After my two friends tried to get me murdered, everyone is suspect. Now if you want the money, then you gotta come with me to get it."

"That's fine by me. Where you got it? In the bank or a stash house?"

"Nah, you misunderstanding me. You gotta come with me to get at Blue Bug in order for you to get it. My whole life savings is at risk, and I don't know, you could be setting me up to get murdered, or to just take my blood, sweat, and tears."

"Are you crazy?!"

"Not at all. The choice is yours. I'll wait a few minutes for you to make up your mind. But once I walk out that front door, the deal is off the table and I promise you that I will catch Blue Bug before he catches me. Either way he's getting put to sleep. Your only dilemma is whether you will cash in on his life insurance policy."

Princess thought about what the young man had proposed, and again, his logic stunned her. She realized that he might actually last on these mean streets longer than the average knucklehead. She reasoned his father had taught him well before his demise. Princess wasn't a stranger to violence or street life. She'd lived in the hood all her life, and now she wanted to move south with her family. With seventeen thousand she could pay down on a large home. At the moment she was collecting $162 a month from welfare, and she wasn't a spring chicken. She was steadily approaching her golden years, and she refused to live and die in Brownsville, Brooklyn.

"You sure do push a hard bargain. OK, meet me back here this time tomorrow."

"Nah, I don't have tomorrow. This nigga gets got tonight. He will not breathe another day on this earth. Living is a luxury, and I'ma revoke his pass."

"I hear that," Princess said, hardly fazed that Blue Bug was about to be murdered. "I gotta make a run upstairs. Meet me in the back alley in twenty minutes. And you better have my money when all of this is said and done. A deal is a deal."

When Princess left, Lil Nut walked over and hugged his mother. "You know you're something else, right?" he asked.

"Shit. You think I was going to allow you to give her all our money?"

Laughing, he replied, "I thought you were going to say twenty thousand. When you said seventeen, I was like, look at Ma, low-balling Princess."

"I knew her greedy ass would take it and wouldn't lose any sleep about taking our last dime. Just make sure you're careful, and if you smell a setup get out of there quick. And if you can't get out of the situation, make sure you take one of them with you. You hear me!"

"I hear you!"

ᴿᴼᴼ

Later that day Lil Nut and Princess rode down Atlantic Avenue toward Cross Bay Boulevard. Blue Bug was living in a predominately Italian neighborhood in Howard Beach. Lil Nut couldn't understand how Blue Bug managed to pull that off, but evidently he had. With his burner resting on his lap, just in case he had to put a bullet in Princess's ass, he was prepared for the worst. The whole ride Princess couldn't keep her mouth shut. Lil Nut wondered if she was talking so much because she was nervous, or if this was who she really was. If it was the latter, then he could understand why Blue Bug got the fuck out of there.

"Do you know that last year all I asked that motherfucker to buy me for Christmas was a fox fur coat, and do you know that he walked up in my house on Christmas morning empty-handed? Yes, he did. He had the nerve to walk into my house empty-handed. So I said to him, 'Blue Bug! I know you got my coat downstairs in your fancy ride. Now stop playing. Go back downstairs and get my coat. Don't play no games with an old woman.' And you know what?" Princess asked, not allowing Lil Nut to answer, "He didn't have shit for me at all. Nothing. And he came in and gave Lady Bug a little funky nameplate. And not one with diamonds, but the cheap, raggedy one with the diamond chips. Can you believe that? My daughter was with his ass for two years, and that's all he bought her for Christmas. That cheap bastard deserves everything he's about to get. Do you think I feel sorry for his ass? Hell no, I don't feel sorry for his cheap ass!"

Lil Nut couldn't understand Princess's sense of entitlement. She was speaking as if Blue Bug owed her something, when the fact of the matter is that he didn't. He made the money and took the risk. Bottom line.

For the next twenty minutes, Lil Nut tuned out Princess. He needed to be focused when he rolled up on Blue Bug. There wasn't any way he could slip up, because if he did, Blue Bug had enough money to hire an army to come after him, and even enough money to put a bounty over his head.

"Turn left at that McDonald's on the corner of Cross Bay and then slow down. His house is on the right hand side of the block," Princess said.

Lil Nut could see that Princess had begun to duck down. And her nervousness made him nervous.

"What? You see him?" he asked.

"No, I don't, and I don't want to. Park over here behind this black Jeep."

Lil Nut did as he was told and cut off his ignition. He was ready to get it over with. He didn't like the white man's neighborhood, and figured that he and Princess stood out like sore thumbs.

"We can't stay parked here," Lil Nut reasoned.

"His house is only a couple feet away. You see the house with the black shutters? That's him."

"I understand that, but if someone walks by and sees us here for a while, they might get suspicious and call the police. Or they might try to attack us on some riot shit. You see what happened with Michael Griffith being attacked here in Howard Beach and chased down until he was hit and killed by a car. That ain't gonna be me."

"Shit. That ain't gonna be me either. What you want me to do? Go and knock on his door and tell him to come outside so you can murder him?"

Lil Nut wasn't in the mood for such sarcasm. But it did spark an idea. He peeled off and began to ride around the neighborhood.

"Whatchu doing?"

"I'm wasting time. It's not dark enough. It should be dark in an hour, and then I got a plan."

"What's the plan?"

"Don't worry about it. You hungry?" he asked.

"Look at my fat ass. What kind of question is that?"

Lil Nut drove to the borderline of Brooklyn and Queens, and he and Princess went into the Lindenwood Diner to get something to eat. Princess ordered a fish dinner and Lil Nut ordered steak and French fries. After they finished eating, he headed back to his destination.

He parked around the corner from Blue Bug's house and told Princess to get in the driver's seat, keep the car running, and be on high alert. She took her orders like a pro, because she knew that within a couple of hours she was going to be rich.

Lil Nut hugged the shadows as he inched down the block toward Blue Bug's house. He knew that Blue Bug's car alarm was always being triggered because of all the custom work he had done to his ride. Blue Bug was too cheap to allow Mercedes Benz to do the work, so he hired a local mechanic, and he got what he paid for.

All it took were a few nudges on the car to trigger the alarm. Lil Nut hunched down and waited for his opportunity. When he heard a front door open and a chirp of the alarm, aggravation sunk in. He assumed that Blue Bug had opened up the front door and simply shut off the alarm.

Lil Nut shook the car, and once again the alarm went off. For the second time the front door opened, Lil Nut heard the chirp, and the door closed and locked. As frustrated as Lil Nut was, he knew that he would break down Blue Bug eventually. When he set off the alarm for the third time, he actually heard the front door open and slam. He knew Blue Bug was coming out, but to Lil Nut's amazement, it was a young, sexy female. And she wasn't an earth. She was dressed regularly in a pair of tight Guess jeans and Reebok sneakers. She wasn't more than eighteen years old.

Lil Nut pounced on her, put the gun to her head, and whispered, "Don't say a word or you're dead. Do you understand me?"

The frightened girl's eyes spoke volumes.

"Is he in there?"

She nodded.

"Is he alone?"

Again, she nodded.

Lil Nut made the girl walk in front of him and lead him into the house. She kept walking through the house until Lil Nut saw Blue Bug sprawled out in his king-sized bed, naked, sipping on a Guinness Stout beer. You could tell that they had just finished fucking. The smell of sex was still lingering in the air. Lil Nut was disgusted that he had the audacity to send the beautiful female outside in the frigid cold to check on his car.

Everything happened fast. Blue Bug looked up to address his female companion and saw Lil Nut instead. In one swift movement Blue Bug tried to go for his gun, but he didn't have a chance. Lil Nut emptied four bullets into his head, neck, and chest. The young girl began begging for her life.

Lil Nut shoved her to the ground and retreated out of the house. Once outside he hugged the shadows again, walking briskly back to the getaway car. He kept thinking of all the things he wanted to say to Blue Bug before he put him to sleep, but it all happened too quickly. The one thing he was glad about was that Blue Bug knew exactly who sent him to meet his maker and why.

"Let's go!" Lil Nut said when he got in the car.

"You did it?" Princess asked.

"Just get the fuck out of here."

Princess began to laugh hysterically. "You one bad motherfucker! When you gonna stop letting people call you Lil Nut? Your crazy, bold ass should just start going by Nut."

ುಌ

That night Lil Nut paid Princess her money and slept peacefully back at home in his mother's house, in his own bed. The next morning his aunt called and told him that Samantha had been burning up the phone lines calling every second of the day looking for him. Lil Nut no longer wanted to be bothered with her. He knew that if he kept her around, she would hold the three murders over his head for life, and as far as he was concerned, he wanted to leave the past in the past.

ↄ◌ↄ

As the preacher said the eulogy for his father, Lil Nut was consumed with grief. Ironically, his two former friends were being laid to rest on the same day as his father. The whole neighborhood was grieving, each in their own way. Lil Nut had bought his father an expensive navy blue suit with a baby blue tie for his burial. He tried to convince himself that his father was in a better place, a place where he could get high all day and not be judged. He still couldn't swallow how dirty Blue Bug did his father, but he did what he had to do. At his wake, he asked that he have a few minutes alone with his father and he really poured out his heart.

"Pops, I really miss you, man. What am I gonna do without your words of wisdom? Do I really have what it takes?" Lil Nut's tears streamed down his cheeks and landed on the sleeve of his father's suit jacket. "I did that, man. I rocked all those niggas to sleep for hurting you and Ma. I'm just sorry that it took me so long, but I feel like I've grown up overnight. I'm a man now. If not in age, then mentally. I promise I'ma make you proud of me and hold down the fort."

When they lowered his father into his grave and began to throw dirt on top of his casket, his mother lost it. She began screaming and hollering, and Lil Nut had to physically restrain her. If he'd let her go she would have jumped on top of the casket to be with her husband. He realized that his father was the only man his mother had known, and it was going to be hard letting him go.

When they got back from the funeral and the limousine dropped them off in front of their building, he bumped into Lamiek's sister, Katina. He went to give her his condolences and she just glared at him. Lil Nut shrugged it off. He didn't give a fuck whether she knew the truth. Her brother had lived by the gun, and he died by the gun. Lamiek was a grimy dude who always had one foot in the grave anyway. Lil Nut just reasoned that he had to give him a little push. Shit, that was what friends were for.

ನ಄ೞ

In the next few weeks as the weather broke, the city formed a task force to combat all the violence that the crack wars were bringing. The mayor of New York got on television to boast about TNT, a covert operation that was supposed to regulate all the drug activity in the urban neighborhoods. Within one week, they had the hood under siege. The TNT squad jumped out of undercover vans, sprayed unsuspecting drug dealers with mace, and threw them into the paddy wagons, hauling the busload of individuals to jail.

Lil Nut realized that he had to change up his operation, and quickly. He'd managed to stay above the law, and he wanted to keep it that way.

One day a few weeks after Lil Nut had returned home, he overheard his mother on the phone with his aunt.

"You mean to tell me that that girl is still calling over there for my son? Now what on earth did that boy do to her? He must have bust her cherry . . ." Julie said.

Lil Nut chuckled at his mother and his aunt with their little gossip conversations. He knew that his life was the only excitement that they both had at the moment. Briefly he thought about Samantha and what they had shared. He wondered if he ever felt anything real for her. He sure hadn't thought about her in the past four weeks since she blew up on him over the phone. But he did have a lot on his mind. He thought about calling her just to catch up. Maybe she could come over and give him some sex.

He waited until his mother got off the phone and then called Samantha. Her father answered the phone.

"May I speak with Samantha, please?"

"Who may I say is calling?"

Lil Nut hesitated for a moment. "This is Nelson."

"Sure, hold on a moment."

Lil Nut could hear her father calling her to the phone. Finally she picked up.

"Hello?"

"Hey, what's up, ma?"

"Lil Nut?"

"Who you think it is?"

She sucked her teeth. "Where have you been?"

"I've been busy."

"Too busy to call me?"

"I'm calling you now."

"You know what I'm talking about. I've been calling you for weeks, and I know your aunt gave you all my messages. After all I've done for you, this is the thanks I get?"

There she goes again, Lil Nut thought. He was right to think they wouldn't work out.

"I thought I did thank you, but if I didn't, thanks. Look, I gotta go—"

"Wait—"

"Nah, I'm busy. I promise I'll call you back," Lil Nut lied.

Samantha began to panic. She knew she'd fucked up and had to think of something.

"Don't hang up before I tell you what I know."

"Know about what?"

She lowered her voice. "GG's been calling me like crazy trying to get me to go over to her house."

"So?"

"So, I can't go over there after you did what you did."

"Why the fuck not? Ain't y'all friends?"

"I helped you murder her boyfriend."

"She doesn't know that unless you told her."

"I didn't tell her shit, but of course she knows. She ain't stupid."

"Weren't you the one who told me she was!"

"I never said she was stupid. I just said that I wasn't stupid."

"Are you telling me that you haven't gone to visit her since her man got murked?"

"Nope."

"Well if she didn't know for sure that you were involved, she knows now. How fucking stupid of you, Ms. Smarty Pants. You were supposed to play it cool. What else is she going to think?"

"Well if you would have called me back you could have told me what to do. I never took the class, How to Behave After You Set Up a Person To Get Murdered 101."

Lil Nut couldn't take her stupidity a moment longer. Inside he was angered and boiling over. Had she been a dude, he would have smashed all of her teeth out. But she was a girl and he didn't hit women. He spoke with her a little while longer and then she finally let him get off the phone. He vowed never to call her again, and prayed that she kept her mouth shut. She was definitely a loose canon.

ɔ୧

It wasn't the headline that caught his attention in the *Daily News*, but the picture that stopped him dead in his tracks. Each morning Lil Nut had a routine of walking to the corner store and buying the *Daily News* and a small hot chocolate. As he flipped through the pages he saw a picture of Samantha, and it wasn't a good article. Apparently her murder was under investigation. Her body was found in the vestibule of her Harlem apartment building with two bullets to the back of the head, and one bullet in her face. After she was shot, the person or persons turned her over and shot her in the face. The police suspected that it was personal. She still had on her jewelry and her purse was still there. The perpetrator had wanted to leave a message.

Lil Nut closed the paper and knew the message. It was from GG and her brother, Chris. GG wasn't going to let go that Samantha had her man murdered. Lil Nut felt bad. He should have protected her, but he didn't. He thought about going after GG and her brother for revenge, but he was tired of revenge killing. He needed to concentrate on making money. And the more bodies that piled up, the tougher the city would be on crime. Soon no one would be allowed to eat if the murder rate didn't decline.

As he walked slowly back to his apartment, he decided that he wouldn't go see her laid to rest, but he did plan on sending a bleeding heart to the funeral home in hopes of paying his respects. Admittedly, this had definitely been a difficult two years. Now he could finally look forward to his future in the crack game.

"Know you heard this before; never get high, on your own supply."

—"Ten Crack Commandments," Notorious B.I.G.

1987

The bass from the boom box radio that sat atop a milk crate spit vibrations through the air. It was the summer of '87, and the weather was in the low eighties.

The new joint from Eric B. and Rakim blared from the speakers.

"This joint is ill right here!" Butter said. He'd finally been released from juvenile detention and Lil Nut had convinced him that it was better to make money instead of taking money. He bobbed his head hard to the beat of the rap that Rakim was spitting.

Butter, Fatman, and Lil Nut all stood on Rockaway and Pitkin Avenue. The Ave was busy since most were en route to and from their destinations. But Lil Nut and his crew were out there to sell crack.

The crew all bobbed their heads and rapped along with Rakim.

"That shit is sick right there!" Butter was amped. Eric B. and Rakim were his favorite rap duo. "I'm saying, can't nobody get with them!" Butter continued to boast.

"You crazy as hell!" Fatman stepped up. "KRS One got that hands down."

"What you been drinking? Lighter fluid? KRS One ain't even in the same category as Rakim," Butter defended.

"Naw, homeboy, I'm telling you," Fatman countered.

Fatman wasn't fat at all. He'd acquired the name when he was just a baby from his mother. He was a fat baby, so the name stuck.

Lil Nut looked over at the pair. Sitting on top of his broad nose was a pair of Cazal's with the glass missing from the frames. You could see his gorgeous, expressive eyes sitting behind the frames. He sported a bubble Kangol hat.

He raised his now five-feet-ten-inch frame from the milk crate he had been sitting on. "Yo, y'all niggas kill that noise and get that dough," he spit at the two.

Butter and Fatman simply looked at each other and walked over to the corner. As soon as they did several customers approached them and they began to do business.

Lil Nut looked up the street and his eyes narrowed as he squinted, trying to see who was approaching.

As the figure got closer he realized it was his new partner, Fuquan. Fuquan and Lil Nut had been friends since day one, but he had moved away a few years back to live with his father. He'd recently moved back into the neighborhood, and he and Lil Nut linked back up.

Since Fuquan came back, Lil Nut made him his partner in the booming crack business and they shared revenue. Lil Nut needed somebody watching his back, considering all the drama he'd recently been through. Last year was a trying time for him. His father was murdered and he had to kill his two former friends, Lamiek and Lite, and also his former boss, Blue Bug. Anybody who was somebody was big time when slinging rock cocaine. However, Lil Nut and his crew were young, small timers, and after he'd given most of his money to Princess, he was really just starting all over. But crack was such a popular drug that anybody who wanted to make a dollar was able to because it was enough bread on the streets for everybody to eat.

Fuquan was all about the paper, and Lil Nut had the brains and the muscle to complete a perfect partnership.

"What's happening?" Fuquan shouted at Butter and Fatman, giving them both pounds and moving toward Lil Nut. "What's up?" He gave his good friend a handshake.

"Yo, you ever find that package?" Lil Nut asked Fuquan.

"Naw, man, I'm telling you my brother got me for it," Fuquan responded.

The package Lil Nut was referring to was the work that Fuquan was holding in his room. It came up missing and Fuquan didn't know what had happened to it. It was no secret that Fuquan's older brother was a hardcore addict, and he had stolen from the house before.

"So what you gonna do?" Lil Nut asked.

"What you mean?" Fuquan asked.

"About the dough we lost." Lil Nut looked at him square in the eyes.

"Man, I ain't fucking with Red like that." Fuquan was serious.

He feared his brother, and so did just about everybody in the Brownsville section of Brooklyn. His brother was out of control. He was considered a crack monster.

"If you ain't gonna say nothing, then I will," Lil Nut said.

"That's on you, homeboy. I ain't fucking with Red like that. And you of all people know better than to fuck with him too." Fuquan pointed at Lil Nut.

"You scared of him, but I ain't," Lil Nut said, plain and simple.

Fuquan was about to respond when someone called his name.

"Fu!" A crackhead walked up on them.

Fuquan turned around and looked the man up and down.

"I need three nicks, man," the fiend with white, ashy lips said.

"See the boys over there." Fuquan pointed to the others on the corner serving several other addicts. "Damn, that shit got niggas foaming at the mouth," Fuquan said and laughed after the man walked away.

"Yeah, man, them cats beam up to Scotty every day, all day," Lil Nut added.

"Beam me up, Scotty. Take me away!" Fuquan joked.

Lil Nut laughed at him while he walked over to a parked car and leaned against it.

"This is where it's at, Nut," Fuquan yelled. "Word up! Ain't noting but cheddar out this bitch, and I'ma rat waiting to get a piece of that cheese!" Fuquan yelled with his arms spread apart. Lil Nut laughed at his friend.

"Hey, Nut." A brown skinned girl waved to him as she walked by.

"C'mere," he said. He licked his full lips and smiled a perfect white smile.

She was walking with her friend, who followed her over to Lil Nut.

"What, y'all don't see me?" Fuquan asked in a jealous manner, because the girls walked by him without speaking.

Both girls looked at him, sucked their teeth, and rolled their eyes.

"Well fuck y'all then!"

"Yo! Don't disrespect the ladies like that! What the fuck is wrong witchu?" Lil Nut raised himself off the car, heated. He hated for any man to disrespect a female, especially in his presence. He had no tolerance for that.

He ice grilled Fuquan with hatred.

"A'ight man, damn!" Fuquan knew not to push the issue any further, so he walked over to the others.

"How you doing, Nut?" Sherri, the brown-skinned young lady asked.

She had a petite frame that had developed nicely. Her sandy colored hair was in a French roll that went around her whole head. She wore door knocker earrings and a small gold rope chain. Her friend was a little taller and much thinner. She was darker, and she wore her hair in corn-rows to the back with beads at the ends.

Lil Nut was still ice grilling Fuquan when Sherri spoke to him again.

"Nut?"

He looked at her and the evil look disappeared from his face. He smiled at her and grabbed her hand. He leaned back on the car and pulled her a little closer to him.

"How you doing, Sherri?"

"I'm good." She blushed.

He spoke to the other young lady. "How you doing, Pam?"

"Hey, Lil Nut." She waved.

"What y'all getting into?" He looked back and forth between the two of them.

"Nothing. We was just gonna go down to the store and get some red Blow Pops."

"Here." He reached into his pocket and pulled out a small knot. He peeled off a ten-dollar bill and handed it to Sherri. "Get whatever y'all want and keep the change."

"Thanks, Nut. You so sweet." She took the money, smiling, but he held on to her hand. She continued to smile.

"Lil Nut, you always take care of us. Thanks," Pam said.

It was true. All the girls loved Lil Nut. Older women adored him as well. He was very respectful to women of all ages.

Sherri kissed him on the cheek.

"Where you gonna be later?" he whispered in her ear.

"I'll be 'round the way," she said, referring to the area where she lived.

"A'ight I'll see you later," he winked at her, still holding onto her hand.

"Thanks for looking out for us, Nut. I know Fu is your boy, but I can't stand him." Sherri frowned.

"If any nigga ever diss y'all, just let me know. I'll put him on his ass," Lil Nut said and meant it.

Just then shots rang out down the street from where they were standing.

"Get outta here, ladies. I'll see you later," Lil Nut said, letting Sherri's hand go and shooing the girls to safety. They didn't hesitate to make their way down the street away from the gunfire.

A rail thin man in a pair of dirty jeans was running for his life. The man chasing him was dressed in a black Adidas jogging suit with a red double stripe going down the legs and arms of the suit. He held on to his three huge rope chains with one hand while he popped off shots with the other hand. The man in the jeans was shot in the leg and limped badly, but he still managed to out run his hunter.

"Oh shit! That nigga finally got caught!" Butter yelled.

"Bust that ass!" Fatman added.

"Yo, ain't that Sticky?" Fuquan squinted to see as he walked back over to Lil Nut.

"Hell, yeah, that's his dumb ass. Somebody finally got with that nigga," Lil Nut said.

No one on the street ran from the scene. Instead everyone watched, waiting to see a murder.

Sticky acquired his name because he was a master thief. He would take anything he could get his hands on. Sticky Fingers was his original name, which was ultimately shortened to Sticky. He was the worst kind of thief, because he was a crackhead.

Three more shots were fired at Sticky, all missing.

"That nigga can't shoot!" Fuquan said.

"Give me the hammer. I'll bust a cap in his ass!" Butter shouted at the trigger man, who whizzed past them.

Sticky dipped in between oncoming cars, allowing him to escape the shooter and certain death.

The onlookers clowned the gunman while he made his way back in the direction from which he came. The look on his face told them that he was pissed.

"Yo, how much he get you for?" Lil Nut shouted to the gunman.

"One cap," the gunman shouted back, out of breath.

"You chased that nigga for one cap?" Lil Nut screwed his face.

"Fuck you, man! Sticky is a dead man next time I see him," he shot back.

Lil Nut laughed and the rest joined in.

"Oh, so you think the shit is funny?" The gunman made a sudden stop, turned around, and headed toward the corner where Lil Nut and the others stood. He was ready to take his frustrations out on the young boys, mainly because he was embarrassed that he didn't catch his target. But what he didn't know was that Lil Nut and his crew weren't your average young boys.

Sensing an altercation, Butter and Fatman walked over to their boys to act as backup.

Lil Nut began to approach the gunman while placing a hand on the butt of his weapon, which he carried in the waistband of his jeans. He gripped the handle.

"What's up?" Lil Nut asked with confidence showing on his face. "You don't want it." He challenged the man.

"You must be high. You don't know who the fuck I am?" the gunman asked.

"I don't give a fuck who you are," Lil Nut spat. "But what I do know is, you must be dumb as shit to let Sticky get you."

The gunman stopped short several feet in front of the crew. Although he had a weapon, he could see that Lil Nut had a gun too, and he didn't know what his boys had. Staying at that distance would give the gunman the leverage and the jump on them if he had to pull out his gun.

"Oh, so you got a slick mouth?" The gunman smirked at Lil Nut, looking him up and down. He opened up his Adidas suit jacket and postured. "So you think you big shit, standing there with your fake-ass gold rope chain." He laughed.

"Naw, nigga, ain't nothing fake 'bout my shit. You the one frontin' like you big time, chasing Sticky down the street for one cap, wild'n out shooting, and ain't hittin' shit!" The crew burst into laughter. "Talking 'bout fake, I see you copped you one of them fake-ass Izod shirts, 'cause ya horse only got three legs."

His boys burst into more laughter. The nosey bystanders had eased their way over to see the show, and they were laughing right along with Lil Nut's boys. This pissed off the gunman.

"I see I'ma have to teach yo' young ass a little lesson, 'cause you obviously don't know who you fucking with," he threatened. He looked over at Butter and recognized him. "Ask ya man. He know me." He pointed to Butter.

"Like I said, I don't give a fuck who you are, and as far as teaching me a lesson, think again. 'Cause I ain't the one to be taught by some wannabe," Lil Nut assured him. "The only man who could teach me shit is six feet under."

"Tell him who I am, Butter," the gunman instructed, not letting Lil Nut's last statement offend him.

"Yo, Nut, man, that's Prodigy. He work for Snookie," Butter

whispered to him.

Lil Nut didn't move a muscle. He continued to grip the gun tightly while he clenched his jaw. He knew who Snookie was. Hell, who didn't? Lil Nut had idolized Snookie when he was much younger. His name was well known in Brooklyn. Lil Nut had heard a lot about him from the older cats in the projects when they sat around and told stories of the pull Snookie had. Not to mention all the police he had on his payroll from the Dirty Seventy-three cops stationed at East New York Ave.

But what Prodigy didn't know about Lil Nut was once the beast inside him was triggered, it didn't matter if Malcolm X himself tried to stop him, he did whatever he had to do, by any means necessary.

"Did I ask you who this clown worked for?" He scowled at Butter. He looked back at Prodigy.

Prodigy looked at the young man and then began to laugh. "Yeah, a'ight kid, I'ma let you slide on this one. Learn to respect your elders," he said and began to walk away, thinking he was sparing Lil Nut's life.

"Show me some respect and you might just get some!" Lil Nut yelled out after him.

"Go fuck ya mother, young boy!" Prodigy kept walking and never looked back.

Prodigy heard the sound, but before he could turn around to see what happened, he felt the heat and then the unbearable burning sensation in his back. He stood there, not able to move. The muscles in his legs began to feel light as a feather, and he could no longer hold his body upright. The pain in his back became more severe by the second. He realized he was shot because he could smell burning flesh, and he could feel the wetness of blood running down his back.

The onlookers all had looks of shock on their faces as they stared at Prodigy. He went down on his knees hard. He felt his knee caps crack when he hit the cement ground, but he didn't feel the pain because his focus was on the pain in his back. It felt like he was on fire. His vision became blurred. He placed his hands on the ground, trying to keep himself from falling farther.

"Oh, shit! Did you see that shit!" someone yelled.

"Yo, that little nigga is ruthless!" another yelled.

"Yo, come on, Nut, let's roll out." Fuquan tried to motivate his friend to move.

Lil Nut stood there, staring at Prodigy, waiting for him to die.

Butter and Fuquan both grabbed Lil Nut by the arm and practically dragged him away from the scene.

Prodigy finally fell face-first to the ground, no longer able to remain conscious. A male fiend slowly approached Prodigy's body. He quickly began to search his pockets and pulled out a knot. This made another male fiend run over and assist with the search.

Two young boys ran over and began to remove his jewelry. The fiends began to protest and an argument broke out. Someone called the cops because a patrol car blared up the street, and the robbers scattered like roaches when the light was turned on.

Lil Nut stayed in the house for a week after the very public murder. He was lying low as a precaution, and at Fuquan's request. Everyone out there that day knew he shot Prodigy. The crew wasn't taking any chances on Snookie coming after Lil Nut. But Lil Nut didn't care. He feared no one. He'd already been to war and came out on top. This shit was lightweight to him.

As the days passed, Lil Nut began to go crazy sitting up in the crib doing nothing. Although he loved the streets and the hustle, he was actually very book smart. While lying low, he read every book in the house at least twice. He read the newspaper every day from front to back, and played every vinyl record his mother owned, and every cassette he had.

Lil Nut was eating Cap'n Crunch cereal out of a mixing bowl when someone knocked on the door. He put the last spoonful in his mouth and walked over to the door. He looked out the peephole and then removed the chain, unlocking the top and bottom locks. He pulled the door open to see his boy Fatman standing there.

"What up?" Fatman asked, slapping hands with Lil Nut.

"What up?" Lil Nut asked with a mouth full of cereal.

Fatman walked in and locked the door. Lil Nut was already back at the kitchen table when Fatman walked into the kitchen.

"What's buzzing on the streets, man?" Lil Nut asked.

"Yo, man, your name is ringing out, man. I'm saying, nobody popping shit 'bout what happened. They saying some respect shit 'bout you," Fatman said with admiration.

"Like what?" Lil Nut asked. He put the bowl up to his mouth and drank the milk, making slurping noises.

Fatman walked over to the refrigerator and opened it.

"You don't live here, nigga," Lil Nut said with milk covering his top lip.

"I'm saying, I'm thirsty and shit. It's hot as hell outside."

"So what? Ask first." Lil Nut continued to slurp the milk from the bowl.

Fatman ignored him and removed the pitcher of Kool-Aid from the refrigerator.

"What they saying about me?" Lil Nut asked again.

"Oh, yeah, they saying you a bold motherfucker to fuck with one of Snookie's boys." Fatman drank the glass of Kool-Aid he had poured.

Lil Nut sat back in the chair and burped loudly.

"And peep this, Snookie ain't even gonna come for you, 'cause word is he was gonna do Prodigy anyway, because he was always fucking up the work." Fatman poured another glass of Kool-Aid. "And check this shit out, word is Prodigy was getting high smoking up the work and then blaming it on other niggas, saying somebody stole the stash and shit like that."

"Niggas is stupid. I'm telling you, if you want to last in this business, you can't be getting high on your own supply," Lil Nut schooled him.

"Word, I hear you."

"I heard a lot of cats who started out making dough, and then the next thing you know you see them in a dope nod off they own shit. Then the next time you see them, they fell off and now they're a fiend." Lil Nut shook his head.

"Yeah, well the way I see it, you did Snookie a favor," Fatman said.

"Cool, so I'ma come back out today." Lil Nut was pleased to hear the good news.

"Fuquan told me to tell you to sit tight for like another couple of days."

"Fuck that! I don't answer to Fu!" Lil Nut put the bowl and spoon in the sink. "Where that nigga at anyway? He ain't been through to see me yet." He turned to look at Fatman.

"That's what I came over to tell you. I ain't seen him in a couple days. After the last package I came and got from you, I went to go get the bread from him, and he said he ain't have it, so I bounced."

"So what he been doing?" Lil Nut was now curious.

"I dunno, man. I went by there before I came over here and he ain't even answering the door."

"He ain't out clockin'?"

"I ain't see him. I ain't gonna lie, I really ain't look for him like that. But I know he wasn't at the spot." Fatman shrugged his shoulders.

Lil Nut stood there leaning against the counter with his arms folded across his chest. He was in deep thought. It wasn't like Fuquan to just disappear like that.

"Where Butter at?"

"Butter around. I got his bread right here with mine. We both sold out."

"A'ight, I'ma throw on my shit, and we gonna go see what's up with Fu," he said, walking out of the kitchen.

Fatman helped himself to another glass of Kool-Aid while he waited for Lil Nut to get dressed.

ᔕᑫ

Lil Nut, Fatman, and Butter walked up into the Howard projects. They were on their way to Fuquan's apartment when Lil Nut saw a commotion taking place. A man was beating the shit out of his girlfriend right in the middle of the courtyard. Lil Nut stopped in his tracks and looked. Butter and Fatman also looked in the direction of the commotion.

"Damn, he whooping her ass," Butter said.

Lil Nut began to walk toward the couple.

"Yo, Nut, where you going, man?" Fatman called out after him.

"Aw, damn, this nigga 'bout to get into some shit. Damn! Come on, Fatman," Butter beckoned as he went after Lil Nut.

Butter caught up to him and grabbed him by the arm. "Come on, Nut, this ain't got nothing to do with you. Just leave it alone. They just a couple of fiends. They gonna be back together as soon as they get some get-high anyway."

Lil Nut snatched his arm from Butter's grip with force.

Butter knew it was a wrap, so he did what any friend would do. He prepared himself to have his boy's back.

Lil Nut wasted no time once he reached the quarrelling couple. The man had knocked the woman to the ground and was stomping out her guts. The woman lay in the fetal position trying to cover her head and face from the forceful blows.

Lil Nut grabbed his gun and pulled it out. He charged the man and clocked him on the back of the head with the butt end of the gun. The man's head split in the spot he received the blow. He instantly threw up his hand to touch his head. He turned around just in time for Lil Nut to crack him in the forehead with the gun. The male fiend stumbled, almost falling to the ground. He tried to stand straight, but he swayed badly. He was dizzy and practically dead on his feet. Finally he fell to the ground hard before Lil Nut could hit him again. The injured man rolled back and forth on the ground in pain.

Lil Nut began to stomp him in the face, stomach, and back. Whatever way the man rolled, Lil Nut was on him, stomping him. He was like a maniac. He was so focused that he didn't even hear the female fiend screaming and hollering for Lil Nut to stop. He was in such a raging trance that he didn't even realize the man was no longer moving. He hadn't even noticed that a crowd had gathered.

"Ain't that the young cat that offed Prodigy?" someone asked.

"Yeah, that's him. That nigga is crazy."

Lil Nut didn't notice this, but his friends did and they felt uncomfortable.

Butter and Fatman charged Lil Nut, getting him off the man. They dragged him away from the horrible bloodbath he'd created.

Lil Nut yanked himself from the grip of his two friends and began to walk on his own. He breathed deeply. Blood covered his hand, the gun he still held, and his Nike sneakers.

Butter and Fatman knew they had to get Lil Nut out of there, and they had to do it fast. Once inside the building, they headed for the elevator.

"Yo, that shit was crazy. What's up with you, Nut?" Butter asked.

"Fuck you mean, what's up with me? You for real? Y'all niggas better chill on stopping me from handling my business. I swear one of y'all gonna catch a hot one one day. And that's my word." Lil Nut's adrenaline was still working overtime.

"It's like this, Nut, we ya boys, and we got ya back. But if you just gonna be wild'n out on motherfuckers just on a whim, then we gotta do what we need to do to getchu up outta sticky situations. Nah-mean?" Butter asked.

"Word up," Fatman cosigned.

Lil Nut stood there staring at his two friends. He understood where they were coming from. It didn't dawn on him before that moment that the actions he took could affect everyone around him. But he couldn't control the beast that lay within him. It had always been like that. His crazy, unpredictable acts were how he got his name.

"Good looking out," he said sincerely, giving his two friends a pound and a hug.

Lil Nut pushed the button for the elevator. They stepped into the elevator and pushed the button for Fuquan's floor.

"Look at my shit!" Lil Nut said, getting mad all over again after seeing his ruined gear. He lifted one Nike sneaker slightly off the elevator floor to get a better look at the damage. "Damn!"

"And them a fresh pair too. You just got them shits the other day," Fatman added.

"Word! Fuck!" Lil Nut hit the elevator wall with his fist, leaving a bloody print behind. "I got that crackhead's blood all over my hands and shit." He looked at his hands and arms while still holding the gun.

"Yo, man, give me that," Butter said, noticing the gun. "You still holding the hammer?"

"Man, I'ma have to get a fucking rabies shot." Lil Nut continued to vent, ignoring Butter's request to conceal the weapon.

The bell rang in the elevator, indicating that the floor requested had been reached. When the doors opened two teen girls stood there in their short shorts and tank tops, sucking on apple Jolly Ranchers candy sticks.

"Hey, Nut," they both sang as if in a love trance.

"Ladies, how y'all doing?" Lil Nut's smile appeared out of nowhere. He poured on the charm as they stepped off of the elevator.

"What happened? Are you all right?" one of the girls asked. The girls were suddenly alarmed when they noticed the blood on Lil Nut and the gun he held. They both approached him and examined him as if they where physicians.

Butter and Fatman simply leaned up against the wall in amazement. Just a few seconds ago Lil Nut was ready to whoop some more ass, and now he looked like the Don Juan of the ghetto.

"I'm good, ladies. I had to open up a can of whoop ass on this nigga. It's his blood, not mine."

"Oh, good." They both sighed with relief.

Both the girls continued to flirt with Lil Nut. Even with all the blood he had on him, they were still attracted to him, especially since he was still holding the gun in his hands.

Butter and Fatman stood there in envy. They had to work hard to get some play from the females, but Lil Nut didn't.

"Uh, excuse me, ladies, but we have to get the king cleaned up, a'ight?" Butter interrupted the overly dramatic scene.

"OK, Nut, where you on your way to?" one of the girls asked. "You headed to Fu's house?"

"Yeah, you seen him?" Lil Nut asked.

"Yeah, he just went into the apartment not too long ago."

"A'ight, thanks, y'all," Fatman said and started to walk toward

Fuquan's apartment down the hall.

"Yeah, good looking," Butter yelled over his shoulder as he followed Fatman.

"A'ight, ladies, I'll see y'all later?" Lil Nut asked.

"No doubt, Lil Nut. We'll be around," one of the girls said.

Lil Nut backpedaled down the hall, checking out the girls' asses as they waited for the elevator to return.

Once at Fuquan's door, Butter and Fatman waited for Lil Nut to get there before they rang the bell.

Lil Nut gave a nod to Fatman to ring the bell. He pushed the bell and it sounded off more like a buzzer. Lil Nut made a gesture for them to step to either side of the door, so if someone looked out of the peephole they wouldn't be seen.

Butter and Fatman had no idea why they were doing this. They just followed Lil Nut's lead. Lil Nut did this out of natural instinct. There was something about the way Fuquan had been missing, and then coming up empty with the re-up money on more than one occasion that made Lil Nut suspicious. Not to mention the fact that no one could catch up to him but the girls in the hallway had just seen him. Lil Nut thought about all of these things, and decided to be on the defensive out of pure street instinct.

"Who is it?" Fuquan shouted when he didn't see anyone through the peephole.

"It's Nut," he said, stepping into view so that Fuquan could see him through the peephole.

Fuquan opened the door to let them all inside.

"What's up, my niggas!" he shouted, giving everybody a pound as they walked in, all except Lil Nut, who brought up the rear. "What the fuck happened to you?" Fuquan twisted up his face at Nut's appearance.

"Man, you don't want to know," Fatman said as he plopped down onto the sofa. Butter followed behind him and sat on the same sofa.

"Yo, you got some shit I could change into? I need to change my clothes and get this blood off me," Lil Nut said, walking past Fuquan while looking him up and down. Lil Nut and Fuquan were about the same size and wore the same size sneakers.

"Yeah, I got something you could throw on. Why you holding that gat?"

"'Cause I need to wipe it off first."

"What happened?" Fuquan's face showed concern.

He looked at the three of them for answers. No one said a word. Butter and Fatman didn't say anything because they were waiting for Lil Nut to speak first.

"Nothing, man. I had to stomp this nigga out in the court over this chick—"

Fuquan cut him off. "Wait, let me guess, he disrespected her," Fuquan said, laughing.

"And you know it," Butter added.

"Naw, he put his hands on her." Lil Nut's eyes narrowed at the slickness of Fuquan's tongue. Any other time he would have joked with Fuquan about his smart-aleck ways, but today was a different day. Lil Nut was having a hard time figuring out where the other half of their money was, and he wanted answers from Fuquan.

"It figures," Fuquan said, no longer making eye contact with Lil Nut. He walked away. "Come on, I'ma get you some fresh gear and a washcloth." He left the room.

"If this nigga ain't got the bread or the product, I'ma beat his ass down too," Lil Nut said to Fatman and Butter. Unfortunately for Fuquan, he meant every word.

"Come on, man, that's our boy. You can't do that," Butter whispered to Lil Nut.

"The fuck I can't. This is business." Lil Nut left the room.

Butter and Fatman looked at each other and shook their heads.

Lil Nut walked into Fuquan's room. Fuquan was in the closet searching for some fresh gear for Lil Nut to borrow. He pulled out a pair of Lee jeans and a Nike T-shirt, and laid them on the bed. Lil Nut stood there stone faced.

"Yo, Fu, Fatman said you ain't got your cut for the re-up."

"I don't. I was gonna come by your crib and tell you. My brother got me again for the shit. I know he did this time, because he took the whole shoebox," Fuquan said as he went to look for a pair of sneakers for Lil Nut to put on. Fuquan had one whole wall lined with sneakers. He tossed Lil Nut a pair of Adidas with shell toes. The sneakers landed next to Lil Nut's foot.

"I let that shit go the first time, and I even took your advice and didn't say anything to Red. But I ain't about to take another loss, and you walking around here like everything is gravy. I hold you responsible for that shit." Lil Nut pointed his finger at Fuquan.

Fuquan was squatting down looking at the sneakers, but quickly stood upright at Lil Nut's statement. "Me? How you figure?" Fuquan walked toward Lil Nut with a serious face.

"How I figure? You are responsible for your half, and this is the second time we lost out on money."

"Yo, we a team. There ain't no I in team. If the team loses, it's a *team* loss," Fuquan said.

"Naw, man, you lose. 'Cause you the only one who keep fucking up."

"How you figure I'm fucking up? My brother keep lifting our shit. What the fuck am I supposed to do?"

Lil Nut stood there staring at him as if trying to see through to his soul. He contemplated what Fu had said, and he thought about how he might be overreacting. Fuquan was his boy, and had been his boy since childhood. Lil Nut knew how Red was. Red was no joke.

"A'ight, man, it's cool. From now on I'm just gonna keep all the shit at my crib," Lil Nut said.

Fuquan breathed a sigh of relief. "Yo, man, you had me thinking I took the shit. I mean I got some of the loot, but not much. But I got something." He tried to make light of the situation.

"Naw, that's a'ight, you keep that. We starting fresh. I'ma let Fatman and Butter rock for a while. You take a break."

"It's whatever, man. I'm wit' it," Fuquan said.

"A'ight, let me get a washcloth so I can get this shit off me," Lil Nut said.

"I gotchu," Fuquan said and walked toward the bedroom door. He stopped and turned around. "Yo, man, thanks, man. We boys for life," he said and walked out.

୨୦୧

Three days later Lil Nut sat on a bench in the courtyard of the Langston Hughes housing projects, where he now lived. He and his moms had moved off of Pitkin Avenue after his father was murdered behind the apartment building. It was just too much for both of them to live with.

While Lil Nut waited for Butter and Fatman to come through with the re-up, he read the latest issue of the *Wall Street Journal*. He had picked up the paper earlier that day when he went to the corner store. The wind was blowing a little harder than normal, but the breeze felt good. Every now and then he looked up, observing his surroundings. Several residents walked by and he acknowledged them with a head nod or a handshake.

He folded the paper and unscrewed the top to a bottle of orange soda. After taking a deep gulp, he burped loudly, then set the bottle back on the bench. He adjusted the two guns he carried—one in the front waistband of his jeans, and the other in the small of his back.

Lil Nut had been thinking about the conversation he and Fuquan had that day in Fuquan's room. He had been thinking long and hard. That was the type of person he was. He analyzed everything. He would pick apart a situation, bit by bit, until he came up with a sensible solution.

He thought about the past mishaps with Fuquan, and the conversations he'd heard on the streets for the past two days. He told Fuquan that he wasn't going to say anything to Red, but after thinking it over, Lil Nut decided to step to Red anyway without Fuquan's knowledge. His plan was to find Red after the fellas came back with the work and he got them situated. However, opportunity knocked on his door sooner than expected. He spotted Red on the other side of the courtyard purchasing drugs from another local dealer.

Lil Nut sat and watched the transaction, and then his eyes followed Red until he disappeared into one of the buildings. Lil Nut looked at his beeper to check the time, contemplating whether he should leave or stay put. He had told Fatman and Butter that he would meet them where he now sat waiting.

Lil Nut hadn't seen Fuquan since that day in his apartment. He wasn't worried too much about that, though, because he now held all the product and money. He just figured Fuquan was still feeling some kind of a way because of the way Lil Nut came at him.

After a few more minutes of thought, Lil Nut got up from the bench. He grabbed the newspaper and the soda bottle. He dropped them both into the garbage can as he walked by it. He was heading in the direction in which Red had gone.

Tim, the dealer who Red bought the product from, was still standing in the same spot he'd been in when Red had approached him.

"Tim," Lil Nut called.

Tim turned around, saw Nut, and threw up his fist in acknowledgement.

"C'mere, man," Lil Nut said.

"Hold up," Tim said, putting up an index finger. Tim served a customer and then placed the money in his pocket. "What's up?" he asked Lil Nut as he approached him. He shook Lil Nut's hand.

"Was that Red that copped from you?"

"Yeah, that was him. Yo, I ain't want to serve him, but he had money. I thought that big nigga was gonna try some shady shit. Feel me?"

"Yeah, I feel you."

"Ain't he ya peoples?" Tim asked, knowing that Red was Lil Nut's partner's brother.

"Yeah, he is. You know where he went?"

"Naw. All I know is he went in there." Tim pointed to the building Lil Nut had seen Red enter.

"Oh, a'ight."

"Oh, wait, hold up," Tim said before Lil Nut could walk away. "Unless he went to the hole," Tim remembered. "Them fiends be going in the basement. They call it the hole."

Lil Nut already knew what Tim was talking about. After all, he lived in those very same projects. He'd never been down in the hole, but he'd always known about it. He wondered why Red would be in the basement of one of the buildings in the projects where Nut lived in. Red didn't usually cop from there.

"Oh, a'ight, good lookin', man." Lil Nut shook Tim's hand again, thanking him before walking off toward the building.

Once inside the hallway, Lil Nut walked to the basement door and looked around. He pressed his ear up against the metal door to see if he could hear anything. When he heard nothing, he carefully pulled open the door. There was a lit light bulb hanging from the ceiling of the stairwell.

He crept down the stairs, making sure he stopped and listened after each step. As he got closer to the bottom, he could hear a lighter being flicked. He then smelled crack burning. He now knew that someone was down there smoking crack, but he didn't know who.

The basement reeked of urine. He had to pinch his nose closed to get relief from the smell. As he traveled along the basement, he made sure he stayed close to the wall, because some parts of the basement were very dark. He could hear mice squeaking as they traveled along the wall. Lil Nut kept moving. Once he reached the rear of the basement the smell of crack got stronger, and then he heard the mumble of voices. There was more than one person down there.

Lil Nut removed one of his guns and held his hand behind his back. He turned the corner, and sitting there on the floor of the basement with a glass pipe up to his lips was Fuquan. Red sat on a crate in front of Fuquan, reloading his pipe with crack. Neither of the men heard Lil Nut approach.

Lil Nut felt his blood begin to boil as he realized that his previous premonition was correct. He was heated that his boy not only had been smoking up the product, but had the nerve to do it in the basement right under Lil Nut's nose, in a building in the very projects where Nut lived. Visions of Lil Nut's father getting high off crack came flooding back and all the beef he had with his friends, Lamiek and Lite. Lil Nut felt betrayed.

Fuquan was sweating profusely as he flicked the lighter again. Lil Nut reached behind his back with his other hand and removed the gun that was concealed in the back of his waistband.

Anger invaded his whole body and he no longer saw his brother in his friend Fuquan. What he saw before him was a man who had betrayed him in the worst way. All the lies Fuquan had told him flooded his brain and infuriated him even more.

Lil Nut cocked the hammers on his guns, and the noise alerted both males to his presence.

"What's up?" Red asked. He stood, still holding the pipe in his hands. "Is you fucking crazy, sneaking up on me like that?" he asked with much bass in his voice.

Lil Nut never said a word. He continued to ice grill Fuquan with hatred. Fuquan couldn't even look his friend in the eyes. In fact, he had the nerve to reload the pipe with a rock and continued to smoke with shaking hands. Lil Nut was filled with rage and anger. Using drugs was the catalyst that had led to his father's murder. Had his pops not been getting high, he would have been on point when the wolves came after him. Milton would have never gotten caught slipping had he not been a crackhead.

"Nut? You don't hear me talking to you, little nigga?" Red bellowed with authority.

Lil Nut simply raised one of the guns and shot Red in the chest, sending him flying to the cement floor.

Fuquan almost jumped outta his skin when the shot was fired. He stood and dropped his pipe to the ground. It crashed, sending pieces of glass flying. He stood there leaning against the wall. He began to cry and plead for his life.

"Nut, man, come on, man, what are you doing?"

"What am I doing?" Lil Nut asked calmly. But it didn't take a rocket scientist to know that Lil Nut was not happy.

"Nut, it wasn't me, man. Red made me do it, man! I was stressing out. He made me do it, I swear." Fuquan cried while snot ran from his nose.

"You were supposed to be my brother. You played me out. I trusted you, and this is how you do me?"

"No, Nut! No, man! I swear it wasn't my fault! What was I supposed to do? He made me do it." Fuquan continued to cry.

"Red ain't make you suck on that glass dick, did he?"

Fuquan lowered his head.

"You were supposed to come to me like a man," Lil Nut told him. His father's advice came out as if it were his own. "Real niggas' don't ever get high on their own drug supply."

Fuquan went down to his knees and continued to beg for his life.

Hearing enough, and no longer having a heart for Fuquan, Lil Nut put a bullet in his friend's head. He then walked over to Fuquan and put two more in his face. He did the same to Red to ensure that they were both dead, and then Lil Nut walked out of the basement.

5

"Never sell no crack where you rest at, I don't care if they want a ounce, tell 'em bounce."

—"Ten Crack Commandments," Notorious B.I.G.

1988

A light mist of rain fell from the sky. It was seventy-seven degrees at eleven ten PM on a Friday night. The blacktop streets shined from the thin mist of rain that covered them. A patrol car slid and then came to a full stop. Radio dispatchers could be heard over the walkie-talkies the police carried.

Onlookers covered the street corners, trying to see what was going on. Lil Nut stood with his crew in front of Akbar's bar. All the patrons from the bar had filtered out onto the sidewalk. Some hustlers continued to conduct drug sales right under the policemen's noses.

"Damn, look at that cat in the car," a male bystander said.

"I think I'm gonna be sick," a woman said to her friend as she turned her head away from the scene.

Two bodies lay twisted in the middle of the street, and another dead body sat behind the wheel of a car. The driver's head lay on the headrest, and it was clear that his face was blown away. Nothing but blood and brain matter was visible. The medical examiners and crime scene investigators hadn't arrived yet, so nothing had been placed over the dead men's bodies to cover the gruesome sight.

"Damn, that dude ain't have a chance," another male bystander said.

"Look at the other two. They had about as much of a chance as the cat in the car," another onlooker commented.

The back of the head of one of the bodies lying on the ground was missing. His brain matter oozed onto the street. The other male had a gaping hole in his back, almost severing his torso.

More police officers arrived, along with television cameras and the news media. The police began to go into the crowd of onlookers and ask questions.

"Let's be out," Lil Nut said as if on cue. He wanted no part of the cameras or the police questioning.

Lil Nut and his crew walked off, making their way through the crowd.

"That's fucked up what happened to Devine and 'em," Butter said.

"Yeah, I bet you it was the Boogie Crew that hit them and shit," Fatman said, looking back at the scene they'd just left. "I know they're the ones that murked Fuquan and Red on some jealousy shit."

"Nigga don't you think if I thought they had something to do with my man getting murdered they wouldn't be breathing right now? Fuck the Boogie Crew. Them niggas' soft. You know I don't have a problem letting my thing go. As I told ya'll niggas last year, I think Fuquan got caught in the wrong place at the wrong time. Shit fucked up. No doubt he probably went down to the basement looking for Red and most likely got played out by some fiend," Lil Nut reasoned. He never did let his crew know he was the one who rocked Fuquan to sleep. He thought it was better this way.

"Yeah, you right," Fatman replied. "I just miss that nigga, that's all."

"We all do," Butter stated.

They were all in deep thought as they walked in silence. Their sneakers, missing the laces, clonked on the wet pavement. Crack vials lay scattered about the sidewalk. Fatman stepped on the vials, crunching them under his feet.

They knew the guys who got smoked just a few blocks back. They were all cool with each other, and had no beefs with their crew. So it kinda hit home to see them dead and disfigured.

The horn of a car sounded off and they all looked up. The window came down and Skinny Lorene stuck her head out of the passenger window.

"Hey, Nut!" she called.

Lil Nut looked over at her, but kept walking. Skinny Lorene was his aunt, his mother's other sister. He hated what she had become. She was one of the many crack addicts on the streets.

"Nut!" she called again.

The fellas all looked at Lil Nut, wondering why he wasn't responding to his aunt's calls. No one said a word, though. They just kept walking alongside and behind him.

A white man who looked to be Italian was driving the old, rusted yellow Vega that Lorene occupied. He crept alongside the crew as instructed by Lorene.

Lil Nut figured the man was probably some trick she suckered into spending his money on some get-high.

All of a sudden Lil Nut stopped walking. His boys all stopped as well. He walked over to the car, which had also stopped and idled in the street.

"Hey, baby boy, you holding?" Lorene asked.

"No, I ain't got nothing. Do me a favor, Lorene, and don't come looking for me in the streets for no drugs. I ain't got nothing," he said simply. He walked away from the car and back onto the sidewalk.

"Oh, so it's like that, huh, Nut? You got you a little money, and you think you all that?" she yelled at him.

As the crew followed behind Lil Nut, the car continued to drive alongside them, and Skinny Lorene continued to yell at Nut out of the window.

"Yeah, all right, I got your number. Nephew or not, you done fucked up!"

Lil Nut was becoming more furious by the second. His aunt was calling him out in front of his crew and a white dude he didn't know.

Lil Nut knew that Skinny Lorene was not the one to fuck with. Even before she became a crack addict, she was ruthless on the streets, always fighting or starting fights. She was of the streets and loved to brawl. After becoming addicted to crack her personality worsened. She'd always been a shit talker, but now she was worse. When Skinny Lorene needed that blast and couldn't get it, she was worse than the devil himself.

Butter tried to reason with Lil Nut. "Nut, man, come on, just serve her before she snitch on us."

Lil Nut kept walking, looking at the ground with his hands shoved into his jeans pockets. His face was twisted. What he was really thinking about doing was pulling his gun from his waistband and just doing away with his aunt and her big mouth. But Lil Nut had too much respect for women, crack addicts included. That was why all women loved him.

Skinny Lorene continued to talk shit to Lil Nut.

"Yo, man, serve her," Nut instructed no one in particular, and then disappeared into the courtyard of the projects where he lived. Fatman walked over to the car and served Skinny Lorene while Butter continued to walk with Lil Nut.

꾸

Early the next morning Lil Nut had just lain down to go to sleep. It was three AM and his body was tired. His head sank into the pillow and he could feel his body floating on the twin mattress. It felt good, and he welcomed the comfort. He was ten minutes into his dream when he heard something hit his window. He knew was dreaming, or that it was the noise from the window fan.

He opened his eyes and looked at the ceiling. He lay still, listening intently, making sure the noise was nothing more than his imagination. He was able to see a roach climbing his bedroom wall from the streetlights that shined through his window. As he watched the bug crawl, he heard the noise again. He knew he wasn't dreaming this time. He sat up in the bed and swung his feet around, placing them on the floor. All he wore were his boxers.

A thin layer of sweat covered his chocolate muscular body, making it glisten. A big keloid scar ran down the front of his chest from where a bullet from a .44 Magnum almost claimed his life. Although Lil Nut survived that night, he had his scar to remind him of it every day.

Who the fuck could this be? he wondered before standing.

He reached under his mattress and pulled out his gun before approaching his window.

Ping! Something hit the window again. He crept along the creaking wood floor and approached the window from the side. He peeked out of the top windowpane and saw Skinny Lorene looking around on the ground. He lowered his gun and lifted the screen on the window. Just as he stuck his head out the window, she tossed another rock up at the window, almost hitting him in the face.

"Word to the mother, you illin'!' he yelled down at her.

"Hey, Nut, you got anything on you?" she asked. She looked up at him with desperation written all over her face.

Standing there, just skin and bones, she continued to look up at Lil Nut with pleading eyes as he thought about his answer.

"I ain't got nothing," he said simply.

"Come on, Nut, I know you got something. I got money." She held up a fist full of wrinkled bills.

Lil Nut sighed and dropped his head. "I said I ain't got nothing."

"That's how you gon' do me? Come on, just let me get three and I won't bother you no more," she promised.

Lil Nut pulled his head in from the window and thought about it. Maybe if he just sold her the three she would go away. He figured if he didn't, she wasn't gonna leave, and depending on how bad she wanted a hit, she was definitely gonna show out. Plus he didn't want his mother to wake up and find her out front at this time of the morning. His mother had banned her from coming around their house.

He began to step away from the window, and was about to go to the stash and get her the three vials when she called out to him again.

"Nut!"

He stuck his head out of the window quickly.

"Chill out!" he said in a loud whisper. "I'm coming."

He knew that this was a bad idea. But he was gonna make sure he told her when he got downstairs that this was the first and the last time he served her from his crib.

Lil Nut threw on a pair of Nike sweats and snuck out of the apartment. He opted to take the stairs instead of the elevator. Once in the stairwell, the smell of urine assaulted his nose immediately. He thought about leaving the staircase and taking the elevator, but that thought left his mind quickly. Either route he took it was going to be one pissy experience. The elevator reeked of urine as well, but not as badly. He walked through the stairwell doors and headed down the hall to the front door.

Before he could get to the front door, Skinny Lorene was standing there peering into the glass part of the door, watching for him. She had her face pressed up against the dirty glass, and when she saw Lil Nut coming, she backed away, looking around frantically as she left fog from her breathing on the glass. Her hands shook and she looked as if she'd seen a ghost by the way her eyes stretched wide.

"Lorene, listen, I'ma do this for you this one time. This ain't no crack house, so don't come back here no more." He looked at her seriously, but respectfully. After all, she was still his aunt, no matter what her crutch was.

"Yeah, yeah, Nut. You got 'em?" She was obviously ignoring his statement as she looked over her shoulder.

"Yeah. How many you want again?" he asked before actually pulling out any capsules from the pocket of his jogging suit pants. He knew what she had asked him for earlier, but he also knew that Skinny Lorene almost never came with the right amount of money for the product she wanted. Then if the dealer would refuse her service because of it, she would have the nerve to wild out on them.

Skinny Lorene began to count the wrinkled bills as if she didn't know how much she had before she came to cop. She made this funny sound with her mouth. It sounded like the noise most people made when their throat itched and they tried to get relief.

Lil Nut looked at her impatiently. He leaned up against the frame of the door, trying to remain calm. He scratched the scar on his chest because it began to itch. He breathed through his nose, sighing impatiently. He watched Skinny Lorene count the money for a third time. He had already counted the money when he watched her count it the first two times. So he knew exactly how much she had, and of course she didn't have enough. He was just waiting to hear the story she was going tell him to be able to get the credit on the product.

Skinny Lorene started counting the money yet again. She kept losing her count because of her delusional state.

She had twenty-three dollars, and the capsules went for ten each.

"I need three of them jumbos," she said, looking around, clearly paranoid.

"How much you got?" he asked, already knowing the answer.

"I got enough, Nut. Let me get the three jumbos," she said with an attitude as she shoved the money into his hand and held out her other hand to receive the crack.

"Lorene, this ain't thirty beans. This is twenty-three," Lil Nut said as he separated the money.

"That ain't thirty? I counted thirty." Skinny Lorene kept looking back over her shoulder onto the street as if she was looking at someone or something.

Lil Nut knew she was high, because he knew the effects crack had on a person. Most crack smokers became paranoid. But he followed her eyes anyway to see what she was looking for.

Parked out on the street was the yellow Vega that she was in earlier that night. Lil Nut knew that was the white man she was with earlier.

"Who that cat you with, Lorene?" he asked as he threw his head up toward the car waiting for her.

"Oh, him?" She turned and looked back at the car. "He just some sucker I met." She turned back to face Lil Nut. "He ain't nobody to worry 'bout." She waved her hand.

"Yo, I don't care who he is. You can't be coming over the crib wanting to cop and then bringing some square with you," Lil Nut told her.

"Yeah, Nut, I know you said that already. You gonna let me get the jumbos or what?" She placed her hand on her hip with authority.

Lil Nut looked down at the money. "Come on," he said.

Lil Nut back peddled into the hallway with Skinny Lorene following him. He just didn't feel right serving her while the man in the car was watching.

"How you gonna play me, Lorene? It's twenty-three here." He held up the bills in the palm of his fist. "Don't try and play me. All you had to say was you was short."

"I'm high as hell, Nut, and I must have counted it wrong. I swear I thought I had thirty there. Can't you let me go this time and I'ma make sure I come to you correct the next time."

Lil Nut knew Skinny Lorene was trying to pull a fast one, but he went into the pocket of his jogging suit pants, pulled out three jumbo capsules, and handed them to her. Skinny Lorene had the nerve to examine them as if he was trying beat her out of her money.

"Damn, these shits is fat as hell. That's what I'm talking 'bout. Good looking out, Nut. I know this shit good too," she babbled.

Lorene wasted no time heading for the door to leave.

"Yo!" Lil Nut called out to her.

She whipped around impatiently. "What?" she asked, her face showing aggravation.

"Remember what I said."

"Come on, boy, damn!" She huffed and stormed out of the building.

༄

The next day Lil Nut met Butter in the courtyard. They were waiting on Fatman, who lived in the Riverdale houses. They sat on one of the benches and kicked it.

"So when we gonna go re-up?" Butter asked.

"Shit, we can go today. I just gotta go get the loot outta the stash," Lil Nut responded. He carefully tucked the laces on his red on white Pumas into the sides of the sneakers.

"So which female we gonna take with us this time?" Butter wanted to know.

They always took a female with them when they were to get more drug supply, so that she could carry the drugs in case the police stopped them. Because they were young boys that dressed well and clearly had money, the police often accused them of being drug dealers.

"I don't know. Maybe we can take Sheila."

"Sheila?! Fuck that, no!" Butter said, displeased with Lil Nut's answer.

"What's wrong with Sheila?" Lil Nut asked as he straightened out the huge gold rope chain that hung around his neck.

"Man, you know what happened the last time we took her with us."

"She a'ight, man. She just like to talk. Don't nobody really fuck with her like that. So when she's around somebody that shows her some interest, she gravitates to them."

Butter stood, placed one foot on the bench, and put his elbow on his knee, leaning on it for support.

"You can't be serious, Nut? The chick is ugly as hell! That's why don't nobody fuck with her ass. I mean she got little ass teeth and big ass pink gums. Her shits don't even look like real teeth, man."

Lil Nut was counting money while Butter talked. At Butter's comment, he stopped mid-count. He raised his head slowly until his evil eyes reached Butter's.

Butter stood upright and stepped back a few steps, realizing he had fucked up with Lil Nut.

Lil Nut simply put the money back in his pocket, pulled out his gun, and put it up to Butter's forehead.

Butter stood there with his head held steady, holding his breath. He was afraid to breathe, knowing all the while that Lil Nut was a crazy motherfucker.

"What I tell y'all niggas about dissin' females? Stop doing that shit around me. Your mother is a woman, my mother is a woman. I ain't feeling that shit, and this is the last time I'm gonna say this. You feel me?" he asked with anger in his voice.

"Yeah, Yeah! Come on, man, chill out, Nut! You ain't gotta do all this. I'm supposed to be your boy." Butter tried to soften the mood.

"Yo!" Fatman yelled, running toward the pair.

They both looked in his direction and could tell something was wrong.

"Yo, this nigga just robbed me!" Fatman said.

"Who?" Lil Nut and Butter asked at the same time.

"Come on!" Fatman took off running with the other two right on his heels.

The three of them ran up Belmont Avenue to Livonia. They stopped at the corner and tried to catch their breaths.

"What the fuck happened?" Lil Nut yelled at Fatman.

"I was on my way down to your crib when this nigga walked up with Sticky. They wanted to cop. I told Sticky to show me the money first," he said between deep breaths. "So Sticky said it wasn't for him. It was for dude. So the dude showed me the money. I pulled out the bag with the jumbos in 'em, he snatched the bag, and they peeled out!"

"Oh, shit!" Butter said.

Lil Nut didn't respond. He just kept looking at Fatman. He was steaming and was ready

to put a bullet in anybody at that moment.

"So where they at?" Butter asked, still breathing hard from the run.

"I dunno. I thought maybe we could catch them if we came back down here," he said.

"Psshh!" Lil Nut sighed and rubbed his hand across his face, trying to calm down. "Why the fuck you had us run all the way the fuck down here?"

"'Cause like I said, I thought maybe we could catch them." Fatman was serious.

"Damn it, man! Use your fucking head. They crackheads. You seriously think them motherfuckers would be standing out here waiting on the corner for us to come looking for them? Give me a fucking break, man! Y'all killing me!"

"Chill out, Nut," Butter said, trying to calm him.

"Naw, that shit is stupid as hell. A fucking crackhead will beat you and dip out of sight. That's how they operate. In and out!" he shouted, walking away from the two.

They searched high and low for Sticky and his friend. They went into crack houses and the whole nine, and still they came up with nothing.

"Lil Nut, man, we out here tryna find these fiends, chasing our tails and coming up with nothing," Butter told him.

"Yeah, we might as well take the L for the team and get something to eat. I'm hungry as shit," Fatman added.

Lil Nut was pissed and could have searched all day, but he knew his friends were right. It was his pride that was getting the best of him. But he just knew they were somewhere inside one of those projects, watching the crew look for them.

"A'ight," he finally agreed, and the three of them went to the pizza parlor.

After eating they walked to Rockaway and Pitkin Avenue where they usually set up shop.

"So, Fatman, you ever seen the cat that was with Sticky before?" Lil Nut asked.

"Naw, man, I ain't never seen him before. He was a white dude."

Just then a brand new 1988 Audi Quattro cruised down the street. It was a bright red color that stood out like a sore thumb. It stopped at the red light at the corner. Everyone in the crew was in a trance, eyes glued to the beautiful hunk of metal.

"That shit is phat as hell," Butter said.

"Word up," Fatman chimed in.

It was as if the driver knew the boys were admiring his car. He sat there at the light revving the engine, and when the light turned green, he peeled out, tires spinning and howling before he jetted from the corner.

"Damn! That shit is fire!" Fatman yelled.

They all walked to the curb and leaned forward, looking down the street to where the Audi was traveling. After the car was out of sight, they walked back to their corner.

Fatman and Butter were chopping it up about the car when Lil Nut interrupted their conversation.

"Fatman."

Fatman looked over at Lil Nut. "What's up?"

"You said dude was white?"

"Yeah."

Lil Nut looked down at the ground, clearly deep in thought.

Fatman continued to look at Lil Nut, waiting to see if he was going to say anything else. When he didn't, Fatman turned back to Butter and they started talking again. The two of them were used to Lil Nut's strange behavior. They knew that when he acted that way, that he was concentrating on something. That was why he was the brains of the crew, because he was wise beyond his years.

ぬ

It was a little after midnight, and Fatman and Butter were playing basketball with a balled up paper bag, trying to shoot it into the garbage can that was chained to the light pole.

"All net!" Butter shouted after he shot a jumper over Fatman's head.

The paper bag hit the tip of the can and fell to the ground.

"Yeah! Now watch and let me school you, young boy," Fatman said.

Fatman picked up the bag and began to squeeze it together with both hands, reshaping it. He backed up several feet from the can to the imaginary foul line.

Butter stood in front him. He grabbed the legs of his sweatpants and pulled them up so that he would have room in them to squat down in the defense stance.

Fatman bent over and swayed from side to side as the two looked each other in the eyes. He faked right, and Butter went to the right. Fatman dipped back to the left, leaving Butter behind. He ran to the garbage can and slam-dunked.

"Unh! Yeah, boyeee!" Fatman yelled as he ran halfway down the sidewalk and back.

"Ah, man, whatever," Butter waved his hand at the boasting Fatman was doing.

Fatman ran over to Butter and stuck out his hand out for a handshake. "Good game, man." His smile was wide.

Butter slapped away Fatman's hand. He went to stand next to Lil Nut, who wasn't paying attention to their little game.

Suddenly they heard sirens approaching at a fast pace. The three of them looked in the direction of the sirens. Four patrol cars came blaring past them. The police cars were driving so fast that the red and blue lights were just a blur as the cars sped past them.

"I bet you they going to Howard," Fatman said, looking up the street.

"Ain't nothing new," Lil Nut said.

A car pulled over to the curb where they where standing.

"Yo, y'all holding out here?" the passenger asked.

"What you looking for?" Butter asked.

"Nicks, or whatever," the man said, hanging partially out of the window.

"How many you want?" Butter asked and walked over to the car.

After serving the man he walked back over to the other two. "Yo, my man just told me that there was a raid at Howard."

"Word?" Fatman asked.

"Yeah, he said everybody got knocked. He said by the time 5-0 finishes, Howard's gonna be bone dry."

"More business for us," was all Lil Nut said before walking off.

Butter and Fatman both shrugged their shoulders and followed him.

As they walked Butter realized they were headed toward Howard projects. Butter looked over at Fatman, and as they made eye contact Butter could tell Fatman was thinking what he was thinking.

"Nut, man, I know we ain't 'bout to step up in Howard?" Butter asked.

"Naw, we just gonna go ear hustle and see what we can find out," he said solemnly.

"What are you tryna find out?" Butter wanted to know.

"Nut, man, we all dirty as hell. That would be suicide to roll up in there," Fatman added.

Lil Nut looked back at the both of them and turned his head back, shaking it as a mother would do when she was disappointed in her child.

"What?" Butter asked, confused.

"What would y'all do if I wasn't around? Y'all gotta keep ya ears to the streets. If I didn't do the things the way I do 'em, we wouldn't even be out here right now. We would be locked up or something. I listen and I watch so that I can stay two steps ahead of these motherfuckers. Feel me?"

"Yeah," Fatman said.

"Word," Butter said, feeling like a fool because he should have known better.

As the trio walked, a horn honked across the street. They all looked over and saw the yellow Vega that Skinny Lorene was in days prior.

The man stuck his hand out of the window, waving for someone to come to him. He pulled the car over to the curb.

They stopped and looked in the direction of the car. The driver beckoned with his hand again. The three of them still didn't know which one he wanted since he didn't say a name. Fatman pointed to Butter, who was standing next to him. "Him?" he asked.

"No, the other one," he yelled, pointing to Lil Nut.

Lil Nut stood there, not saying a word. He was trying to see if his aunt was in the car, but she wasn't. The man blew the horn again and waved.

"You want me to get him?" Fatman asked, sensing that Lil Nut didn't want to serve the man.

They knew that this was the same car that Skinny Lorene was in the previous night. Fatman also knew that Lil Nut was very particular about who he served. He left that up to the crew most of the time.

"Naw, I got this one," Lil Nut said and stepped off the curb. For some reason he wanted to see the man up close and personal.

He waited patiently until the several cars traveling down Rockaway drove past. Butter and Fatman followed Lil Nut across the street.

Lil Nut walked onto the sidewalk and over to the passenger side of the car. The window was rolled down. The white man leaned over to the passenger side and reached for the handle of the door to open it for Lil Nut to get in.

"Yo, I ain't getting in. What's up? Whatchu' want?" Lil Nut asked the man.

"I want to cop a little something, my man." The man tried to sound down.

Lil Nut was bent over at the waist with his hands in his pockets, looking into the car.

There was silence for a few moments while the two held eye contact before Lil Nut spoke again.

"Hold up," he said.

Fatman and Butter were standing back in the cut, waiting on Lil Nut. He walked over to them.

"Come on," he said, walking away from the car.

The white man in the car craned his neck to see where they were going. The three of them stepped out of sight just on the side of the building.

"What's up?" both Fatman and Butter asked Nut once they were on the side of the building.

"Yo, he wanna cop, and I ain't feelin' him," Lil Nut explained.

"What, you think he 5-0?" Butter asked.

"I dunno. There's something about him. I'm just saying, I ain't feelin' him, and y'all know how I get down."

"Yeah, we do," they both chimed in.

"So what you wanna do? You want me to serve him? I mean I served him before, and ain't nothing happen. I don't think he po-po," Fatman said.

"That's on you. I ain't serving him." Lil Nut walked back around to the front of the building.

"Fuck it. I'll serve him," Fatman said and shrugged his shoulders.

"How much you want, man?" Fatman asked when he walked up to the car.

Lil Nut and Butter had walked several feet away from the car, waiting for Fatman to finish the transaction.

"Let me get eight jumbos," he said to Fatman, but kept his eyes focused on Lil Nut.

"A'ight, hold up." He dug in his pocket and pulled out a small Ziploc sandwich bag containing crack vials. Fatman got down in a squatting position next to the car so that none of the passing cars could see the transaction. He counted out eight vials and then stood. He placed the bag back into his pants pocket and stepped forward to the passenger's side window. He leaned on the windowsill of the door, resting his elbows on the sill. His hands dangled inside the car.

The man handed him eight ten-dollar bills and Fatman dropped the eight vials onto the passenger seat. He then stepped back from the car, smoothly shoving the money into his pocket.

"Good looking out," the man said before pulling off.

He honked the horn at Lil Nut as he drove past. Lil Nut just watched as the car drove past.

Fatman walked over to where Butter and Lil Nut were standing.

"What's up?" Butter asked. "Everything a'ight?"

"Yeah, it's cool," Fatman said.

The three of them walked off.

Once they reached Howard, they agreed that their customer was right. It looked like a raid or the biggest heist of the century. There were at least fifty police cars and seventy police officers in and around the projects. There were several paddy wagons and some were already loaded. The three friends stood in a crowd of onlookers and watched the scene play out.

After fifteen minutes or so of this, Lil Nut had enough.

"Let's break out," he told his boys.

Lil Nut gave Butter and Fatman a pound as they left him and walked to their homes. It was well after one AM. He kept his hands in his pockets while he walked toward the entrance of the projects. If the police stopped him at that moment he would've gone to jail for a long time. He was holding all the money from the sales of that day, and the remaining drugs that were left.

Nearing the projects' entrance, Lil Nut saw the yellow Vega when it bent the corner after he walked across the street. He could see the car in his peripheral vision. Before he could turn into the project entrance, the yellow Vega pulled up and honked the horn to get his attention. He stopped and turned around, but before he could make a move to go over to the car, one of the local residents that had been standing around with some of his friends called out to him.

"Nut!"

Nut turned around to look at the man who called him.

"Yo, c'mere right quick," the man said.

Lil Nut threw up an index finger to let the yellow car know he would be with him in a minute.

"What's up?" Lil Nut asked the man who had called him, shaking his hand.

"What's good, baby boy?" Skip asked.

Lil Nut gave a pound to the other two men that stood with Skip.

The three of them were much older than Lil Nut, and they were the muscle of another drug lord. They also sold drugs for the kingpin.

"Yo, who that cat?" Skip wanted to know.

"This cat that cops from me," Lil Nut answered.

"What, he followed you home or something? I know you not selling outta these projects?" Skip asked, reminding Lil Nut that the crew he worked for had that particular project on lock, which meant that no one other than anyone from their team could set up shop there.

"Naw, I ain't clocking outta here," Lil Nut told them.

"I seen that honky somewhere before, but I can't think where," Skip said, staring at the car.

"Yeah, me too," one of the other men chimed in, staring down the man.

The four of them stood there staring at the car before Lil Nut spoke.

"Let me go see what he wants."

"Yo, Nut, man, I ain't feelin' no good vibes from that cat. Tell him to step, 'cause ain't nothing here," Skip ordered him.

Although Lil Nut wasn't down with their crew, he grew up there and was known in those projects. In fact, the older heads looked out for him and respected his hustle, just as long as he wasn't hustling on their territory.

"Yeah a'ight," Lil Nut said, walking off.

As he walked to the car he looked over his shoulder, back at Skip and his crew, and as he suspected, they were watching him.

He walked onto the sidewalk to the passenger's side of the car and leaned down, looking into the car.

"What's up, my friend?" the man asked and smiled at Lil Nut.

"What's up? Yo, seriously, why you come 'round here?"

"I need to score some more drugs. You got the best shit in town, and I wanted what you got. I need ten this time."

Lil Nut just continued to stare at the man.

"You don't be with my aunt anymore?" he asked out of nowhere.

"I haven't seen her in a while. I came here with her one time before to score. In fact, that was the last time I've seen her, Lil Nut," he said, smiling.

"You don't know me like that to call me by my name," Lil Nut told him seriously, getting angered because he knew no one but his aunt could have told this man his name.

"My bad." The man held up his hands. "My name is Danny." He held out his hand for a shake. Lil Nut just looked at Danny's hand as it was suspended in mid-air.

"OK, I understand," Danny said and placed his hand back on his lap. "Can I score?"

"Naw, I ain't got nothing."

"Come on, Lil Nut. Hook a brother up," Danny said in his best b-boy talk.

Lil Nut frowned. "You need to watch your back riding around here in this loud ass-colored car. You might get jacked. I ain't fuckin' with you, man," he said.

"Come on, man, just sell me the ten and I won't come back tonight."

Lil Nut looked up over the top of the car at Skip and his boys. They were still watching.

"Naw, man, I ain't got nothing," he said to the man and stepped back a few steps away from the car.

"Aw, come on, Nut, I need to get the ten. Listen, I'll tell you what. Let me get twenty and I definitely won't come back," the white man said in a last desperate attempt.

"I'll get up with you tomorrow," Lil Nut said and stepped around the back of the car to cross the street.

"Oh, that's how you gonna do me, Lil Nut?" Danny yelled out the window after him. "As much money I done spent with you, you gonna play me out like that?" Danny asked, calling him out in front of Skip and his crew.

Lil Nut kept walking. He became angrier as he listened to Danny yell out after him. *Crackheads*, he thought.

"Yo, bounce!" Skip yelled to Danny.

"Yeah, you better roll the fuck up outta here, motherfucker, before you get your shit split!" one of Skip's boys warned.

"I'm tryna do business with my man, Nut," Danny yelled back at them.

"Nut don't do that kinda business, so bounce," Skip said, now walking toward the streets.

"Yeah, what the fuck you think this is? This here is a clean neighborhood. Don't none of that shit go on here," another of Skip's boys said.

"So I guess you three are on neighborhood watch, huh?" Danny asked with a smirk on his face.

"Yeah. Why, you got a problem with that?" Skip asked. Skip and his two boys began to cross the street and approach the Vega just as Danny slammed his foot on the gas pedal.

The Vega coughed first before jerking forward and peeling out.

ಸಲ

It was about eleven AM the next day when Lil Nut walked out of his building. He began the walk through the courtyard on his way to the store to get the daily newspaper. He was scheduled to meet up with Butter and Fatman at about one o'clock.

As soon as he stepped foot through the entrance of the projects about ten unmarked and marked cop cars came screeching up in front of the building. They pulled their cars up in different directions, having no concern for the cars that were traveling down the street. Several cop cars actually drove into the projects.

"Freeze!" several of the cops yelled.

Lil Nut stood there for a moment looking at the chaos surrounding him. He was thrown to the ground with other people that happened to be passing by. Everyone got searched. The paddy wagon pulled up and the officers began to load it with anyone that they caught with paraphernalia. Lil Nut watched as the officers brought Skip and his crew out in cuffs and loaded them into the wagon as well.

Lil Nut was searched and they found nothing. "This one's clean," the officer that searched him told a cop, who looked to be in charge of the bust.

"Let him go," he told the officer as he walked back into the projects.

Lil Nut went on his way to the store. Once there he stopped at the payphone and paged Butter. When Butter finally called him back he told Butter to meet him in front of the Tilden projects. Then he called Fatman and told him that he and Butter would be there shortly.

Twenty minutes later the three of them were talking about the raid.

"These motherfuckers is going crazy. First Howard and now Langston," Butter said.

"I'm sayin'. Word up," Fatman concluded.

"Somebody talking," Lil Nut said.

"You think so?" Fatman asked.

"Word up. Just look at how they know exactly when to hit and what apartments to hit." Lil Nut looked at the two of them before continuing. "Them niggas be clocking outta they sets. That's how they know where to hit at."

Both Butter and Fatman stood there listening intently.

"You see why I don't serve outta Langston. I always take that shit away from where I rest at. That's why I tell y'all niggas don't serve nobody from y'all's cribs either."

"Word," Butter said in a low tone, now realizing why Lil Nut had always told them that in the past.

Fatman became uneasy. "Yo, I served Sticky and that cat that beat me outta my shit in front of my projects."

"Word, that's right," Butter said. "Yo, where ya shit at?"

"I got it stashed at the crib in my room."

"You gotta get that shit up outta there. They probably gonna hit Riverdale next," Butter said.

"Naw, they gonna hit Tilden next," Lil Nut said.

"Well I'm good then," Butter said. "I gave you all I had left yesterday," he told Lil Nut.

"I'ma go get my shit and bring it to you, Nut," Fatman said, getting off the bench.

"Yo, chill. They ain't gonna do nothing now, 'cause they gotta get paperwork and all that shit together first," Lil Nut said. "You still got time. I need to go back to Langston to see what's going on. Let's be out."

Butter followed behind Nut, but Fatman was feeling some kind of a way. He wanted to get rid of the drugs first to ease his mind. He was scared, and he didn't want the others to know that he was. Reluctantly he followed them.

As they approached Langston housing projects, they could see the aftermath of the raid. Garbage cans were turned over and garbage was everywhere. People were still standing around talking about the raid.

"They got all them drug dealers," one lady said.

"I'm glad. Good for they asses!" another woman added.

"Yeah, it's about time. Kids play out here and they don't care. You think they wouldn't want the kids to see that kinda shit. But nooo!"

"I know that's right, girl! These niggas don't have any home training." She laughed, and the two women gave each other a high five.

The crew walked right past the cackling women and into the building that Lil Nut lived in. Once inside his apartment, they went straight to his room. Butter plopped onto the bed and Fatman leaned up against the wall next to a poster of Chuck D from Public Enemy.

Lil Nut leaned against his dresser. He noticed the worried look on Fatman's face.

"What's up, Fatman?" he asked him.

"I'm good," Fatman said, looking down at the floor.

"I think we need to chill for a minute till I can find out what's up out there," Lil Nut told them.

He wanted to wait until things died down before they continued with their business.

"I'm thirsty," Fatman said, expressing no interest in what Lil Nut was talking about. He walked out of the room and into the kitchen to get something to drink.

"What's up with that guy?" Butter asked Lil Nut.

Before Lil Nut could respond, a loud bang sounded. He and Butter jumped to their feet and ran out of the room. When they ran into the living room, they saw Fatman on the floor, face down, being handcuffed. Three officers tackled Butter and Lil Nut, slamming them to the floor.

After being cuffed, Lil Nut watched as the team of cops ransacked his mother's apartment. He knew she was going to have a fit when she got home. As the police searched the apartment, two officers left to take the boys down to central booking.

Twenty minutes later the police were done with their search.

"What we got?" the officer in charge asked.

"Nothing."

"Nothing?"

"Yeah, absolutely nothing. The place is clean," the young officer said before walking out of the apartment.

ເⓍ੭

Lil Nut sat in central booking, handcuffed to a table.

The door to the interrogation room opened and in walked Danny, the white guy with the yellow Vega.

A smirk came across Lil Nut's face.

"What's up, Nut? I'm Detective Delveccio," he said, taking a seat in front of Lil Nut. "So where the shit at, Nut?"

Lil Nut didn't say a word. He continued to ice grill the detective.

"I know you the brains behind ya little crew, Nut. So where the drugs at?" Detective Delveccio asked again.

But Lil Nut sat in silence. He knew the code of the streets.

"Your boy Fatman is gonna go down for a long time. He sold to me, an undercover officer."

Lil Nut still remained silent.

"Oh, yeah, your boy Butter is in there singing like a canary. He said you the brains behind it all. He said you the one who gives the orders. He says it's all you." The detective pointed to Lil Nut.

But Lil Nut knew better. He knew his boys wouldn't sell him out. Or at least that's what he thought.

Truth be told, the detective was just toying with his mind. Lil Nut was correct in thinking that his friends wouldn't rat him out. The detective was reaching, reaching for anything to get Lil Nut.

"I'm clean. You got nothing on me," Lil Nut said with confidence.

"Oh, but I do, young man," the detective lied. "You know Lorene Bolden, don't you? Oh, yeah." He laughed. "How could I forget. She's your aunt, right?"

Lil Nut continued to mean mug the detective.

"Yeah, she copped from you that night, right?" the detective asked.

"Did you see her cop from me?" Lil Nut asked.

"No, but she confirmed it when she came back and got in the car with me."

"That's hearsay," Lil Nut said.

"Hearsay my ass. She copped from you, and you know it." Detective Delveccio was getting annoyed with Lil Nut's smart mouth.

Lil Nut just smiled at the detective, realizing he was getting under his skin.

"Where she at? If she can testify to that, then you got yourself a case, detective."

Pissed was an understatement for what Detective Delveccio was starting to feel about Lil Nut. He had been trying to find Skinny Lorene and couldn't. He was going to use her to testify not only against Lil Nut, but several other dealers. But she had come up missing, so he got out there on his own, hoping the dealers would trust him and still sell to him without her. Most of them did, but Lil Nut never sold to him directly. Without his boys or Skinny Lorene testifying against Lil Nut, the detective knew he would have to let him go.

Detective Delveccio stood as calmly as possible and left the room. One hour later a uniformed police officer stepped into the room. He unlocked the handcuffs from around Lil Nut's wrists.

"You're free to go," he told Lil Nut.

Five minutes later Lil Nut walked out of the precinct a free young man. But the same could not be said for Fatman. Fatman had sold to an undercover officer, and drugs were found in his room at home. He would do five years in jail. Butter was released and met up with Lil Nut at Langston a little while later.

"That's fucked up what happened to Fatman," Butter said. He and Fatman were close.

"Yeah, it is, but I told y'all cats before don't sell where you rest at," Lil Nut said plain and simple, realizing he needed to take his own advice more often.

He had gotten away this time, but what would happen the next time?

"That God damn credit, dead it. You think a crackhead payin' you back, shit forget it!"

—"Ten Crack Commandments," Notorious B.I.G.

1989

"Listen, kill all that noise. I ain't tryna hear that shit. Pay me my money!" the dealer told the crackhead.

"I'ma have your money on Friday. I get paid on Friday. I told you that," the crackhead responded.

"How the fuck you gonna ask me for more credit and you already owe me?"

"I swear I got you on Friday. Don't I always come to you straight?"

"Yeah, you do, but you two hundred dollars deep, and I can't give you no more credit. Pay me whatchu' owe!" the dealer shouted.

This was the conversation Lil Nut heard as he walked to the store. Lil Nut had that Brooklyn swagger in full effect. He was on his way to the store to get something to eat. He glided past the two arguing men with a touch of gangsta in his walk.

It had been a year since Fatman got locked up, and two years since he'd killed Fuquan. To this day no on knew who killed Fuquan and Red. Now his crew was down to two. He missed his friends, but his business had taken him to a new level in the crack game. He and Butter had recruited runners to work for them after their near jail experience.

It was a cold winter that year, but it didn't stop the fiends and the crackheads from plowing through the snow chasing that next hit. Lil Nut was rocking a brand new Triple F.A.T. Goose coat and a pair of Forty-Below boots. He had the legs of his jeans crunched down on top of the boots. No Brooklyn cat would ever be caught dead with the legs of his jeans stuffed inside his boots. Lil Nut looked like new money.

"What's up, Nut?" one of the boys standing around the store asked him.

"What up?" Lil Nut said as he stepped into the store.

As soon as he completed his purchase and stepped out of the store, shots were fired. He looked in the direction of the gunfire and saw the dealer who had been arguing with the crackhead earlier pumping bullets into the man's face. The man slid down the wall after the first shot, but the dealer wasn't satisfied. He began to pump bullet after bullet into the man's face. The man's head hit the brick wall every time a bullet entered him. The shells from the 9 mm gun discharged and fell to the ground. When the clip was empty the dealer took off, quickly running away from the scene.

While others on the street came to investigate the killing, Lil Nut shook his head and walked off in the opposite direction. He wouldn't have used that type of a gun, because it left shells for the police to gather as evidence.

The hulk was out, so that meant it was cold as hell and Lil Nut hunched his shoulders as the wind whipped around his body. When he reached one of the buildings of Ocean Hills projects, he climbed the stairs two at a time. He walked into the hallway on the second floor and rang the bell at the second door. He waited patiently, using his thumbnail to clean the dirt from underneath his other nails.

Finally Butter came to the door and opened it.

"My nigga, what's up?" He smiled at Lil Nut.

"What's up?" Lil Nut walked into the apartment and saw Butter's girlfriend, Tamia, sitting on the sofa watching TV.

"Hey, Nut," she said, glancing up at him.

"What's up, Tamia?" Lil Nut asked as he walked through the living room and into the back guest bedroom.

In this room was a pull-out sofa, a table and two chairs, a television, and a stereo system. This was the room where Butter entertained his company and conducted business. Lil Nut sat in one of the chairs and waited for Butter to join him.

Finally Butter entered after several minutes. In his hands he held two shoeboxes. He placed them on the table in front of Lil Nut. Lil Nut opened the boxes and saw stacks of cash wrapped in rubber bands. Each stack contained ten thousand dollars. Lil Nut removed the stacks, counting each one. In total there were twenty stacks, ten in each shoebox, equaling two hundred grand.

"Not bad for two weeks' work, huh?" Butter asked. He smiled as he retrieved a beer from the small refrigerator that sat in the corner of the room.

"It's all good," Lil Nut answered. It was indeed a great two weeks. It would normally take them a month to make two hundred gees. But since Lil Nut's connect came up on a new and more potent product, business was really taking off. "So how we looking on the product?"

"I checked with them little niggas last night, and as of last night, we out," Butter told him.

"Yeah, well I meet with the connect today, and as soon as I do, I'll come through with some more of the new shit," Lil Nut said.

He grabbed ten of the stacks and stood. He placed five stacks into a plastic bag and rolled it up, placing it in the inside pocket of his coat. He did the same with the other five stacks. While he did that Butter lit up a joint and began to smoke. Lil Nut looked up at him when he smelled the marijuana. He shook his head and continued what he was doing.

"I'm out, man," he said to Butter once he was finished.

"A'ight, B, I'll get up witchu when you get back," Butter said as he blew smoke from his mouth.

"Yo, man, you need to leave that shit alone."

"Ain't nothing wrong with smoking a little cheeba," Butter said.

"I'm telling you it's fucking up your focus," Lil Nut said, exiting the room before Butter could respond.

Nut walked through the living room where Tamia still sat in the same spot she was in when he arrived. She was watching the new video show called *Yo! MTV Raps.* A video by MC Hammer was playing on the television. Lil Nut stopped, looked at the video, and shook his head, laughing at the pants the rapper wore.

"Later, Tamia," he said before stepping out of the apartment.

On the train ride to Harlem, Lil Nut's beeper began to vibrate. He removed it from his waistband. Checking the number, he saw it was the connect letting him know that they were still on to meet at one PM. He and the connect had code numbers that they used to communicate.

Lil Nut put the beeper away and sighed. He was relieved to know that everything was still on, especially since he was holding a hundred gees on his person. In the past the connect had called and canceled or changed the time at the last minute, and Lil Nut would have to turn around and go back home. He thought about getting a car every time that happened, but quickly pushed the thought out of his mind when he saw black dudes constantly being pulled over by the police.

An hour or so later, Lil Nut walked up into the connect's spot. He was greeted by the bodyguards and frisked. He was then escorted to a back room of the apartment where the connect sat on a sofa with two Dominican beauties.

"Lil Nut, my friend." The heavily accented Dominican man greeted him with a huge smile.

"Luis, what's up?" Lil Nut smiled back, shaking the man's hand.

Luis didn't get up from the sofa because of his obesity.

"Vamoose, chicas," he said, shooing away the two women, but not before he hit each of them on the butt after they rose from the sofa. The two women giggled and left the room. The bodyguard closed the door and allowed Luis and Lil Nut to have their privacy.

"How are you, my friend?" Luis asked again.

"I'm good," Lil Nut answered.

"Business good, no?"

"Business is real good," Lil Nut agreed.

"Good, good. You a good man."

"You too, Luis."

"So what do you come for today?"

Lil Nut pulled out the plastic bags from his pocket. He took out the stacks of money and threw them onto the coffee table that sat in front of them. Luis reached into the cigar box that sat on the table. He grabbed a cigar and wet it, placing it in his mouth. Lil Nut continued to pull stack after stack out of the plastic bags. Luis lit the cigar, sending huge amounts of smoke streaming into the air. Lil Nut threw the last stack onto the table, balled up the bags, put them back in his coat pocket, and sat back on the couch.

"Yeah, I see, business is good." Luis nodded his head, impressed. "OK, we do big business."

"No doubt," Lil Nut said.

"Hector!" Luis called out.

The bodyguard Hector entered the room again. "Come, Hector," Luis beckoned.

Hector walked his huge, fat body over to the table and stood in front of it.

"Take dis money and get my friend his stuff."

Hector did as he was told without saying a word.

"So, my friend, you still no have no car yet?"

"No, I don't need a car," Lil Nut told him. Lil Nut was getting tired of Luis's nagging. He had heard that he needed a car a thousand times. Everyone told him he should get a whip. But he never wanted to bring unwanted attention to himself, and a car would definitely do that. Besides, he never obtained a driver's license.

"Ah, but yes you do, my friend. You no can ride the train with this kinda money and product. It's too risky. I can no take risks." Luis looked at him seriously.

Lil Nut got the picture. He understood exactly where Luis was coming from. If he got busted, Luis didn't want to take the chance of Lil Nut snitching on him. But Lil Nut was not a snitch.

"Yeah, I feel you, Luis. I will look into one soon," Lil Nut told him.

"Good. For now, how you get home? Not train, no?"

"Naw, I usually take a cab home when I come to cop."

"Tsst, tsst." Luis made the noise with his mouth, letting Lil Nut know he wasn't pleased with that idea. "I give you ride home this time, my friend. But remember before you come next time, drive your own car."

Lil Nut nodded his head in agreement.

"I notice when you come, you come alone. You have security, yes?" Luis asked as he tapped the ash from the cigar into the ashtray that sat on the arm of the sofa.

Lil Nut shook his head.

Luis tried to turn his huge body to face Lil Nut, but failed. So he turned his head instead. "A man can live alone, a man can eat alone. But a man in this business can no be alone. He needs someone he can trust to have his back. You need to have muscle to help protect you," Luis said while the cigar hung from the corner of his mouth.

"I can take care of myself, Luis, and in this business you can't trust everyone."

"True, son, but me no say trust everyone. Me say someone. There has to be someone you can trust. If you take care of your peoples, they will take care of you."

"I am my own muscle," Lil Nut told him with confidence.

"No, no, young man. Who will watch your back? I no see eyes in the back of your head." Luis looked behind Lil Nut's head. "No, you are businessman, take care of business. It's OK to be able to protect yourself when the time comes. But it is important to have people around you to take care of you." He blew a cloud of smoke from his mouth. "You see Hector?"

Lil Nut nodded as Hector walked in on cue, carrying a large brown shopping bag with handles.

Luis removed the cigar from his mouth before he spoke. "Hector will never let anything happen to me. He will fight to the end to protect me. Hector loyal to me," Luis said, looking up at Hector.

"Always," Hector bellowed before leaving the room.

"See?" Luis pointed toward the door after Hector. "You need loyal men on your team. Do you have loyal men on your team?"

Lil Nut figured this was one of those trick questions that Luis so often liked to throw at him.

"Of course, Luis. I was tryna respect you and not bring nobody else with me. I thought you wanted it that way."

"Sure I do, but if you have people you can trust and is loyal to you, then you can bring them with you to watch your back."

Lil Nut thought about it, and the only person he would bring would be Butter. But since Butter had started smoking weed, he felt that Butter had lost some of his focus, and he didn't want to take any chances.

Luis's driver dropped Lil Nut off in front of Butter's apartment building. Butter was sitting on his car out front talking with one of their runners when Lil Nut got out of the car with the brown shopping bag full of cocaine. Lil Nut stepped away from the car and watched it pull off.

"Who was that?" Butter asked when Lil Nut approached them.

"That was the connect's driver," he said.

"What's up, Nut?" the runner asked.

"What's up? You a'ight?" Lil Nut asked.

"I'm good, man. It's all good," the boy responded.

"Cool," Lil Nut said while walking past Butter.

Butter jumped to his feet. "A'ight, man, I'll get up with you," he said to the runner. He shook the boy's hand and ran to catch up with Lil Nut. "Yo, when you gonna let me meet the connect?" Butter asked Lil Nut. "We partners and I should be able to meet with him too."

Lil Nut walked up the stairs and Butter followed Lil Nut into the apartment where Tamia was still sitting on the sofa watching videos.

"I don't know, man. He really don't like too many people knowing about him. He don't trust a lot of motherfuckers." Lil Nut told Butter that to stop him from asking anything further about the connect.

"So hook me up. Let him know I'm ya right-hand man."

"I don't know. I'll think about it." Lil Nut sat down at the kitchen table and prepared to cook up the cocaine for crack distribution.

Butter stood there in the kitchen watching Lil Nut.

"Yo, man, sit yo ass down and help me do this shit," Lil Nut said, noticing Butter standing there doing nothing.

Butter was feeling some kind of way. He felt he was an equal partner and should be able to meet with the connect as well. But Lil Nut was ignoring his request. He reluctantly sat down and began to help Lil Nut.

✿

Three days later Lil Nut got a page on his beeper and he grabbed it from the counter. He looked at it and saw that it was a 911 call from Butter. He picked up his phone and called him.

"Yo, I'm on my way to come get you," Butter said. "This cat owes me a gee and he was supposed to come see me last week. He been ducking me, but I got word where he at." Butter sounded amped.

"A'ight, I'll be outside," Nut said. "How long before you get here?"

"Ten minutes."

"A'ight." Lil Nut hung up the phone. He scratched the hairs on his chin that were growing in. *That damn credit,* he thought. They had more money owed to them in credit than he liked.

Exactly ten minutes later Butter pulled up in his BMW 325i. Lil Nut jumped into the passenger's seat of the luxury car. The first thing that hit him was a cloud of weed smoke. He immediately rolled down his window to get some relief. When he did this, protests came from the backseat as well as from Butter.

"Yo, Nut, roll that window back up. You letting all the smoke out," Butter said.

"Yeah, Nut, we need the smoke to stay in the car," a voice said from the backseat.

Lil Nut turned around to see two of his young runners in the backseat sucking on a joint.

"What the fuck is wrong with you?" Lil Nut screamed at Butter. "And you wonder why I won't let you be more involved on the business side. It's because of dumb shit like this." Lil Nut was pissed.

"What, man? Come on, lighten up," Butter said, looking over at him. Butter was leaning over to the right in a gangsta lean with his driving arm resting on top of the steering wheel.

Lil Nut didn't even realize at first that the two young boys were sitting in the backseat because of the amount of smoke in the car. "It's shit like this that can get us locked up. What the fuck, man!" Lil Nut yelled. "Roll these fucking windows down and put that shit out before I put a bullet in all y'all motherfuckers!"

The teens in the back put out the joints with a quickness. They had never experienced Lil Nut's short temper before. They'd only heard about it from the streets before joining the team. Butter rolled down the window and turned up the music on the radio. Soul II Soul's "Back to Life" blared from the woofer speakers.

Butter pulled the car over when he saw another vehicle pull out of a parking spot. He parallel parked the car, killing the engine. He reached into the middle console and pulled out a .45, placing the gun in the inside pocket of his raccoon jacket. Lil Nut checked the contents of his guns and cocked them.

"Stay here," he said to the young boys.

They both looked at each other in shock, and then they both looked at Butter for assistance. Butter had told them they could rock with them when they found the cat that owed the money. But Lil Nut obviously had other plans that didn't include them.

Butter shrugged his shoulders. "We'll be back," he told them as he got out of the car right after Lil Nut. Lil Nut stood on the sidewalk and waited for Butter.

"Who is the nigga?" he asked with a serious face, still disgusted with his behavior.

"That nigga Freddie."

"Where he at?"

"He s'posed to be in the first-floor apartment," Butter said.

Lil Nut walked back over to the car and opened the back door.

The teens in the car looked at him with fear in their eyes. "If y'all little niggas do anything stupid, I'ma take this gat"—he showed them the gun he held in his hand—"put it in ya mouth, and pull the trigger. Y'all feel me?" He mean mugged the two of them.

They both nodded their heads in agreement, because they were too afraid to speak.

"Let's roll," he said to Butter and began to climb the stairs.

Once inside he held the two guns down to his side and slightly in back of himself, trying to conceal them. They passed a dope addict sitting in the hallway on the floor shooting up. He had his pants down around his ankles and sat on the floor in his dirty underwear while he looked for a vein in his thigh. He wasn't concerned with Lil Nut and Butter, because he was too busy concentrating on the blast he was about to receive from the heroin.

"Knock on the door," he told Butter.

Butter knocked. They heard noise behind the door. Lil Nut and Butter stood on either side of the door so no one could see them out of the peephole.

"Who is it?" a female yelled.

"It's Pete. Is Freddie here?" Lil Nut asked in a deep voice.

"Oh, hey, Pete," the female said. "Freddie, Pete's here!" she yelled out to Freddie before opening the door.

Lil Nut looked at Butter and shrugged. He never thought it would actually work. But fortunately for them, Freddie had a brother named Pete.

Once the door opened and the woman realized Lil Nut and Butter weren't Pete, she was about to protest until Lil Nut put his .357 in her face. Whatever words were going to fly out of her mouth quickly got stuck in her throat. Her eyes got larger and she stood stone still.

"Get her," Lil Nut told Butter. Butter grabbed the woman, wrapped his arm around her neck, and placed the gun to her temple, walking her back into the apartment.

Lil Nut looked down the hall to make sure no one was watching. He stepped into the apartment and closed the door behind him, locking it.

"Theresa!" Freddie called out from the back room.

Lil Nut's demonic eyes burned a hole right through Theresa. From the look he was giving her, she knew not to say a word.

"Who else is here?" Lil Nut whispered to her. She shook her head from side to side, because she really couldn't talk.

As Lil Nut crept along the living room toward the back room he heard footsteps approaching. Butter quickly moved the woman over to the side so she wouldn't be seen by whoever was coming their way. Lil Nut stood back on the side of the doorway, waiting as well.

"Theresa! Did you say Pete was here?" Freddie yelled as he walked through the doorway.

All Freddie felt was a sharp pain hit him across the bridge of his nose, blinding him. He saw nothing but a bright light before his focus came back. Blood poured from his nose. Another blow to the forehead sent him sailing back through the doorway. He hit the floor with a loud thud.

Lil Nut stood over him. Freddie had passed out. Lil Nut kicked him hard on the side of his head. The female yelped as she witnessed this act of torture.

"I dare you to make another sound," Butter warned her as he tightened his grip around her neck.

Freddie came to and looked up at Lil Nut. "Where's my fucking money?" Lil Nut growled at him.

"Yo, man, I ain't got it right now! But I swear I'ma get it to you tomorrow!" Freddie panicked.

"Bullshit! You been ducking me for weeks!" Butter cut in.

"No, I told you that I would have it to you by the end of this week!" Freddie tried to save face.

Lil Nut placed his foot on Freddie's neck to hold his head steady. "How much you got on you now?" Lil Nut asked through gritted teeth.

"I ain't got nothing, I swear!"

Lil Nut pumped two bullets into Freddie's face with no remorse. He then turned to Butter. "Do the bitch and let's be out," he said, walking past them.

Butter was in a state of shock. This was the first time he ever heard Lil Nut say anything negative about a woman. In fact, Nut had never used the word bitch in his presence.

By now the woman was in tears and began to whimper loudly. Butter held her head down on the couch, placed a pillow over her head, and fired three bullets into her through the pillow.

They all drove in silence once Nut and Butter returned to the car. No one uttered a word. Butter dropped off the two runners first.

"All I know is this shit's gotta stop. No more credit for no one," Lil Nut said.

"Nut, we got some loyal customers who do pay their debts," Butter said, trying to reason with him.

"Fuck that! Now we just lost a gee from that punk-ass nigga that we ain't never gonna get!"

"Yo, man, we stack bread every week. A thou ain't shit for us," Butter said.

"Nigga, bread is bread, no matter how you slice it. I ain't in the business to be giving that shit away!" Lil Nut was furious. "Yo, let me explain something to you. I'm in the drug game to stack paper and then get out. All these motherfuckers owing us bread it's gotz to stop. I'm not gonna be hustling backwards. Not for you or anyone! My pops taught me better than that. Milton probably spinning in his grave over this foolishness that's going on. I gotta be rockin' niggas' to sleep over kibbles and bits. I didn't get in the game for this, Butter. I'm not going to be doing this shit for all my life. From here on out, it don't matter who you are, male or female, if you cross me over my paper, I'm sending you to the other side. No questions asked."

"Is that why you had me do the girl?"

"Charge that shit to the game."

"What about all these years you saying that your parents taught you not to disrespect women? I always admired you for that."

"Butter, that's old school. It's 1989. Like I said, male or female, it don't matter to me no more. I'm tired of being nice to motherfuckers. My name gonna start ringing bells and niggas gonna start respecting me one way or another."

Butter's beeper sounded off. He checked the number and it was Tamia calling 911.

"Shit, that's Tamia calling me 911. She probably don't want shit," he said.

Lil Nut didn't see the logic. "Why would she page you 911 if she don't want nothing?"

"Because she always doing that thinking I'm out with another chick," he said with a frown on his face because the beeper was going off again.

Lil Nut didn't reply. He just wanted to get back to Butter's apartment, pick up the product, distribute it to the runners, and go home. He was still pissed.

They pulled up and parked in front of the projects up the hill. Before Lil Nut and Butter could get out of the car, Tamia came running out to the car, hysterical.

"Why the fuck you ain't answer my pages?" she screamed.

Tamia was only five feet two and Butter was five eleven. Tamia jumped up and down, swinging at him. Lil Nut simply leaned up against the car and watched. What he was waiting for was Butter to put his hand on Tamia.

"Chill out! What the fuck is wrong with you?" Butter blocked the blows Tamia threw at him.

"These motherfuckers came up in the apartment and robbed you blind! They took everything!" she screamed.

"What?" both Lil Nut and Butter yelled at the same time. They took off running toward the building. Once inside the apartment, they saw that it was ransacked. Lil Nut went straight for the closet in the back room where he stashed all the crack they had cooked and bottled. It was gone, every last bit of it, as well as the money in the shoeboxes.

"Fuck!" Lil Nut yelled.

Butter was searching the apartment as well. He had his own personal stash, and it was gone too. He sat down on the floor with his knees bent. He rested his elbows on his knees and put his head in his hands.

"Y'all motherfuckers left me here, and these bitch-ass niggas came up in here and robbed us!" Tamia continued to shout. Because of her light complexion her face became flushed red.

Butter simply ignored her. He was used to her bitching. However, Lil Nut was furious, and all Tamia's shouting did was throw more lighter fluid on the fire. Out of nowhere Lil Nut snatched up Tamia and slammed her against the wall.

"Who was it?" he asked in a low whisper. Tamia looked into his expressive eyes that she always thought were pretty, and quickly looked away. His eyes no longer held beauty. Lil Nut palmed her face and made her look him in the eyes.

"Who did it?" he asked again.

"I don't know, Nut! Get off of me! Butter, you better come get your boy!" she yelled.

But Butter was still sitting on the floor with his head in his hands.

"How these motherfuckers manage to walk up in here and take all my shit, and you not see who they are?"

"I didn't say I didn't see what they looked like. I told you I didn't know who they were." Tears began to fall, because she realized Lil Nut was really crazy.

"Maybe you do know who they are. Maybe you set us up," he said, breathing his hot breath in her face.

"That's bullshit! Why would I do that?" She tried to break free of Lil Nut's strong grip, but to no avail.

"I don't know, but I will find out, and if I find out you had anything to do with it, you a dead bitch!" He shoved her to the floor next to Butter.

Tamia bumped into Butter when she fell to the floor. Butter looked up at his friend. He'd done it again. He'd disrespected a woman. But what Butter didn't realize was that the beast within Nut was starting to rise.

Lil Nut stormed out of the apartment and down the stairs. As he practically jumped down the two flights of steps, he pulled out his two guns. He kicked open the front door of the apartment building and stepped out into the courtyard. Lil Nut put his gun to the head of anybody who looked suspicious. He was losing control.

As Lil Nut terrorized the complex, Butter managed to stand to his feet.

"Butter, how could you let your boy disrespect me like that?" Tamia asked through her tear-filled eyes.

Butter simply walked into the bedroom and closed the door.

༄

Lil Nut closed the door to Butter's Beamer. Butter had let him borrow the car to go see the connect. It had been two days since the robbery, and he and Butter were no closer to finding out who stuck them for their money and product. Tamia was still insisting that she had nothing to do with the robbery, but Lil Nut didn't believe her, and he made Butter keep an eye on her.

After all that had happened, the business still had to be run, and bills needed to be paid. But Butter had no money left. Lil Nut was a little smarter than that, though. He had a little nest egg stashed away in a wall safe at his apartment, but it wasn't enough to start the business back up from scratch.

Lil Nut took a deep breath and walked up the front steps of the three-family building. Before he could ring the bell, Hector opened the door for him. Lil Nut stepped inside, knowing the routine. He raised his hands and Hector proceeded to search him. Lil Nut was then escorted into the back room where Luis normally was. Sure enough Luis was sitting in his usual spot on the sofa.

"My friend! How are you?" Luis greeted Lil Nut with a smile.

"What's up?" Lil Nut asked without a hint of humor showing in his eyes.

"Why so serious?" Luis asked.

Lil Nut didn't respond. Instead he sat next to Luis. Luis waved Hector and another bodyguard out of the room.

"What brings you here today, my friend? Don't tell me you finished already?"

"No," Lil Nut said, not making eye contact with Luis. What Lil Nut was doing was contemplating, thinking things over, which he had done for two days. He was coming to Luis to ask for credit. He wanted to get some cocaine on consignment, and pay him back when they sold all the product. He had never asked Luis, or anyone for that matter, for credit before in his life.

"Luis, listen, we got robbed. Everything that we had, the loot included, is all gone. I wanted to ask you for a favor," Lil Nut said, finally looking Luis in the eyes.

Luis simply stared at Lil Nut, waiting for him to continue before he spoke. Luis knew there was more, so he waited quietly.

"I was wondering if you could spot me a couple of bricks and I will pay you back," Lil Nut said.

Luis simply smiled and reached for a cigar. He took his time, wet the cigar, and then lit it. Lil Nut waited patiently for Luis to speak.

"Hmm . . . credit. You want me give you two kilos of my coca?"

"No, not give. Front me the two keys," Lil Nut corrected him.

"Ahh, front, sí. So you want to get credit and when will you pay me back?" Luis looked at him.

"I don't know exactly when, but I know it will take me a little over thirty days to get you all your bread," Lil Nut assured him.

Luis burst into a roaring hearty laugh. Lil Nut just looked at him. He didn't see the humor in what he just said.

"Listen, my friend, if I give you credit on two kilos, you will pay me in two weeks." He held up two fat fingers.

Lil Nut's eyes became wide. "Two weeks? I can't guarantee that I'ma sell two bricks in two weeks," he said.

"Oh, but you need me. It's only business, my friend. It's up to you." Luis shrugged his shoulders and reared back on the sofa. He laid his head back and blew smoke from the cigar into the air. His huge stomach sat up like Mount Everest.

Lil Nut sat there thinking about the proposition.

"A'ight, Luis, two weeks."

"No problem, my friend. Hector!" he called out.

Hector opened the door almost immediately. "Get our friend dos,"

Luis said.

When Hector came back with the brown paper bag, Lil Nut stood. Hector handed him the bag.

"Listen, my friend, two weeks and two weeks only. I will come looking for you, and will find you. Do you understand?" Luis was serious.

"Yeah, no doubt," Lil Nut answered as he walked toward the door that Hector held open for him.

Lil Nut and Butter packaged the product at Lil Nut's apartment. After Lil Nut put the last Ziploc bag filled with crack vials into the duffel bag for storage, Lil Nut walked into the living room where Butter was watching TV. Lil Nut sat on the couch.

"Yo, let me ask you something," Lil Nut said.

Butter looked over at him, giving him his undivided attention.

"How much money is out there on credit?"

Butter looked back at the TV for several second as he calculated the numbers in his head. "'Bout twenty-five," he answered as he looked back at Lil Nut.

"Twenty-five what?" Lil Nut sat up. "I know you ain't telling me we got niggas out there owing us twenty-five thousand? Please tell me I ain't hear that!"

"I'm saying, yeah, give or take a few hundred."

"Get the fuck outta here!" Lil Nut jumped to his feet. "You killing me, Butter! That's bullshit! You fucking with that weed and that shit got you fucked up. You fucked up the work by giving niggas credit. I thought you had shit under control. That's why I let you do you." Lil Nut paced. It took all he had in him not to snap Butter's neck in two. Over the years he had desperately tried to control his temper, but under the circumstances, he knew he wouldn't be able to hold on for much longer.

"The shit is ridiculous, Butter!" Lil Nut yelled.

"Yo, man, come on. I'm good to our customers. That's why they keep coming back. I give them breaks because they're loyal. We blew up like this because I treat them with respect," Butter said, defending his actions.

"You must be smoking crack. They crackheads, Butter! Ain't no loyalty in a crackhead, nigga! You out here respecting a drug addict, and they raping me for my paper! They ain't committed to nobody but that glass dick!"

"We gon' get the money back, man," Butter said sadly. The way Lil Nut was degrading him was starting to make him feel like less of a man.

"Nigga, you shot out! That shit's a rap! We will never get that loot back. But you gonna wear this one." Lil Nut pointed to him. Butter looked at him with confused eyes. "Yeah, you," Lil Nut confirmed when he saw the question in Butter's eyes. "You gonna get out there with the rest of them little niggas and grind to get this paper up. We got two weeks to pay back the connect, and frankly I ain't gonna let you fuck up the work. My life is on the line, and I ain't fucking with them Dominicans like that," Lil Nut stated with authority.

"So you got the shit on credit?" Butter wanted to know.

"Yeah, I did." Lil Nut walked over to the window and looked out. "And ain't you or nobody else gonna stand in the way of me paying it back."

There were several minutes of awkward silence.

"I wanna know who the motherfuckers that owe," Lil Nut said as he turned back to Butter. "Do you even know who owes?"

"Yeah, but some of my customers are straight cats. They ain't no real crackheads."

"They smoking crack, they crackheads. Let's roll out, 'cause somebody gonna pay me my cash, or they gonna pay with they life." Lil Nut walked out of the living room.

Butter knew that Lil Nut was serious. He also knew that one of his customers was law enforcement. He had made a deal with the officer. If Butter gave him crack when he wanted it, the officer would make sure that no heat was brought down on the operation.

What am I gonna do? Butter wondered. What he definitely wasn't gonna do was tell Lil Nut about that particular customer. But what he knew he had to do was get on point with the figures, because Lil Nut was about his business, and he wouldn't be caught slipping.

ᔤ

Two men sat at a card table in a bedroom. One was speed balling, shooting up a mixture of cocaine and heroin. As he concentrated on carefully pushing the drug into his vein, the other man held a butane torch to the end of a crack pipe. The smoke from the melted crack swirled around in the bowl like a tornado.

Suddenly the bedroom door busted open and hit the wall behind it with a bang, startling both males. They jumped to their feet. Lil Nut stood in front of them holding two semi-automatic weapons.

"What the fuck are you doing?" the man with the needle still stuck in his arm asked.

"Coming to collect on a debt," Lil Nut said nonchalantly.

Neither of the two men said a word. They both looked at each other. They knew they owed money, and Lil Nut was not the only one they owed to.

"Well I ain't got it. It's on you, homeboy. You just gotta do what you gotta do," the vein shooter said with cockiness.

Lil Nut shot the man in the groin. The man grabbed his crotch and began to yell in pain. Lil Nut shot him again, but in the neck this time, silencing him. The crack smoker released his bladder as he stood there, watching his friend die. He breathed heavily, but never said a word. His eyes were fixed on the gun that Lil Nut held.

Lil Nut simply riddled the crackhead with bullets before turning and leaving with Butter on his heels.

For three days Butter and Nut rode around strong-arming the people who owed them for their money. Several were roughed up, and in total three were left dead.

"Nut, man, we gotta ditch the car. By now I know somebody knows we been busting off and put a call in to 5-0," Butter said.

Lil Nut sat stone faced, looking straight ahead.

"Nut? You hear me?"

"Ditch the car then, and we get another one," he said matter-of-factly.

Butter sighed, because he was the one who would have to steal the car. He would much rather get one of the young boys to do it. But he knew Lil Nut wasn't gonna go for that.

"Something ain't adding up," Lil Nut said.

"What?"

"The cats that we went to see for the loot, well the bread ain't adding up right. We already collected forty-one hundred, and with the jokers that are dead and the one other cat we got to see, that debt equals nine hundred, so that would mean that one cat owes twenty grand. Please don't tell me one cat owes twenty grand by himself," Lil Nut said, finally looking back over at Butter. "I know you ain't that stupid to let one motherfucker owe us twenty gees!"

Butter began to get uneasy. He adjusted himself in the seat and kept looking straight ahead. He frowned and pretended to be counting. But Butter knew he had to come up with something fast.

Before he could respond, his beeper began to vibrate. He snatched it up and looked at the number. "It's Tamia. She paging me 911. Maybe she knows something. I better call her back," Butter said quickly. As quickly as he possible he pulled the car over to a payphone.

He fed the phone box with coins and dialed the number from the beeper.

The caller answered on the first ring. "What do you think you're doing?" the caller asked.

"It's not me. I told you this shit was gonna come back and bite me in the ass," Butter said, watching Lil Nut watch him.

"Well you need to take care of that problem, and fast," the caller said.

"Officer Ryan, I can't do this anymore. You gonna have to give me something. He ain't slow. He already knows something don't smell right. This nigga gonna kill me if he find out." Butter tried not to show on his face that the conversation was of some concern since Lil Nut was watching him like a hawk.

The officer told Butter where to meet him, and that he would take care of Lil Nut. Butter didn't want to do that to his friend, but with the warpath Lil Nut was on, Butter knew it was just a matter of time before he became a victim of Lil Nut's killing spree.

"What she say?" Lil Nut asked when Butter got back into the car.

"Man, she called me because she thinks she pregnant."

"Congratulations," Lil Nut said with no enthusiasm.

They ditched the second car Butter had stolen after they succeeded in collecting the money that the last customer owed them. Now it was time for Butter to fess up and tell Lil Nut who owed twenty thousand dollars, but he didn't know how. All he knew was that he had to say something. He contemplated leading Lil Nut to the police officer so that he could kill Lil Nut, but they had been friends for a long time, and he just couldn't do it. So he figured if he told Lil Nut about the officer, they could get rid of the cop together.

As they walked Butter looked over at Lil Nut. He could see that stress was all over Nut's face. Butter could tell that his friend was under a lot of pressure, and he knew it was from the debt he now owed the connect. Nut's stress was all his fault, and he knew he had to fix this situation on his own, so he decided to meet the cop by himself and kill him.

"Nut, man, I'ma meet you back at your crib. I'm gonna run by the spot and check on Tamia right quick," he lied.

"We need to get this paper, and we need to collect from the young boys too," Lil Nut told him.

"I know, man, I gotchu. Word up. Just give me a minute to check on her so she can stop bitching, and I'll get up with you," Butter assured him.

Lil Nut looked into Butter's eyes to see if he was sincere. "A'ight, man, hurry up." Lil Nut headed toward Stone Avenue while Butter went in the opposite direction.

Nightfall was near and it was dusk by the time Butter reached the alley where the cop told him to bring Lil Nut. He made his way down the alley. Butter walked past the back door of a restaurant and traveled deeper into the alley. He was beginning to think the cop wasn't gonna show when he heard a noise. He whipped around to see the black cop dressed in all black.

"Yo, man, why you playin'?" Butter asked, startled.

"Where's your boy at?" Officer Ryan asked.

"He . . . he . . . comin' through," Butter stuttered.

The officer twisted his lips in disbelief. "What kinda fool you take me for, boy?"

"Word up, he coming."

The officer removed his service revolver and pointed it at Butter. "I don't like dishonest motherfuckers," the officer said.

Butter looked at him like he was crazy. In his mind the officer was nothing but pure evil.

"Man, why can't you just give me some of the loot and we can keep the deal going as is? I mean, he don't know." Butter tried to reason. "I mean, I'm sayin', do you even have some of it that I can take back to him?"

"Oh, I have it. In fact, haven't you wondered why I haven't contacted you to get more?"

Butter thought for a minute. He realized now that the cop hadn't called him to get more drugs for a while, and he used to get crack from Butter every day.

"Yeah, I do now. What, you went to rehab and quit?" Butter laughed nervously.

"Funny, but no. I robbed you while your girl was home alone."

"Oh shit! You got us for all our shit. That's fucked up!" Butter was getting pissed.

"Oh, word? So it was you who took my shit?" Lil Nut asked from behind the cop.

The cop turned around and fired a shot that missed. Butter dove to the ground. Lil Nut shot the cop in the hand that held his gun. The officer dropped the gun and grabbed his injured hand. Lil Nut shot him in both legs, one bullet causing him to drop to his knees.

Butter was shitting bricks. He wasn't sure how much of the conversation Lil Nut had heard, because he never saw him enter the alley.

Lil Nut walked up on the cop as he lay on the ground, breathing heavily. "Your credit is dead," a demonic Lil Nut said before he unloaded the remainder of the bullets into the officer.

He and Butter ran to the end of the alley and peeked out before making a mad dash up the street.

On the walk home Butter discovered that Lil Nut didn't hear the entire conversation. What he heard was the cop tell Butter he broke into the apartment. Butter was relieved and swore that he would take this secret to his grave.

"So how did you know where I was?" Butter asked after they were back at Lil Nut's apartment.

"Because I know how much you love Tamia, and if she really told you she was carrying your seed, you would have been amped. But what really clued me in was when you said you was gonna stop by your crib. I watched you walk away, and you weren't headed in the right direction. At first I wasn't gonna follow you, but then I said fuck it. Then I lost you and was walking around for a minute until I heard the voices echoing out of the alley. That's when I snuck up in there and heard the convo."

Butter told Lil Nut that the cop was bribing him for money, and he had to pay the cop once a week, so that was why his debt was so high. Lil Nut seemed to accept that answer, and Butter was relieved that he had escaped with his life.

ന്ദ

Two weeks later Lil Nut had managed to get the money up to pay back Luis.

"Mmm . . . you surprise me, Little Nut," Luis said.

"Why?"

"Because me really not think you could do it. I had to test you, my friend. Now we do real business, and anytime you need credit, there will be no time limit for you." Luis smiled at Lil Nut and patted him on the back.

"Naw, not me. That credit shit is dead in my book."

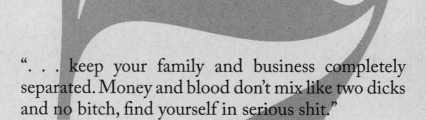

". . . keep your family and business completely separated. Money and blood don't mix like two dicks and no bitch, find yourself in serious shit."

—"Ten Crack Commandments," Notorious B.I.G.

1990

It was surprising how just a few months of steady hustling in the crack game could get the crew back on their feet. Lil Nut began to take things more seriously and wanted to treat the crack game like a business. Yes, he'd always wanted to get money and took that seriously, but now he wanted his hard work to sustain. He'd seen niggas getting locked up and getting sentenced to football numbers—double digits—on drug charges. And he'd also seen motherfuckers getting murdered over this here crack game. In fact, he'd rocked to sleep more than his share of niggas, and he was just approaching his twenty-first birthday.

Lil Nut stood in his boxers looking out the window of his project apartment. Melissa, his new girlfriend, was sound asleep in his bed, and his mother was in the kitchen making breakfast and gossiping on the phone with her sister, Mary. Lil Nut thought about his future, and then reflected on his past—his friends, enemies, and most of all his pops. He sure did miss him.

He walked into the kitchen and gave his mother a kiss on her cheek. She looked up, smiled, and pointed toward the food on the stove.

"Hold on a minute," Julie said to Mary. "Nelson, go ahead and make you and Melissa a plate for breakfast."

Lil Nut looked at the bacon, eggs, and grits and smiled. He loved his mother. He watched her on the phone and noticed that her hair was graying and she'd put on some weight over the past couple of years. He wondered if she was happy living without her husband. Lil Nut tried to give his mother all the amenities to keep her occupied while she stayed cooped up in the house each day. Her most prized possession was her fifty-two-inch color television. Starting from noon until four o'clock she watched her soap operas, Court TV, and then primetime sitcoms.

"Ma, hang up the phone. Tell auntie that you'll call her back. I need to talk."

Julie didn't hesitate to please her son. "Mary, I'll call you back later. I need to talk with my son."

Lil Nut fixed a plate and sat at the table next to his mom. A lot of thoughts had been running through his head for a while, and he wanted to share them with her.

"Ma, I want to get us up out of here, move us somewhere nice where we don't have roaches crawling up and down our walls, and motherfuckers pissing in the elevators. Whatchu think about that?"

Julie thought for a moment before responding. "Nelson, I've lived in Brownsville all my life, and I would love to get out. But my eyes have seen more than I would wish on anyone. Now my daddy was a number runner, and back in the sixties he was the man. When I was nine years old he moved me and your grandmother out of our rent stabilized apartment and bought us a house over on State Street. We didn't live in that house for more than two years before Daddy couldn't make the mortgage payments, and we were evicted. Nelson, I'm too old to be evicted from anybody else's property."

"Ma, running numbers is old school. The type of money I'm making is practically guaranteed money—"

"There ain't no such thing when it's illegal tender."

"You mean to tell me you think that there won't always be crackheads?"

"Of course there will be, but your slot ain't always guaranteed. There are too many pitfalls out here lurking around. You got little young boys trying to make a name for themselves that might want to try and take you out. You got stickup kids, five-oh, and snitches. How you gonna keep beating those odds? That's why I keep telling you to save up enough money and then open up a legit business."

"Ma, I hear you, and that ain't gonna be me. I'm not one of these knuckleheads out here—"

"Oh really?" she interrupted. "That's why you got a twenty-thousand-dollar car parked outside the projects? You don't think that was a knucklehead move? Your father is probably turning in his grave."

Julie was disgusted when Lil Nut went up on Northern Boulevard in Queens and dropped twenty-one thousand dollars in cash on a used Mercedes Benz 190E 500. She knew that he was making one of the ultimate mistakes young drug hustlers made, and she feared that his actions were already setting the stage to either get him noticed by the police, or murdered by the competition. His foolishness was the main reason she wasn't leaving her apartment. With or without her son, she knew that she'd always be able to afford this roof over her head.

"It ain't even that serious. You know how badly I've wanted a Benz. I've been working hard toward this for six years. You telling me that I can't reward myself? I'm supposed to just keep using my bread to make other motherfuckers happy? I didn't see you telling me to invest my dough in a business when I came through with your new TV. I spent three gees on that. I didn't hear you complaining that the money could have went to something else when I copped you that mink coat for

Christmas. Did you?" Lil Nut accused. He felt that his mother was being hypocritical, and he wasn't above calling her out.

Julie shook her head. "I know I didn't raise a dumb nigga, but that's exactly what you sound like. In all your years of slinging that drug, the same drug that destroyed our family, I ain't ever asked you for shit!"

Lil Nut looked at his mother incredulously. "Are you fucking kidding me? That's all the fuck you ever did. You had me paying our rent when I was just a little young dude of fifteen. What the fuck you call that?"

Julie refused to take her mind there, so she found it easier to call her son a liar.

"Look, you better get outta my face with all your lies. In fact, you and your bitch can get the fuck outta my house. My name is on that lease, and my name alone!"

"Oh, you think you really saying something? A'ight, bet. You think I won't jet and be out?" Lil Nut brushed past his mother, went straight to his bedroom, and woke up Melissa. He shook her forcefully, startling the sleeping beauty. "Yo, wake up. I need you to go to a Realtor and find us an apartment."

Yawning, she replied, "What? What's going on?"

Lil Nut was already pulling thousands of dollars from one of his stashes. This was his pocket money. He tossed five thousand dollars at Melissa and repeated his wishes. "I want you to go to a Realtor and find us an apartment. I want something plush in a residential neighborhood, and I don't want no roaches! And you better make sure my name is on that motherfucking lease."

ഇരുഇ

Six weeks later Lil Nut and Melissa were renting the ground floor apartment of a Cobble Hill, Brooklyn brownstone that didn't have any roaches. He was a little pissed that the landlord wouldn't allow his name to be on the lease because he didn't have any credit, but it was all good. The living room even had a working fireplace, plush carpet throughout the two-bedroom apartment, and ceramic tiled floor in the compact kitchen. It was more than they both could have imagined. His tricked out Benz didn't stand out like a diamond in a minefield on these streets. The tree-lined block was filled with high-end luxury cars. Lil Nut felt like he had finally arrived.

When the couple finally got the keys to their apartment they didn't have a stitch of furniture, so they made love in front of the fireplace on the plush carpet. When they awoke in the morning Lil Nut gave Melissa five thousand dollars and told her to get busy shopping for furniture. Meanwhile, he had work to do.

Back around the way Lil Nut stood politicking with Butter and his cousin, who everyone called Peter Piper. Peter was Skinny Lorene's son, and he was a thorn in Lil Nut's side because he was always begging, just like his mother.

Butter and Lil Nut had their cars parked in the lot of Howard projects with Ice Cube's new album, *AmeriKKKa's Most Wanted*, blaring from Butter's Beamer. Slowly the west coast was taking over the rap scene with their explicit gangsta lyrics. The three began a friendly game of dice.

Lil Nut blew inside his hand that held the dice and giggled.

"Blah-ow," he yelled and then rolled a six and a four. "Yo, y'all gotta come through and see my crib."

"Yeah, I heard you up and moved out, leaving Auntie Julie upset. Why you had to go and do her like that?" Peter Piper asked.

"Nah, she was beefin' and shit. You know I don't like all that arguing and shit. She was trying to make a nigga feel low, like I wasn't shit. So I figured I could show her better than I could tell her."

"I feel you," Peter Piper replied as he picked up the dice.

"Yo, I've been meaning to tell you about this nigga I met at the rink the other night," Butter began.

"What rink? Empire Skating Rink?" Lil Nut asked.

"Nah, the rink in New Jersey. That shit was nothing like Empire. You know when you walk in Empire you see around-the-way girls and the same old head hunters ready to snatch your chain. We gotta keep our gat close by just to get our skate on. But with the rink in Jersey you look out and see a sea of beauties. I swear each girl in there has long hair touching her butt. I mean *real* hair, long and silky, and they wear the tightest jeans as their hips be swaying from side to side." Butter began demonstrating their movements and they all burst out laughing. He continued. "But what I like most about the rink is that all the dudes in there holding serious paper and making serious moves. You know real recognize real."

"You know those Newark niggas on some real grimy shit too," Peter said. "They just as bad as us Brooklyn cats."

"You ain't listening. It's none of that bullshit in there. Those ain't Newark niggas. Those niggas are from Harlem."

"Harlem?" Peter Piper asked.

"Yeah. When you pull up in the parking lot all you see are Mercedes, Lexuses, Beamers, you name it. And all those niggas in there are about getting money. So I was talking to this nigga named Remy, and he was peeping my style. He know I'm from Brooklyn, and he was saying that not many of them niggas in there would want to fuck with me because we're known for that grimy shit, but he got a connect in D.C. that could get us that powder white for a low number."

Lil Nut was furious. Butter was going against the grain fucking with an outsider. Lil Nut was a creature of habit, and he didn't like no other boroughs, because each borough had their own code. He was a thoroughbred from Brooklyn, and he didn't trust no niggas from

Harlem.

"What the fuck you doing discussing our operation with other motherfuckers?" Lil Nut yelled. "I hope you didn't think I would be OK with that?"

"Damn, Nut. What the fuck is up with you?" Peter piped in.

Nut's head swung around to face his cousin. "Who the fuck was talking to you? Your bum ass don't have a pot to piss in, nor a window to throw it out of. You don't even have an operation to discuss!"

Peter gritted his teeth to keep from responding to his cousin's disrespect. He knew that his cousin was a hot head, and Peter wasn't built to go to war with him. Butter finally decided to squash the situation.

"Nut, man, sometimes you got to listen and just see where I'm going with this. You know those uptown cats get paper. And you know we get paper too. But we both said that we wanted to start pushing weight, 'cause that's where the real paper is at. I don't want to be out here hustling when I'm thirty. At that age I want to be married and chillin' in a big ole house without a worry in the world, talking shit about how I beat the game and the game didn't beat me. But just eating off our little runners ain't gonna cut it. It might take us a week to pull in five gees. We could make five gees off each brick, and move ten bricks a week."

Lil Nut thought about Butter's logic and was a little pissed that he didn't think of it himself. He decided to ignore his gut feelings about those Harlem niggas and take a chance on Butter and his newfound friend. Lil Nut had a lot to prove to his mother. He wanted to show her that he wasn't just an airhead, and could make enough money to legitimize his business. Nut decided that once he made five hundred thousand in the crack game, he would retire.

"So you trust this motherfucker?" Nut asked.

"Hell, yeah. He seems solid. And he's heard of you too. So that means he knows you ain't no joke, so if he ever tried any funny shit, he knows he'd have to look over his shoulder night and day, and I know he ain't built like that."

Lil Nut was flattered that his name was ringing bells, but he also knew that those uptown cats were just as ruthless as he was. They'd cut up a nigga and leave him in pieces over that paper. Harlem had their fair share of murders that were getting news coverage, just as much as Brooklyn. Just last week the streets began buzzing about a rich Harlem nigga who had murdered his best friend over that paper. Everyone thought that nigga was foul to kill his peeps like that, but Lil Nut understood his logic. He'd already murdered three of his friends.

"Fall back from that Remy for a while and let me think on him. I'll let you know my thoughts on whether we should fuck with him or not. Meanwhile, we still got a business to run. Shit, I got bills to pay. My rent so high you'd think I was paying mortgage."

"Speaking of business, cuz, I was wondering if you could put a nigga on and give me some responsibilities so that I could make some paper," Peter said.

"Nah, you can't work for me." Lil Nut didn't mince his words. His father told him many years ago to keep his business separated from his family.

"Why?"

"No reason."

"No reason?"

"Why you looking at me all stupid?" Nut asked.

"Because it's not like I'm asking for a handout. I'm asking to work for mines. And since you fam and you already got your organization set up, I want to know why I can't eat too?"

Lil Nut had had enough bickering for one day. He pointed his finger in Peter Piper's face and yelled, "Nigga, you wanna eat, then make your own plate. I built this here and I run it the way I fuckin' want."

Lil Nut didn't stay around long enough to hear Peter Piper gripe. He hopped into his Benz, revved the engine, and skidded his tires as he sped away. The hood loved a good car screech, and Lil Nut and his crew never failed to disappoint.

Lil Nut casually walked into his apartment after what he called a hard day at work. Melissa was in the back room with their bed covered in books. This was her second year in college, and she was studying to be a child psychologist. Lil Nut figured that with all those books she was reading, she could shed some light on his street dilemmas. But she couldn't. When it came down to his business, all she managed to do was make him paranoid.

"I see you didn't get a chance to clean up or cook," he said.

Melissa hardly looked up from her books. She gave him a glance and then replied, "No, I was busy."

Lil Nut tossed his baseball cap onto the bed, just inches from her notes. Again she glanced up and then cut her eyes at him. For some reason her actions irritated him. He decided to pluck her nerves by pushing her buttons.

"Melissa, get up!" he demanded. "A nigga out working hard all day to provide you with a roof over ya head, and the least you could do is fix me a fucking plate of food and clean the fuck up this messy-ass house. Damn, what I gotta do? Replace you?"

His words stung. Lil Nut didn't know how to sensor himself. Melissa jumped to her feet and began grabbing all of her books off the bed and shoving them into her book bag. Frantically she ran around, pushing past Lil Nut in an attempt to clean up the apartment. The last thing she wanted was to be replaced. She had a crackhead mother and no father she knew of, so her future without Lil Nut was bleak. Tears slid down her high cheekbones because her feelings were truly hurt.

Lil Nut hopped on the same bed she'd just gotten off of and kicked off his sneakers. He watched her for a while, in amusement, until his conscience got the best of him. He realized that he was treating the two women that meant the most to him in the world cruelly. He decided to make up.

He got up and began to help her out by washing the dishes. Still the house was quiet, because Melissa refused to talk.

"How you doing in school?" he asked.

Melissa hesitated for a moment because she really didn't feel like talking, but she responded anyway.

"I'm doing good."

"Oh, yeah? What you got on your last test?"

"Which one?"

"Anyone. I don't know. Fuck it. All of them."

"I've been getting mostly Bs and a few As."

"You can't get all As?"

She wanted to reply that if he gave her a chance to study, she could, but instead she said, "I guess I could. I just got to study harder."

Lil Nut liked that answer. Melissa was a good girl. She didn't know it, but that response was going to earn her a car. She needed a car anyway to get to and from school. Most times he gave her cab money or dropped her off, and then she'd take the train back home. But his girl shouldn't have to be taking the train. Besides, he was hearing about how mad Queens and Harlem niggas were buying their girls cars. Shit, those Harlem niggas were buying chicks cars when they reached their sixteenth birthday. Melissa was twenty. Yeah, he'd go and get her something this week.

"Yo, tomorrow I was thinking about inviting Butter and them niggas over to see our crib. That's why I wanted it to be clean."

Melissa stopped cleaning. "Baby, I don't think that's wise."

"What's not wise?"

"I don't think you should let anyone know where you rest your head at. That could be dangerous. Keep your street friends in the streets. Where you live should be your sanctuary. I've been seeing so many home invasions on the news lately. And you yourself have heard stories about stickup kids coming in and killing the whole household to get at the stash."

"I don't keep any real money here—"

"Then they'll just kill us quicker," she interrupted.

"Ain't nobody dumb enough to try me. They know I will let my thing go in a heartbeat."

"Baby, these people are good at catching you when you're vulnerable. I don't want us to make the evening news. Please, promise me that you won't let anyone know where we live. And when you drive home you got to make sure you're not being followed."

"But Butter is my man! He wouldn't try to do me dirty. I know where his moms lives!"

Melissa was aggravated. Lil Nut wasn't hearing her at all. His bullheaded nature was so difficult to deal with. At that very moment she realized that as soon as she got on her feet she would leave him. Yes, she loved him, but she loved her life more.

"OK, Nut. As always, I guess you know best."

Lil Nut grabbed her in a bear hug and gently kissed her on her neck. He felt her melt in his arms as her tension began to subside. "All right, I hear you. No company. You feel better?"

She nodded and smiled.

"And no more crying like a big baby. I didn't even say anything to your ass, and you crying like a baby."

ကၡ

Three days later as Melissa walked home from school she didn't notice all the familiar cars parked outside her ground floor apartment. But she did hear an array of voices from inside as she put her key in the lock. Her heart began to palpitate. Her instincts told her to do an about face and run for her life. But then she heard a hearty, distinctive laugh, and knew that it was her man. Pushing open the front door, she was accosted by a cloud of weed, and a living room full of men. She peered into a sea of unfamiliar faces, and then at her knuckleheaded boyfriend. He had a Corona beer in one hand and a blunt in the other. She wondered when he'd begun smoking weed. Slowly Melissa began seeing Nut change before her eyes, and she didn't like the man he was becoming. She understood that it was a new era and that he had a lot of pressure on his shoulders, but smoking weed to escape reality just wasn't like the man she fell in love with. She decided that she'd have to have a heart-to-heart talk with him.

Anger shot through her body as she stood stone still from shock. It was ninety degrees outside and her idiot boyfriend was showing off by having the air conditioner up on full blast with a fire burning in the fireplace. The television was on mute, showing a basketball game, and bottles of beer and liquor littered the sitting area. She should have known not to trust him.

"Whaddup?" Lil Nut asked, acknowledging her.

She didn't say a word. She just did a beeline directly for their bedroom, and slammed the door. As far as she was concerned, he'd just signed both their death certificates.

After most of the company left, Lil Nut, Butter, and Peter Piper sat around talking shit before the conversation turned to business. Once again Peter Piper tried to get on payroll.

"Motherfucker, do you think I talk just to be talking?" Nut asked. "I said hell motherfucking no!"

"A'ight, Nut. I ain't gonna ask you no more."

"Please do me that favor," Lil Nut replied, antagonizing his cousin. Then he focused his energy on Butter. "So you saying that this kid Remy is where we can make a quick come up?"

"Word up. I think we should give him a chance, feel him out, and take our operation to the next level. If we want to make real bread, then we gotta move weight."

Lil Nut nodded. "When the next time you gonna get up with him?"

"I'm going to the rink tomorrow night. You should come through and I'll make the introduction."

"OK, set it up."

ာၶၚ

The next night Lil Nut realized that Butter didn't exaggerate at all when he described the rink. When they pulled into the jammed packed parking lot, all he saw were high-end cars. It looked like a car show. He looked at some of the vehicles, and saw that pretty ladies were pushing the hot whips. He couldn't believe his eyes when he saw this red-headed cutie pushing a 1990 Acura Legend four door! His eyes followed her as she parked, walked to her trunk, and pulled out a pair of custom skates—white with pink wheels. She then switched her sexy ass inside the roller derby. Lil Nut was amped. He was already having a good time, and the night hadn't even started.

When he stepped out of his Mercedes Benz 190E 500, he looked down to make sure that his clothes were proper. Within the first five seconds he saw a lot of hotties, and he wasn't leaving here tonight without a few new numbers. Butter and Peter Piper both rode in his car, and they were just as amped.

"See? What did I tell you?" Butter bragged. "These honeys are top of the line."

"You ain't never lie," Lil Nut retorted.

The three men went inside and Butter and Peter Piper both got skates. Lil Nut didn't skate, but he did like to watch. He wished that he was coordinated, but he just wasn't. Instead he stood listening to the music and watching the hot dance moves and tricks being done on the floor.

Out of all the potential women, he couldn't take his eyes off the sexy redhead. She was skating her ass off, and Lil Nut could tell that she was popular. She skated every song with a new dude. When she skated off the floor to go to the refreshment stand, Lil Nut was right there to greet her.

"What's your name, shorty?" he asked.

The redhead looked Lil Nut up and down, and replied, "Well, it ain't shorty. Let me get a Pepsi," she told the woman behind the counter.

Sassy little bitch, Lil Nut thought. He knew the type. She thought that her shit didn't stink. She was probably used to getting any nigga she wanted, and most likely she already had a dude. That was how she was pushing that Acura. Despite her miserable attitude, Lil Nut still wanted her.

"My bad. What's your name, beautiful?"

Tossing her hair over her shoulder, she turned slightly to face him. She wanted to get a closer look at the stranger. She knew almost every person in that skating rink, and she knew he was new. She could tell that he was a dealer just from his gear alone. He was wearing a pair of new Nike sneakers, white-on-white, and a velour white Nike sweatsuit. But that was not what gave away his hustler status. The gold Rolex watch, and gold and diamond chain did that. He also had a certain swagger, a cockiness that said that he wasn't broke. She decided to give him some play.

"My name is Ria."

He smiled. "Ria, that's a pretty name. You got a man, Ria?"

"I might."

"Well, Ria, my name is Nut, and I'm going to take you from your man."

Ria giggled. Obviously this guy didn't have a clue.

"Do you know who my man is?" she asked. Without waiting for him to answer, she continued. "Because if you did, you would know that he pays the cost to be the boss."

"Well how much I gotta pay to be your lieutenant?" Lil Nut joked and actually got Ria to smile. When the counter girl came with Ria's Pepsi, Lil Nut reached in his pocket and pulled out a knot of money. Holding it just long enough for her eyes to see the hundred-dollars bills as he flipped to find a twenty, he paid for her soda and told the attendant to keep the change. Normally he wouldn't have tipped her shit, but he was trying to make an impression. He did. Ria began opening up.

"Where you from?" she asked. "I've never seen you around here."

"I'm from Brooklyn."

"Oh, we've been getting a lot of guys from Brooklyn coming here lately. I hope it don't get all wild and they have to shut it down."

"You act like Brooklyn don't have any class."

"Don't play innocent with me. Brooklyn is wild as shit."

"And where you from?"

"Uptown."

"And where your man from?"

"He's from uptown too."

"What's his name?"

She hesitated before she replied, "Shue."

Shue. Lil Nut had heard that name. It definitely rang bells. Word was Shue had a lot of paper. He was damn near a millionaire from what the streets were talking. He was twenty-four years old, and half black and half Chinese. From what Lil Nut had heard about the guy, he bought a large mansion somewhere on the low in New Jersey, and his chick lived with him. Shit. She was a tall glass to fill. Lil Nut wasn't nowhere near on the level of her man. Well at least not yet.

Lil Nut's eyes began to scan the room for Butter to see if he'd gotten up with Remy yet. Right on time he saw both figures walking toward him.

"Ria, I got some business to handle. You think I could get your number and call you some time?"

"Well I can't give you my home phone number, because I live with my man, but I got a beeper. Beep me and I might call you back," she said flirtingly.

Remy noticed the exchange between Ria and Nut, and he was less than thrilled, but he said nothing. Shue was his man, but he was on a paper chase. He was trying to get as many clients as possible to expand his drug operation. He needed niggas who was buying weight, and from what Remy had heard, these Brooklyn niggas were making it happen.

"Nut, this is Remy. Remy, Nut," Butter introduced.

Both men exchanged a handshake before they moved to the side and began talking business.

"It's like this, man," Remy began, "I got a connect in D.C. that be giving me the lowest number around, and his shit be uncut and powder white. Right now he got a few clients in Oakland, California, B-More, Philly, Detroit, and New York. Through me he got uptown on lock. I want to expand and start fucking with Brooklyn, but not just any nigga in Brooklyn. That's where Butter comes in. Y'all from Brooklyn, so y'all can maneuver and sell the product without taking the risk I would be taking. Y'all go through me, and then resell it to Brooklyn. Together we can all make a killing."

Lil Nut was feeling Remy's logic. He was on board with the plan.

That night when he went home he made love to Melissa, but he was thinking about Ria. First thing in the morning he was going to beep her. And he could only hope that she would beep him back.

ↄᴏ

Lil Nut finally had to break down and hire his cousin. Butter was in D.C. with Remy, and the girl they'd hired to drive down to D.C. and get the four kilos of cocaine had been put in the hospital by her baby's daddy, who beat her ass after he found out she fucked his man. Lil Nut didn't know who to be more angry with—the girl, or her man for putting his hands on her.

"Nut, I need you to get someone here as soon as possible," Butter told him over the phone. "I'm sitting like a duck with four pies around a bunch of motherfuckers that I'm not really feeling. These D.C. niggas are ruthless. They calling this city the murder capital, and from watching the news each night, they ain't lying."

Lil Nut could hear the panic in his voice. He was doing all he could do to get someone fearless enough to drive from D.C. to New York with four kilos of cocaine. If he was less of a man, he would have asked Melissa.

"I gotchu, man. Just chill. Let me call you back."

"A'ight, call me right back."

Nut began pacing while thinking, and then, bingo! "You still want a job?" he asked Peter Piper as soon as he got him on the phone.

"Oh, no doubt. I thought you'd never ask."

"How long will it take you to get to my house?"

"I'm dressed and could leave right now. It'll take me forty minutes on the train. But if you pay for my cab, then I could be there in fifteen minutes."

"A'ight, I got your cab money. Listen, is your license clean?"

"Yeah, yeah, it's all good," Peter Piper lied.

Just as he stated, Peter was there within fifteen minutes, and ready to work an unknown job. All he knew was that he needed the money.

"I need you to take the Camry, drive down to D.C., and meet Butter," Nut explained.

"That's all? I can do that."

"Let me finish. You gotta drive down there, pick up four bricks, and get them back here safely."

Peter Piper thought about the job. "How much?" he asked.

"You make five hundred off each brick."

The prospect of receiving two thousand dollars just to drive was unbelievable to Peter. It sure beat standing on a corner doing hand-to-hand transactions. But Peter Piper needed to be sure he'd see the whole two grand. "Who pays for my gas and tolls?"

"I'll cover all that."

"What about my food?"

Nut was getting impatient with Peter's pettiness. "Motherfucker, didn't I just say I got all that?!"

"OK, I hear you. Then I'm yours. Anything you need, just tell me what I got to do."

Lil Nut ran down the particulars and ended with a few warnings. "Make sure you do the speed limit. Don't pull over for shit. Fill up the tank in New York. When you get to D.C., before you pick up the bricks, make sure you fill up again. As soon as you get back to New York, bring those joints straight here. Don't do nothing stupid like drinking and driving. And if you do get pulled over, make sure you cut off the radio.

Don't be having no loud rap music blaring. Say, yes, sir and no, sir. Your reason for driving up and down I-95 is that you just dropped off your sister at college. You got me?"

"Piece of cake."

Lil Nut called Butter back and told him to sit tight, that he was sending Peter Piper. Butter didn't much care who he sent to pick up the bricks, just as long as he didn't have to bring them home. He didn't want no part in driving dirty through three states.

After Lil Nut got his business squared away, he decided to take care of Melissa. He told himself weeks back that he was going to buy her a car to get around in, and there wasn't any time like the present. He knew his woman deserved a car, especially after he saw how big those chicks were doing it at the rink in Jersey.

So far he hadn't caught up with the sexy Ria yet, and he was a little tired of her reindeer games. Each time he beeped her, she'd return his call, whispering. He couldn't ever make out what she was saying, and each conversation only lasted a few minutes. He didn't know if this was game she was playing, or if her man had her on lockdown like that. Shue. That pretty boy looking motherfucker had done good when he found Ria.

As he perused the car lot he was torn between getting Melissa a Honda Accord or a Maxima. The black Accord was somewhat standard looking, but the dealer kept telling him that Hondas were good cars. The burgundy Maxima with the beige leather seats and light tint on the windows seemed more feminine. Could the Maxima compare to Ria's burgundy Acura Legend? Never. But it was a start.

Lil Nut drove off the lot after giving the dealer twelve thousand dollars in cash, and headed over to his mother's house. He hadn't gone to see her since he moved out, and he was sure she was missing him. The longest he'd ever been away from home was when he was shot up over his coat. Instinctively he fingered his chest, outlining his bullet wound. The night he got shot felt like many moons ago.

He pulled up in front of the housing project and things seemed different. He couldn't believe that he once felt safe inside the low-income housing development. He was also surprised that no one had ever tried him in his neighborhood.

He hopped out of Melissa's new ride and went upstairs. He could hear the loud blaring of the television as soon as he got off the elevator. He stuck his key in the door like he still lived there and walked inside.

"Ma?" he called.

"I'm in here," she replied as she sat in the living room smoking a Newport. She was engrossed in *General Hospital*, but was equally excited to see her son. She knew it was only a matter of time before he came back around to see her. They were best friends.

He sat down and peered at the nonsense on the TV. "Whatchu been up to?"

"Oh, just taking it day by day. I went to church on Saturday. You know me, same routine."

"That's good. I've been busy making a few moves."

"Like what?"

"Well, I bought Melissa a car, and I also hired Peter."

That news was enough to make Julie click off the television and give Lil Nut her full attention. "You did what now?"

"I bought Melissa a car, and I hired Peter to make a few runs for me."

She exhaled. "I sure wish you would have called me first."

"Why?"

"Before you went and hired your cousin. His mother is a fuck-up, and the apple don't fall far from the tree."

"I hear you. You sound like Pops, but it was an emergency. From the rip I knew that hiring him was only temporary, and once he's done with this run, I'm going to let him go."

Julie inhaled deeply on her cigarette and then exhaled. "You know what? He ain't gonna go quietly, and then I'm gonna have to hear Lorene's mouth."

"Tell her to call me and I'll handle her."

"Oh, I can handle her. I just don't want to. Now tell me about this car you bought for Melissa. What did you get her?"

"I bought her a Maxima."

"Just as I thought. You don't love that girl. I mean, she's smart and sweet, but you're not in love with her, and the longer you keep her around, the more you'll end up hurting her. Now I like Melissa, but what I like don't matter. You need to turn that girl loose before you mess her up totally and make it hard for her to ever trust a man. She loves you. And no matter how much she'll try to convince herself that she can live without you, she won't want to. You gotta let her go and find you a trashy girl until you find the one."

"Ma, what are you talking about? I'm starting to think you going crazy in your old age."

"I ain't crazy. I'm wise. Just wait and see that everything I've done told you will come true."

"And you know all of this because I bought her a Maxima?"

"That's exactly how I know."

Lil Nut left his mother's house a little while later, but not before leaving her one thousand dollars to go food shopping and pay her bills. It was always enlightening speaking with her, if not amusing.

ഗ്ര

Peter Piper was a sight for sore eyes. Butter had never been so happy to see someone in his life. He had to admit that although he was trying to play it cool, he was a little shook. All those niggas out there in D.C. were crew, and he felt like an outsider. Even though they seemed to welcome him with open arms, something just didn't feel right. He decided that as soon as he went home he'd have a sit-down with Nut and tell him that he'd have to start riding down I-95 with him, because he needed a nigga to watch his back.

Butter had Peter Piper meet him at a mall in Woodbridge, Virginia, not too far from D.C. Once they made the exchange, Butter looked at Peter's gas odometer.

"Yo, why you ain't fill up before you came to meet me?"

"I wasn't thinking about all that. All I was thinking about was meeting you."

"Nah, it ain't even your fault. Nut should have told you the ropes before you got on the road," Butter replied.

"That nigga be slipping. He ain't tell me shit," Peter Piper lied. "All he care about is barking orders and his bitches."

"That nigga be fucking up all the time. This shit could have cost us." Butter had mad bass in his voice. Down in D.C., Butter was the boss, and it felt good to diss Nut for a change.

"You mean it could have cost *me*, but I'm straight. I'ma let it do what it do. I got this." Peter wanted to seem like he had shit on lock, just in case he could get a quick promotion. He figured if he got on Butter's good side, then perhaps he could guarantee Peter a job. "You the brains behind this here shit anyways."

"True that," Butter agreed, but decided to keep it short. He knew when somebody was gassing him up. Besides, he had something else on his mind that was fucking with him. "Yo, yesterday I was at this basketball game in D.C., and you know Rasun?"

"From Flatbush?"

"Yeah, kid. He got murdered yesterday in broad daylight in the middle of a basketball game. The kid walked right up to him and blew his brains out."

"What? Get the fuck outta here. He's dead?"

"Yeah, man," Butter replied. "And it was a young kid too."

"From where?"

"From D.C. I'm telling you, they don't play out this motherfucker. That shit still got me shook."

"Shook? You know it ain't no shook hands in Brooklyn," Peter Piper joked. "Don't worry. With me by your side, I could always have your back down here, you know. All you gotta do is talk to my cousin."

Butter thought about it for a moment, and then replied, "As soon as I get back up top, I'll let him know what's up. Be good, man, and drive safe. I'll see you on the other side."

Not only did Peter Piper get back on the highway without stopping for gas, he also wasn't doing the speed limit. Peter was very absentminded. It didn't take him long before he saw the flashing lights behind him as the flashing light on his gas tank began to blink. He was still in Virginia, just about to enter D.C.

He didn't have any choice but to pull over.

The two state troopers sat in their patrol car for a long moment before they both got out to approach Peter Piper. Both walked cautiously toward the car with both their hands on their service revolvers. You could hear "Just Don't Bite It" by N.W.A. blaring through the windows.

"Son, turn down that music and shut off your ignition!" the husky trooper demanded.

Peter quickly snapped to attention, clicked off his radio, and shut off his car. Suddenly his hands began to tremble.

"Yes, sir," he replied. Suddenly Lil Nut's instructions came gushing back. He watched as the troopers looked around in his empty backseat before delivering an arsenal of questions.

"Where are you coming from?"

"I, ummm . . . I'm coming from dropping off my sister at college."

"College? License and registration, please," the trooper replied. "Which college? Northern State?"

Peter Piper began searching for his license and the vehicle's registration. "Yes, sir. Northern State. I graduated from there myself two years ago."

Both troopers began to relax.

"Is that right?"

"Yes, sir."

"And where are you from? New York?"

"Yes, sir."

"Do you have any guns or narcotics in the car?"

"No, sir. I've never touched drugs or a gun in my life."

"Could we check your car?"

Peter Piper swallowed hard. "Of course. Anything you want."

By this time Peter had handed the trooper his license. He was defeated.

"Nah, that's all right. I'll take your word for it. You seem like a good man. If your license is clean"—the trooper waved the license up and down—"then I'll let you off with a warning. But if you have any points, then I'm going to give you a ticket for speeding. Is that fair enough?"

"Ummm, can't you just let me off now with a warning? I promise you my license is clean, and I was only speeding because I'm about to run out of gas. See?" Peter Piper pointed toward the light on his odometer. The trooper peered in and then looked at his partner. His partner shook his head.

"Nah, I still got to run your license. That's protocol. But as I said, if it's clean, then I'll give you a break. I'm not a complete dick."

Both troopers walked back to the car. Peter didn't know how to handle the situation. One part of him wanted to bolt and jet down the highway, risking being shot in the back. The other part of him wanted to start the car and make a run for it, no gas and all. Ultimately he realized he wasn't built for either escape, so he prayed that they would only come back and issue him a ticket, sending him on his merry way.

Again the troopers approached his vehicle, only this time their guns were no longer holstered. They were both pointing their guns directly at Peter's head.

"Step out of the car and put your hands behind your head," one trooper yelled.

"What? What did I do?" Peter asked, playing dumb.

"You're driving on a suspended license. Get out of your vehicle and put your hands behind your fucking head!"

Peter's body went slack. He had to be dragged out of the car, tossed to the ground, and then handcuffed.

"Check the trunk," the trooper instructed his partner.

Within two minutes Peter heard, "Bingo! We need backup."

Peter was thrown into the back of the police cruiser and then taunted.

"What were you going to do with all those drugs? How much street value is all that shit worth? You know you had me going with that no-sir-yes-sir bullshit." The trooper let out a hearty laugh. "I think you just got me and my partner promoted."

Peter Piper saw his life pass before his eyes. In a panic-laced voice, he replied, "I'm not who you want. I could tell you who the head nigga in charge is!"

"Never keep no weight on you. Them cats that squeeze your guns can hold jobs too."

—"Ten Crack Commandments," Notorious B.I.G.

1991

Bentley's was the nightclub to be at on Christmas Eve. All the moneymakers were going to be there. From rappers to hustlers, to even professional fighter Mike Tyson, everyone was getting it in. For Christmas Nut treated himself and upgraded his Mercedes 190E to a brand new Mercedes convertible 300 SL, silver with cream interior. He'd dropped ninety-five thousand on that ride, and it was brand new. No more used cars for him. Butter also dropped an obscene amount of money on a purple Porsche. But when Peter pulled up in a candy apple red 525i BMW, jaws fell open. Had the crew not been so caught up in their own hype, they would have realized that spending large sums of drug money on luxury cars was nigga nonsense.

"Yo, whose dick you done sucked to get that?" Nut asked. He knew that he paid well, but not nearly enough for Peter to stunt like that. After Peter had successfully come back from his run to meet Butter in Washington, D.C., Butter had a heart-to-heart with Nut and convinced him to let Peter stay on. Butter felt safer with fam watching his back. He was a little intimidated with how D.C.—the murder capital—got down, therefore Peter got and stayed in the game and began making his own money.

Peter grinned wildly. "You feelin' me, right?"

"Hell, yeah, I'm feelin' you. You gonna get mad pussy tonight when we roll through. You finally look like one of the crew," Butter replied.

"I know, and I'm feeling right tonight."

"So where you get the ride?" Nut asked. "Don't let me find out that you been tapping my stash. Fam or no fam, I'll put your lights out."

The crew squirmed. Leave it to Nut and his threats to put a damper on things.

"Nah, I'm not stealing. This here a rental. I got it from Larry off Lincoln Ave."

"Black Larry?"

"Yeah, him. He's a smart dude. He got that good credit and shit, and he's leased about twelve luxury cars, and then releases it out to broke niggas like me for a day, week, or month."

"Word?" Nut replied.

"Yeah, so I got this for two days."

"And how much he charging you?"

"Six hundred dollars—"

"Damn!" Nut responded. "That is a smart dude. He's about to cake up. I bet the car companies are leasing him the cars for four, five hundred a month tops. Then he's turning around and releasing them to y'all thirsty motherfuckers for a ransom. I'm fucking pissed I didn't think of that myself."

Butter interjected. "But that shit can't be legal. That's some fed shit if he gets caught. That's that white-collar crime type shit that you don't want any part of."

"How the fuck he gonna get caught? Unless jealous niggas start snitching. You ain't no snitch, right, Peter?" Nut asked.

"Hell motherfucking no! What type of stupid-ass question is that?!"

"Nigga, calm down. I'm just trying to make a point to this scary nigga," Nut said and pointed toward Butter. "A'ight, if y'all done wasting time on bullshit, follow me," Nut instructed as he hopped in his ride. Each man revved their rides and followed in procession through the Brooklyn streets until they reached the Brooklyn Bridge to the FDR drive toward Manhattan.

As Nut drove he thought about his afternoon with Ria. He'd bought her a diamond tennis bracelet that she absolutely loved. It took a while for them to start fucking around, and she didn't come cheap. Shue was still her man, but Nut felt her heart belonged to him. As soon as he got up enough paper to fully support her the way she was used to being taken care of, she was going to leave Shue. In the meantime, she had the wettest pussy Nut had ever fucked.

He would spend tomorrow with Melissa. She'd already graduated with her associate's degree and decided to continue on to get her bachelor's. Even though she had all the circumstances to make her a street chick, Melissa tried her best to be different. She wanted stability, an education, and a good man. *Two out of three isn't bad,* Nut thought.

It wasn't that he didn't love her. He just couldn't love her the way she wanted him to. He knew in his heart of hearts that if he got jammed up and had to do any time in prison, Melissa was that ride-or-die chick, and would do the time with him. Ria, on the other hand, would be ghost, and he knew that. But he didn't care. He just wanted to keep Ria for as long as it lasted. Besides, he didn't plan on getting hemmed up. He was too smart for that. And when he was in doubt about any situation, he always had the ten crack commandments to keep him away from the pitfalls.

As the crew pulled up in front of the club, each car behind the other, they sat there idling their rides to allow everyone to see them. Nut's phone rang. It was Melissa.

"What's up, baby?" he asked.

"I miss you," she whined.

"I know. I'll be home soon."

"I don't know why I can't ever go out with you when you go out to party. It's Christmas."

"I already explained that these clubs are no place for a lady, especially my lady."

Melissa knew that was bullshit, but she didn't want to start an argument with her man, not on Christmas Eve.

"OK, baby. I'm waiting up for you in something red and naughty," she purred.

Nut wished the vision could get his dick hard, but it didn't. "Yeah, you wait up for Daddy, 'cause I'm gonna put you to sleep."

He disconnected the line, peered out his window one last time to make sure all eyes were on him, and then proceeded toward the parking garage. Once inside the large club, the trio headed straight to the bar. It was already well after midnight, and the club was jam-packed. No mink coats were checked at the door. Each man and woman lugged their luxury frocks on their forearms or on their backs.

Nut found a spot at the bar and ordered three large bottles of Moët. The large buckets filled with chilled Moët cost nearly one thousand dollars each. As the men began popping bottles, the vultures—women— and a few bum-ass niggas came out the woodwork. Every couple of yards he spotted a different group of men—Queens, New Rochelle, and uptown. His eyes scanned the room for Shue, but he wasn't anywhere in sight. He saw Remy and Alonzo, but that was it.

As the night continued, the party began jumping. Everyone was drunk and singing along to all the songs DJ Kid Capri played. Nut spotted her first—red skin, red hair, fuchsia-colored lips, and a chocolate-covered full length mink coat dragging across the floor. Hovering over her was Shue—pale skin, dark hair, Chinese eyes, and a jet black three-quarter mink coat. The mere sight of him turned Nut's stomach. Then he remembered how Ria had sucked and rode his dick earlier. The two secret lovers spotted each other from across the room and made eye contact. Ria was slick with hers. She winked at Nut and he nodded and took a sip of his drink. Instinctively he rubbed his dick.

A litany of women pranced all around Nut, trying to get his attention. He flirted a little, passing out glasses of champagne and talking closely in their ears, mostly because he wanted to get Ria jealous, and partly because he was on the prowl for new pussy, and the ladies were looking scrumptious. Good enough to eat, only Nut didn't eat pussy.

Slowly Ria made her way over to where Nut stood, but not without going unnoticed by Remy, who by now was only a few feet away from Nut, Butter, and Peter Piper. They took a few minutes to talk business, but didn't get into anything heavy.

Remy knew the game. The first lesson someone should have taught Shue was never to treat a ho like a housewife. When Shue met Ria she wasn't shit. She grew up in a foster home and was rumored to have fucked her foster dad when she reached the age of twelve. She'd been fucking ever since. Shue took her away from all of that and gave her a plush, opulent lifestyle, and she repaid him by fucking all the major players in the game. Although Remy knew that Shue wasn't any angel, a man is gonna be a man regardless, and he felt his friend deserved a good girl.

"I wanna link up tonight. Can you get away?" Ria asked as she pretended to be ordering a bottled water from the bar. Nut was surprised by her question.

"I can do what the fuck I want. If you can get away, I'm down."

"OK, when you leave here, meet me at the Hyatt."

Nut couldn't wait for the party to be over. Instead of going home, he got his usual suite at the Hyatt, and just as she said she would, Ria met him there. She came stumbling in, kicking off her stilettos and slithering out of her mink coat.

Nut was sitting quietly on the edge of the bed with his hands clasped tightly together. He was in deep thought. He didn't like sneaking around anymore. He didn't like how he felt when he saw Ria come in with Shue. And now he didn't like the realization that she wouldn't leave Shue until Nut could make more money.

"Yo, how the fuck you get away from that nigga twice in one day?"

Giggling, she stumbled toward the bed and dropped down to her knees. Nut could smell the liquor oozing out of her pores, and he wondered if he smelled as badly. Hunched in between his legs, she hiccupped and then held her head to get it to stop spinning.

"That bastard is so stupid." Again she hiccupped. "I broke the code to his SkyPager and heard this bitch confirming that he was coming over tonight after the party. When he told me in the club that he had to go take care of important business, and for me to go home, I wanted to spit in his face. Instead I got even."

"Oh, that's what you call what we doing? Getting even with your man?"

"Nah, it ain't even like that. I mean, fuck him. He ain't shit anyway."

"If he ain't shit, what does that make you for being with him?"

"Whatchu trying to say?"

Nut was calm and steady. A lot was going through his mind. "I'm just asking you a few questions. If you know that he's checking for someone else, then why are you still there?"

"That bitch ain't really no threat. He been fucking with her for years now. He even bought her a car, a little raggedy bullshit Honda. Nothing too slick. That bitch been wanting to take my place for years, but I ain't gonna let that happen."

Nut pushed her hands off him. "Whatchu mean you ain't gonna let that happen?"

Ria thought about her words and did a remix. "I mean she ain't gonna take shit from me. I'd walk away first. That's what I plan on doing, walking away from Shue and directly into your arms, if you'll have me."

Ria reached up and planted a wet, juicy kiss on Nut's full lips. Nut welcomed her kiss, but he knew that it would be the last. He was a lot of things, but he was nobody's trick.

Nut woke up in the morning to Ria's legs wrapped around his waist. He'd definitely overslept. As the sun streamed through the hotel room and his head was no longer clogged from the alcohol, he realized that he'd made a stupid mistake. He'd let Ria control his actions, therefore dictating his life. If her man wasn't out fucking some other bitch, then she wouldn't have wanted to be with Nut, and Melissa wouldn't have had to spend the night alone worrying about where her man was. Nut knew that she would be worried sick, and also furious at the prospect of him cheating.

He cut on his beeper and she'd beeped him 911 more than thirty times. It could have been more, but they just didn't register. Nut pushed Ria's legs off him and hopped in the shower. As he lathered up he tried to think of a good excuse to tell Melissa once he walked through the door. Whatever it was, he knew she wouldn't believe him, but he just wanted it to sound plausible.

He called Butter and Tamia picked up. "Let me speak to Butter," he said.

"Well good morning to you too."

"Good morning. Now can you put Butter on the phone?" Nut had never liked her. He always thought that she had too much mouth, so he took satisfaction in hating her.

"Merry Christmas, kid," Butter said. "Where you at, 'cause I know your ass ain't been home. Melissa been calling all morning. Shit, since six this morning."

"Damn! I was hoping that you could have covered for me and said that I passed out on your couch."

"Well I could have if you told me your whereabouts last night. And that reminds me, that's some dangerous shit just breaking out like that for a broad. That same broad could be setting you up, and no one would be the wiser."

"I don't need a lecture right now. I know Melissa gonna be flipping."

"Yeah, she's gonna be pretty pissed."

Nut hung up the phone, got dressed, and miraculously Ria didn't wake up. He started to tell her goodbye, but then decided against it. He grabbed his keys and his coat, and then bounced.

All the way home his stomach was uneasy. He knew he did a dummy move. When he got home he expected Melissa to be up in the living room ready to cuss him out. Instead, she was buried in bed.

"Ma, what's wrong?" he asked.

"I'm not feeling well."

"Really? What's wrong?"

"I'm just not feeling well."

Nut sat on the bed and looked stupid. "Don't you want to open up your gifts?"

"No, I don't. I just said that I'm not feeling well. I just want to be left alone."

"Well are you going to go with me to my mom's?"

"I don't feel like it. You go."

Nut knew not to push her. He wished that if she was about to start beefing about his whereabouts, she'd just get on with it. He really didn't feel like carrying this through the whole day.

"Last night I got so drunk that I fell out at Peter's," he said.

"Umm, humm, that's nice."

"Yo, what's wrong with you?!" he screamed.

Calmly, she replied, "I just told you, I'm not feeling well."

Melissa ignoring Nut and not showing him attention by acting all crazy somehow had him stressed. It was early in the afternoon, and now he didn't have shit to do. He expected to sit around all day with her, and then in the evening go visit his moms. All his friends were with their girls. His other girl was with her man, and now he didn't have shit to do. *Fuck it,* he thought. He went into the living room and began flipping through the channels.

Meanwhile . . . on the other side of town

"I'm telling you, you better give us someone and fast, or else we're pulling you back in," the federal agent warned.

"I know. I'm working on it," Peter Piper replied.

"Your time has expired. We want Nut and his whole crew. If you don't set it up so that we bust his black ass with no less than five keys, then you're going away for life, my amigo. I promise you that."

"Come on, man, you gonna threaten me like this on Christmas?"

"I'm not your man! And you better be glad that you're out celebrating Christmas, you fucking snitch! Now bring me your fucking cousin. You got five days."

Peter Piper hung up the phone and wiped a bead of sweat from his forehead away. He didn't know how he'd gotten into this situation, and he surely didn't know how to get out. He wasn't built for such a high level of stress. He was a simple man with simple needs. He didn't need a mansion on the top of a hill. A starter home would do. He didn't need to fuck the best looking bitch. An average chick worked just as well for him. He didn't have to own a fleet of luxury cars. He'd settle for a lease. And in his pursuit of the American Dream, he'd gotten jammed up.

He wanted to hand them Nut on a silver platter and then leave town and start over. Nut never did shit for him, so he wasn't losing any sleep over his decision. The only thing that bothered him was what if Nut beat the case and got out? He'd surely be a dead man walking. The mere thought sent chills down his spine.

ᖆᏇ

"So you're really leaving me, huh?" Nut asked Melissa the next day.

"Yes, I really am," Melissa responded as she ran around frantically packing her things. Nut watched her as she pulled out suitcase after suitcase, stuffing them with her shoes and clothing. What amused him was that he wasn't supposed to be home. He'd left home for the day, walked a couple of blocks, and then changed his mind and came right back in the house. He watched as she packed every article she had in the house, including all the jewelry he'd given her throughout the years.

"Why? I'm saying, why you out? What a nigga do?"

She stopped packing momentarily. "Nut, you know that it hasn't been working between us for a long time. I know about your chick Ria from Harlem, Crystal and Lisa in Queens, and Stephanie in the Bronx. I know about all of them because I broke your code on your SkyPager a long time ago. But even as I listened to all the messages your stable of women left you, I never cheated on you. I still loved you through all of that. But now I'm done."

Nut wanted to scream at her for breaking his code, and tell her that it was good for her. Whatever she heard was her fault. She shouldn't have gone looking for shit, because when you looked, you just might find it. But instead he said, "Those bitches don't mean shit to me."

"That's why you don't come home at night? That's why you leave me here crying all the time, because those bitches don't mean shit to you? Maybe I'm the bitch that doesn't mean shit to you."

"Nah, I love you. You know that."

Melissa shook her head to fight back tears. "You don't even sound convincing."

"So you were just going to leave me like that? Without letting a nigga know?"

"I gotta do what I gotta do."

Her response infuriated Nut. He felt as though he was pleading a good case. He'd just told her that he didn't love any of those other women, and that he loved her, but it seemed as if she was taking him for granted. "Look, I ain't gonna beg you to stay. If you wanna leave, then get the fuck out. Another bitch will be glad to take your place. But leave all the shit that I bought you at the door. Money, car keys, clothes, everything! Bitch, I ain't no trick."

Melissa's eyes welled up with tears. She was hoping that she could pawn all of the jewelry he had given her and sell her mink coat so that she could support herself until she finished college and got a good job. Now that she couldn't take anything with her, she was frightened. She had managed to stash away three thousand dollars, but that wouldn't carry her far. She'd eat that up in carfare and lunch money in no time. Plus, she had met a nice girl at school who agreed to rent Melissa a room in her apartment. That alone was four hundred dollars a month.

Melissa fought back her tears and remained stoic. He wasn't worth her tears. She'd cried over him too many nights. Instantly she stopped packing, tossed her car keys on the dresser, and walked off with only the clothes on her back. He could have everything. She didn't care. One day she'd earn her own money so that she would never have to be disrespected again by a man.

ฌฌ

"Yo, Nut, I just got those pies from Rem. Where you gonna be, 'cause I'm coming through," Peter Piper told Nut. It was the day before New Year's Eve.

Nut was feeling fucked up. Melissa had left him and he decided to stop fucking with Ria. Word around town was that Ria and Shue got engaged Christmas morning. The trifling chick hadn't called him since he walked out on her six days ago. While she was having a very merry Christmas, his shit was totally fucked up. He sat on his sofa feeling sorry for himself, wondering who he could call over to help ease his pain. If he called any one of his regular chicks on the side, they'd come with a million questions. He didn't feel like talking. He wanted someone new. Someone anonymous.

"What the fuck you calling me for?" Nut asked. "You know I don't touch them things. Call Butter."

"I did. I've been paging him for hours, and he hasn't gotten back to me. I need a place for these to sit while I go and service a few niggas in Queens. You know, I gotta make that money for us, and I can't keep those niggas waiting on Butter. They'll go cop from someone else."

"Now what you talking 'bout?" Nut was only half listening. Peter had lost him at Queens.

"I got ten joints on me, and I gotta go to Queens to hit a nigga off with two pies. I'm not cruising the pavement with extra joints. That's like hustling backward, right?"

"Again, why the fuck you calling me? Drop those shits at your crib."

"Nah, baby bruh. What if I get into it around my hood? How I look bringing eight joints through the projects? I just need a place for these to rest until I come through, and since Melissa ain't there, these will be safe."

"You know I don't keep pies where I rest at. That goes against one of my rules, yo."

"I know, but we're a team, and I'm pulling my end here. I'm out here grinding and ain't nobody out here helping—"

"Man, stop fucking whining like a little girl."

"Nut, man, you're killing me. I'm like two blocks from your crib. I'm driving around in circles and shit."

"A'ight, come through," Nut replied reluctantly.

Nut got up, let Peter in, and returned back to his position on the sofa. The living room had a carpet picnic laid out that consisted of Chinese takeout, a six pack of Corona, a large bag of popcorn, M&M's, and two blunts, freshly rolled. Nut was watching an old video of the Mike Tyson versus James Buster Douglas fight, and he was irritated by anyone's presence. He was truly in a funk.

"What's up, man? I see you doing you," Peter Piper sang.

"What the fuck you so happy about?"

"Huh? I'm not happy. I'm working," Peter replied as he placed the heavy duffel on the couch. "You sure you're all right?"

"Nigga, don't I look all right? Ain't nobody stressing."

"I know you're not. I was just checking, that's all," Peter replied. "OK, I'm out. I'll be back for that in the morning."

"Don't just leave that shit sitting there," Nut said as he stuffed a handful of M&M's into his mouth. "Put it in the closet or some shit."

Peter did as he was told. "Yo, so what time you leaving tomorrow?"

"You know I don't go out on New Year's Eve. That shit's cursed. Too many motherfuckers be getting murked or locked the fuck up. Just swing through early and get that shit out of my crib."

"No doubt."

"And don't make me have to call ya ass!"

Peter was twenty-seven years old, way older than his cousin, and far too old to be spoken to like he was a child. Inwardly he despised Nut, and he was exhilarated at the thought that Nut's time was coming.

"You won't have to call me. Those joints will be out of here before noon. I put that on my life."

ကာ

The next morning Nut woke up feeling miserable. He was filled with angst and agitated, and he couldn't explain away his emotions. He couldn't sit still for shit. He tried to blame it on how he felt about New Year's Eve. Then he told himself that it was because he was missing Melissa. Finally he decided to call his mother.

"Hey, Ma."

"Nut, what you doing up this early?"

"I'm over here stressing."

"Stressing? About what?"

"I don't know."

"Well where's Melissa?"

He paused. "Ma, we broke up the other day. She walked out on me. What happened to good women like you?"

"Now don't go blaming that girl for y'all breakup. I was a good woman to your father, but he was also a good man to me. You can't have one without the other. I told you to let her go a long time ago and you wouldn't be feeling no pain. I'm sure she's feeling just as sad and lonely. Why don't you come over here and spend the day with your old momma?"

"I would, but you know I don't travel on New Year's Eve, but I'm going crazy in this house."

"Well take a walk around your neighborhood and sort out your thoughts. You can't be cooped up in the house all day. It's still early. Ain't nothing lurking outside this early."

"Ma?"

"What?"

"I love you."

"I love you too, baby."

Nut hopped in the shower, and as he rinsed off, he decided to take his mother's advice and take a walk around his neighborhood. The crisp air was exactly what he needed to clear his mind.

After getting dressed he headed out. There was a small playground a few blocks from his house, and that was his destination. With his hands stuffed deeply into his pockets, he tried to clear his head.

Sitting on a nearby bench, he watched a white couple play on the swing with their small daughter. Nut thought it was too cold to have a child out on some metal swing, but they were jumping around and acting all jolly like the cold didn't affect them. White people were weird. Sporadically the father's eyes darted back and forth to Nut. Nut turned away because he didn't want to intimidate anyone. He knew how it looked. He was a black man in a predominantly white neighborhood in a kiddie park without any kiddies.

The father gave one more suspicious glance, and Nut knew it was time to leave. He walked to a nearby corner store and decided to call Butter and curse him out for not picking up his telephone, and for not beeping back Peter last night.

"Yo, nigga, where the fuck you been?" Nut asked.

"I been chilling. Why? What's up?"

"Nah, Peter said he was trying to get in contact with ya ass all day yesterday."

"What the fuck that nigga talking about? He came through yesterday and dropped off five joints. He's supposed to come through and pick that shit up."

"Word? What the fuck going on with that stupid nigga?" Nut was pissed. He didn't know what Peter was trying to pull, but Nut was going to bust his ass once he got his hands on him.

"I don't know what's up with him, but you better watch him. Make sure his count is right. That nigga was a little too happy yesterday," Butter stated, recalling his visit with Peter. "He might either be on that shit, or shaving off the product and cutting small deals on the side."

"You think that nigga could be getting high?"

"I don't know. Anything's possible. But as I said, he could be stealing too. You never know. He coming through your crib and telling you a story about me for what reason? Either he smoking that shit and it has his mind going crazy, or he's guilty of something. You feel me?"

"Yeah, I feel you. Check it, when he comes through in a couple hours I'ma put pressure on that nigga and squeeze out the truth. You know I'm not one to fuck with."

"True, true."

Nut hung up and put pep in his step. He couldn't wait until Peter came through so that he could get to the bottom of his actions.

ಎಲ್

Melissa had camped out all night in a borrowed car, waiting for Nut to leave the house. At first when he kicked her out with only the clothes on her back she told herself that she wouldn't beg him to help her. But then reality sunk in and she convinced herself that she'd earned everything he bought her. She washed his funky socks, ironed his heavy jeans, cooked, cleaned, sucked his unfaithful dick, and never refused to fuck him when he wanted to be fucked.

When Nut left on foot with his car parked directly in front of her former car, she sat still, thinking that he was only going to the local store. After twenty minutes without him returning, she wondered if he had a bitch in neighborhood and was knee-deep in pussy. She wouldn't put that past him.

Melissa used her house key and crept back into the apartment. It was filthy. She didn't want any of her clothes, but her jewelry was important. Her livelihood depended on it. As she ran around her former apartment looking for her valuables, her heart nearly stopped when the front door was kicked in and a succession of loud noises followed.

Oh my God, they're gonna kill me, Melissa thought as the gunmen came in and tackled her to the floor.

ᔕᑫ

Nut couldn't wait to get home so that he could wait on that stupid motherfucker Peter, but he slowed his quick pace when he heard the sound of sirens as he approached his apartment.

"Are they at my motherfucking crib?" Nut screamed. His heart began to thump loudly. "They are at my motherfucking crib! What the fuck is going on?"

Nut dipped in the cut and watched the commotion from across the street with the other bystanders. His apartment was completely sealed off as numerous police officers, under cover detectives, DEA, and FBI all littered the scene, which was being treated as a crime. There wasn't any need for Nut to stick around. Besides, he was the only black man standing in the crowd. Just as he was about to bounce, he saw a figure in the back of one of the squad cars. Within seconds he realized it was Melissa.

What the fuck was she doing in the back of the squad car in front of his house? Nut was boggled.

Nut arrived at his mother's apartment within ten minutes. He hopped out of the cab and raced upstairs. Just as he entered, his beeper began going off with numerous unknown numbers all paging him 911.

"Ma, you won't believe what just happened."

Julie heard the panic in her son's voice and jumped to her feet. Her first thought was that he was shot.

"What? Are you hurt?"

"Ma, they just busted my crib."

"Who did?"

"I don't know. 5-0 and the feds."

"What? How they get on you?"

"Ma, I don't know what's going on. And they had Melissa."

"Melissa? How they had her? Is she snitching?"

"I guess so . . . I don't know. I don't know shit. All I know is that they had her in the back of a police cruiser."

"Nut, that don't sound right," Julie began. She wished she could have said more, but she didn't have any insight on the matter. All she could do was ask questions. "But you don't keep nothing in your apartment anyway. Right? They didn't get shit, did they?"

Nut hung his head low.

"I usually don't, but Peter came through yesterday with eight bricks."

"What!" Julie screamed. She smelled a rat. Eight bricks would ensure that her baby spent the rest of his life in prison. "You know I told you not to trust that slimy bastard!"

"You thinking what?"

"I'm thinking that he set you up to get knocked off."

"But why? What would he gain by getting me locked up? I'm the hand that feeds him. Nah, I think this has to do with Melissa. What the fuck was she doing there?"

"Did she know you had those things?"

"No. But I'm sure she's mad that we broke up."

"Nelson, listen to yourself. You can't see the forest from the trees. Your nerves are bad right now. Sit down and think this through. You'll see the truth once you calm down."

Nut knew she was right. He went into his old room and lay down on the bed. He just needed five minutes, although he couldn't quite get a handle on his concentration because he felt that any second the police would kick in his mother's door with an arrest warrant.

He went over the situation a million times in his head. Who'd have something to gain if he were locked down—Peter or Melissa? He kept coming up empty. In his mind neither one of them had a motive. He decided to call Butter and tell him the news, and also tell him to get rid of his beeper and not to talk over the phones.

The phone rang and was picked up, but Nut didn't hear anyone on the other end.

"Hello?" he asked.

"Yes, who's this?" an unfamiliar voice asked.

"No, who's this?"

"Who would you like to speak to?" the voice asked. Immediately Nut knew. His heart sank as he slammed down the phone. Butter had got knocked.

He had his mother call his aunt's house just to see if any strange events had occurred there. He wanted to know if Peter had gotten knocked too. Lorene picked up. His mother chatted with her briefly about the soap operas and then hung up.

"It's Peter," Julie assessed. "You and Butter's cribs get knocked, and nothing happens to Peter."

"I think you're right," Nut replied. His didn't have a clue how or why, but all he was thinking about was when. When the fuck would he get his opportunity to murder his cousin? "You better prepare yourself to break out your black dress. I'm about to rock your nephew to sleep."

"Fuck 'im," Julie replied.

"Shoulda been number one to me, if you ain't gettin' bags stay the fuck from police (uh-huh). If niggaz think you snitchin', ain't tryin' listen. They be sittin' in your kitchen, waitin' to start hittin'."

—"Ten Crack Commandments," Notorious B.I.G.

1992

Nut was a nervous wreck on lockdown inside his mother's apartment. He never went back to his crib after New Year's Eve. By now the news of Melissa's and Butter's arrests were flowing through the grapevine. The gossip mongers were having a field day. Nut purposely didn't shut off his pager just to see if Peter would beep him to a known number. That call never came. Peter left word with Skinny Lorene that when he heard about the two houses getting busted, he jetted out of town in fear that he would get busted too. Of course neither Nut nor Julie believed one word of his alibi. And Lorene wasn't any help. He kept asking her where the fuck her son ran to, but she said that she didn't know, and didn't want to know.

Just to make sure, Nut finally emerged from hiding and went on a stakeout in areas he knew Peter frequented. After days of looking for him, Nut found zip zero.

જીલ

"How did she look? How's she holding up in there?" Nut asked his mom a few days later.

Nut couldn't wait for Julie to sit down. He had a slew of questions, and he couldn't get them out fast enough.

"Hold on. Let me take off my shoes and get comfortable, and I'll tell you everything you need to know. It's a lot."

Nut had sent his mother to visit Melissa and Butter. They were both being housed at M.C.C. in lower Manhattan, right off the Brooklyn Bridge. The feds had them, and that only made him more fearful. Everyone knew that the feds had a 98 percent conviction rate.

Finally Julie sat down and began. "You know I always said that I liked Melissa, but now that I've gone to see her, I'm mad at myself for not seeing how much she truly loved my son. You once asked me why she wasn't as good to you as I was to your father. I'm about to say something that might sting a little, but it's the truth. And I always speak the truth with you. That girl is ready to give up her whole future because she loves you. They've been begging her to snitch on you, and she refuses. They told her that they know those drugs in that apartment weren't hers, but since she was the only one caught in the house with the drugs, and because the apartment was in her name only, unless she testifies against you and says that they're yours, she's facing a life sentence."

Julie shook her head at the mere thought of being behind bars for life. "Now as much as I loved the ground your father walked on, and he was my husband and the father of my only son, I would have never made that sacrifice for him. Never in a million years."

"Damn, Ma. Why you gotta put it like that? Don't you think I feel bad already?"

"I know you do, but I'm just saying. That girl has an education and could have had a bright future. I mean, she doesn't even have any kids. And the way things are looking for her, she won't ever have any. Life means she will die behind bars."

"You talking like I need to turn myself in." Nut's round, expressive eyes hooded over in anger. He didn't like the way the conversation was going.

"That's your choice. But I will say my piece. That girl didn't have one dollar in those keys. She never sold drugs or controlled your drug money. She was simply in the wrong place at the wrong time. You made your own choice about which road you wanted to take in life, and I supported you in your decisions. You compared her to me. Now I will compare you to your father. Your father wouldn't have allowed me to spend one day in jail over some shit he created."

"Awww, come on now, Ma. That's not fair, and you know it. What am I supposed to do? Just turn myself in and say let her go? I didn't set her up. I didn't even ask her to come back there. What the fuck was she even doing there? Did you ask her that? She's probably lying anyway. What if they're using her and all of this is really a game? What if she's not really locked up, and they just placed her there to feed you the bait? She could be in some witness protection program or some shit!" Nut knew he was reaching, but he couldn't wrap his mind around the guilt trip his mother had laid on him.

Ignoring his conspiracy theory, Julie said, "She needs a lawyer, a good lawyer. Who do you know that would have a shot at getting her as little time as possible, maybe twenty years? I hope you do plan on paying for her lawyer?"

"Of course I'm going to pay for the lawyer." Nut was spent. He felt like he had the world on his shoulders. "Get in contact with Jacob Sheinberg and see how much he charges for a case like this. He's good, Ma. He's represented so many niggas and got them off. I'm telling you he can get her off too. She's innocent."

"OK, I'll give him a call in the morning."

"What about Butter? What he say?"

"Butter don't really know anything. All he knows is that Peter dropped off five bricks and the next day the police were kicking in his door. They also got one hundred fifty cash of his stash."

"What the fuck was he doing with his stash where he rest his head? Didn't we learn our lesson the hard way back in the day? He's a fucking knucklehead."

"I don't think you're one to be name-calling."

Nut couldn't believe his mother's slick mouth. He wondered if she always spoke like this, just not to him.

"So I guess that means I'ma have to pay for his lawyer too?"

"He said those boys are trying to lean on him hard. They've already offered him a sweet deal if he turns you in. So if I were you, I would come down from my throne of pointing fingers and playing king, and dig into my pockets and play Santa Claus, because if you don't, you'll be spending next Christmas behind bars."

ꦢ

The new year came in on a lousy note, but Nut figured that it could have been worse. He could be the one locked away in a cage. Life went on. He still had a business to run, and with lawyer fees, he was scrambling to make it happen. He needed to keep Melissa and Butter optimistic about their futures, as well as keeping their books fat. His mother was the go-between for him, and she was becoming just as expensive. Not only did he cover all her bills, but he also had to hire her a driver to take her wherever he needed her to go. She said there wasn't any way she was standing on anybody's corner hailing a taxi. And the train and bus were out of the question.

It was all worth it, though. He made sure his mother went to visit both Melissa and Butter weekly to get any and all updates. Melissa's lawyer wanted fifty-five thousand dollars just to retain him. And he told Nut that it would cost another two hundred grand if the case went to trial. That wasn't including if he needed to hire any experts or fly any witnesses in from out of town.

Butter's attorney wasn't as costly, but he wasn't cheap either. He charged Nut a thirty-thousand-dollar retainer fee, and was urging Butter to take a plea bargain. If Butter took a plea of twenty years, he'd be out in eighteen. Butter told Julie that he didn't want to gamble with a life sentence. The deal wasn't on the table yet, but his lawyer, Allen Shapiro, was hoping to negotiate that with the prosecutor. If he was successful, then Nut would owe Shapiro an additional ten grand.

All his years of hustling were going down the drain on this one case. He'd spent year after year trying to save money to go legit. Now he needed all that money to pay for lawyers, and he was pissed. And if he thought that nothing else could go wrong, he got a double dose of bad news when he ran into Remy at Willie Burgers on 145th and Eight Avenue.

"Yo, Nut, man, you gonna live a long time, my nigga," Remy said and gave him a pound. "I've been trying to holla at you for weeks now. I know you've been getting my pages."

"Yeah, no doubt, but you know my man got jammed up. And I'm not fucking with that number no more. It's hot."

"I heard all about that. You know I know. But I needed to get at you, 'cause it was an emergency. I asked Ria if she had another number on you, but she said nah."

The name stung. Nut's mind raced on the fact that Remy knew he knew Ria. They'd never made their relationship known. Nut tried to play if off.

"Ria? Why would you think she could get at me?"

"Oh, I just thought y'all were cool, that's all. But when you didn't come to her wedding, I figured that I must have been bugging."

Now he was really miserable. "Yeah, you must've been bugging. But what's up? What did you wanna holla at me about?"

"That debt you owe."

"What debt?"

"Peter took fifteen keys on consignment."

"OK, and? That's Peter's debt."

Remy looked at Nut like he was crazy. "Nah, kid, it don't go like that—"

"First off, I'm not your fucking kid—"

"Excuse me, my bad," Remy corrected. Although he was uptown in his neighborhood, he hadn't expected to get into any beef. He was just passing through to get something to eat, and left his hammer in the car, but he was most certain that the Brooklyn kid was strapped, so he tried to calm things down.

"No doubt," Nut said. "As I was saying, I don't do consignment. Ever. I stopped doing that credit shit when I was a little young nigga. Peter had the paper to pay you—"

"It's not me y'all owe. He went straight to the top and got those joints from Luis, and he used your name."

"So if this doesn't concern you, motherfucker, why the fuck you all up in our business?" Nut went berserk. He began patting down Remy, checking for a wire. At this point he trusted no one. If his own cousin could do him dirty, anyone could, including his own momma. That's exactly what his pops told him back in the day. And what made the matter worse, was that Nut hadn't used Luis in years. Why would his name still be good for credit with him? "You wired, motherfucker? You working for the feds?"

Remy was able to get Nut off of him and began copping a plea. "Nah, I'm not wired, man. You my man. I was just trying to look out.

Niggas out here gunning for your head, and I was just trying to put you on."

Nut shook his head. Maybe he was out of order. But he knew that Remy took pleasure in spilling the beans about Ria and Shue getting married. And also delivering the news that Nut had a tab over his head.

"Yo, how much that motherfucker saying I owe?"

"Last I heard it was two hundred eighty-five thousand, plus ten gees a week until you pay the tab."

Nut hopped in his car and sped off. He wasn't safe in those Harlem streets. He'd taken a loss for the money he gave Peter to buy those keys, and Peter didn't even buy the fucking keys. He realized that Peter took his money and walked away with close to three hundred grand, and Nut still had to come up with another three hundred grand? How the fuck was he gonna do that? He figured that he must be the dumbest motherfucker walking around. Never in his imagination did he think that his cousin could pull something like this off right under his nose.

Thinking that he'd hop on the West Side Highway and cut over to Chambers Street to make his way toward Brooklyn, Nut had a change of heart. He needed to go see Luis, face-to-face, and see if he could work out something. He knew that Luis had a lot of muscle, and neither he nor his moms was safe if Luis put a bounty over Nut's head. Nut made a U-turn and headed back up top.

When he arrived he was told to wait in the vestibule while Hector patted him down for weapons and two gunmen stood guard. After an intense stare down, Nut was allowed to walk through the narrow corridor to the spacious living room where Luis sat.

"Amigo," he sang. "So good to see you, no?"

"Nah, not really."

"Whatsa matter?" he asked in his broken English.

"Word out on the street that I owe you a lot of paper."

"Sí, true." Luis nodded his head vigorously. "And you will pay me, no?"

"I want to pay you, but it's like this. I already paid for those pies. I gave the bread to my cousin Peter. I told you a long time ago that I didn't want nothing else on credit."

"But he no pay me."

"Yeah, I heard all of that. But like I said, he took my dough, and now I got to pay his debt?"

"No, not his debt, papi. Your debt. He come and use your name."

"But I never told him to do that. I wish you would have called me first before you gave him that product on consignment."

Luis waved his hands in dismissal. He didn't care about Nut's gripes, nor did he care to hear a grown man whine. The drug business was serious shit, and he had little patience for those who couldn't keep up. Either you swam or you sank. End of story.

"Me no make calls. I told you that your name was good here, no? He used your name. You have to be the general over your army."

Nut shook his head. He knew where Luis was coming from, but he still wanted to see if he could work out a deal. "I hear you. So check it. I wanted to know if we could work something out. I'm sure you heard what happened within my organization. Shit is a little tight right now—"

Luis was insulted. He didn't understand why the young fellow was still talking nonsense. He yelled, "I . . . don't . . . make . . . deals! I make money. You have tree"—he put up three fat fingers even though he had slaughtered the word—"tree days to bring me my cash. All of it, or you will not make it to the fourth day. You understand me, no?"

Nut understood perfectly well. He was fucked.

☙☙

The next day Nut went back uptown and dropped off sixty-five grand. It wasn't anywhere near what he owed, but he wanted Luis to know that he was going to make good on his debt. At this point, Nut knew anyone could get touched, and he feared for his mother. Between lawyer fees and repaying this debt, Nut was almost tapped out. His crew had dismantled and he needed to recruit some new little soldiers so that he could start making that paper again. In the meantime, he still had a score to settle.

He'd heard that this girl named Felicia that lived in Howard projects had gotten hired by the telephone company as a customer service representative. Once Nut heard that, a light bulb went off, and he put the word out that he was looking for her. He drove to her job on West Street and waited for her to come downstairs. Slowly she came switching toward his car all dressed up. She definitely wasn't wearing business attire. She'd gotten dressed extra nice in hopes of snagging one of the most sought after ballers in her neighborhood.

"Hi, Nut," she sang.

"What's up, Felicia? You looking good."

Her grin stretched from ear to ear. "Thank you. My sister said that you wanted to speak to me in private, and that you was coming up here today to see me. What can I do for you? 'Cause I'm prepared to do anything you want."

Nut wanted to tell her to be easy. If she didn't pour it on so thick, maybe she could have had a shot. "That's what I like to hear," he said instead, "so check it. I need you to get me a copy of all the calls from a particular number. I need the record log. Can you do that?"

Felicia aimed to please. "That won't be a problem."

"And if I find a particular number that interests me, could you get me an address?"

"Yup. All that information is right there, but if it's an out-of-town number, the address won't show up."

"Damn," Nut swore. There wasn't any guarantee that he was going to be interested in a New York number.

"But there are ways for me to get an out-of-town address as well. All I'd have to do is call their phone company service, give them a fake ID number, the real telephone number, and tell them that the person is applying to get a phone in their name in New York, and we're calling to verify whether they've given us all the right information. You know, shit like that."

Nut loved a good schemer. Perhaps he would keep her around.

"Sounds like a plan. But keep this between me and you. Here"— Nut shoved the telephone number into her hands—"do that for me. And if you come through, there'll be a couple of dollars in it for you."

"You don't got to pay me shit."

"You just gonna look out for a nigga?"

"If you want to do something, then take me out to dinner. Your money ain't good here."

Nut liked her style. She was definitely pushing up and going for hers.

"You got it, sexy. Let me drive you home."

ଊଊ

Nut was in a trancelike sleep from a long night of sex, drinking, and smoking weed. Now that Melissa and Butter were jammed up, he had a large tab over his head, and his cousin had beat him for three hundred thousand, he'd sat around all day impaired. His mother came into his room and vigorously shook him awake.

"Nelson, wake up!" she demanded. As soon as he pried his eyes open she tossed a heavy stack of papers near his head. She'd received a copy of the discovery papers from Melissa's and Butter's attorneys.

"It's official. Peter 'Piper' Brown has been named as the government's informant."

Even though the news wasn't shocking, Nut was still surprised. He shook his head in disgust. Julie turned and walked back out of the room, but you could hear her loud and clearly ranting and raving about how much of a loser Skinny Lorene and her son Peter were. Then she came back in the room and said, "He don't deserve to breathe the same air as you! How could he snitch on his own flesh and blood? He's just as trifling as my sister. Did I ever tell you that she tried to give your father some sex when we were younger? Yes, she did. But of course my husband didn't want none of her rotten twat. When he told me I marched right over to her house and beat her ass!"

Vaguely Nut remembered that incident. He was really young, but the memories came flooding back.

Julie walked off again, and Nut lay there in deep thought. He still couldn't understand what made his cousin turn snitch. On any given day he could have loaded up the car with Nut's money and just kept driving. Why did he have to go out like that and involve those peoples, and then to take the drugs from Luis and leave Nut susceptible to getting murdered behind his shit was unfathomable. The anger welling up in Nut's stomach was about to explode.

Finally Nut had enough strength to get into the shower. When he emerged his mother had made him a steak and French fries.

"How's Melissa holding up?" he asked.

"She's all right. She's tougher than she looks. She's been going to church inside the prison and has faith that Jehovah will see her to freedom."

"And what do you think?"

"I think that all things are possible when you have faith."

Nut agreed. "Did she ask about me?"

"Not one word."

"Did she ever tell you what she was doing back at the crib after she'd already left me?"

"I just told you that she doesn't mention you."

"Well next time you go up there tell I said what's up? OK? Can you do that for me?"

"I sure can."

As he sat at the table eating his mother's good cooking, a familiar number came through on his pager. It was Felicia. Immediately he called her back.

"You got something for me?" he asked.

"Yes. I was able to get the printout this morning. Do you want it today?"

"Hell yeah. Come to my crib when you get off work."

"I can't wait," she flirted.

Nut decided that he'd have to fuck Felicia and probably toss her a few dollars to get her hair and nails done, but that was it. When she brought him his aunt's telephone bill printout, he noticed there was a number that showed up constantly in Delaware. They didn't have any family out there, nor did she have any friends out there, so he knew that the only person she could be talking to for hours at a time was Peter. Now all Nut needed was the address.

Nut almost walked a hole through his mother's rug pacing up and down waiting for Felicia. Right after work she came tapping on his door. He opened it and gave her a once over. Her lips were all glossed up and her short hair was done nicely. She wasn't a beauty queen, nor did she have a voluptuous body, but she did look a'ight.

"Hey," she said.

"Whaddup. Follow me back to my room. My moms is here, so be quiet. She's sleeping."

"OK," she whispered.

"Damn, not that quiet," he said, clowning her.

Inside the safe haven of his room, she pulled out the paper with the address. He looked down at paper and realized that soon he'd get a small fraction of revenge.

"Whose address is that anyway?" Felicia asked.

"See, just when things were going so well. Don't ask any questions about my business. You got that?" Nut's voice was loud, firm, and intimidating.

"I thought you said your mother was asleep?"

He laughed because he knew she was talking slick. "Come here," he said and pulled her to him. She came willingly. "Take off your pants and do it quickly."

Giggling, she stepped back and took off her pants and panties. Lil Nut reached inside his jeans and pulled out his massive dick. Then he reached into his pocket and pulled out a condom. With this chick he definitely wanted to wrap it up. Felicia climbed her bony legs on top of Nut and began to ride his dick. He had to literally wrap his large hand over her mouth to keep her quiet. He did not want Julie hearing him fucking a strange girl. When they were through he tossed her a hundred dollars and sent her on her way. Even if he wanted to, he couldn't wipe that smile from her face.

The next morning Nut had moves to make. He got a little shorty from his building named Head who was starting to get a name for himself to follow him in Melissa's Maxima. They both drove down to Northern Boulevard so that he could sell his Mercedes 300 SL back to the dealer. Last year he'd paid ninety-five thousand for that car. Today he collected forty grand. Talk about depreciation. Had he moved a little quicker, his car wouldn't have had to go. Originally the plan was to sell Butter's Porsche, but the feds got to it first and confiscated it.

After that Nut and Head road uptown in the Maxima and gave Luis another fifty grand. Although the deadline to pay the money in full was tomorrow, Nut knew that they wouldn't murder him, not when they saw him trying to pay. He was more important alive than dead.

From the outside looking in, with Nut selling off assets and the feds breathing down his neck, he looked fucked up. But he still had his hustle mentality, and about thirty grand to work with. If he properly flipped that he could make thirty grand into three mill. Shit, he was a little nigga who started out with nothing and banked well over a million dollars in this crack game. Nut was down, but he definitely wasn't out.

With no time to waste, Nut got on the road. He decided to take the little wild dude with him, just in case he ran into any unforeseen problems, but then he remembered that he needed to do this type of dirt alone. No telling who that young nigga might tell.

He knew that he was taking a huge chance getting on 95 South with a loaded 9 mm, but he had to do what he had to do. There wasn't any other way, and there wasn't no way he was letting Peter get a pass. No fucking way. The heavy rain pounded on the top of his car as his tires glided across the sleek black pavement. His headlights illuminated the almost vacant roads as he made his way into a desolate apartment complex. Nut had everything he needed for his stakeout. He wasn't an idiot. He needed to know if there was some sort of police guard looking out for Peter's snitching ass. And he also needed to know whether Peter had any gunmen living with him, a girl, any kids running in and out. All those things were crucial before he went in there blazing.

The first sighting of Peter made Nut's skin crawl. He watched as the canary motherfucker walked from his apartment to another building where they had a laundry room. Peter didn't have a worry in the world. He didn't appear to be paranoid. Nut never saw him looking over his shoulder or peering around corners. He almost had a skip to his steps.

After twelve hours of watching Peter, he knew how he was going to catch him slipping. After eighteen hours, he was ready to rock him to sleep.

In the wee hours of the night, Nut climbed to the third story by using the balconies. It was so silent in that area that the only sound that could be heard was the crickets making that annoying noise. The noise was distracting.

Nut lifted the lock on the balcony and crept inside. The apartment was spotless. It almost looked brand new. The moon illuminated the living room, making it easy for Nut to find his way to Peter's bedroom where he was sound asleep. Nut pulled out his burner and stood over his cousin for a long moment. He really wanted to wake him up and ask him why the fuck he did what he did.

Finally Nut picked up a pillow, placed it over Peter's head, and pulled the trigger. The muffled gunshot wasn't enough to alarm anyone. Peter's body rocked from the impact, but that was the extent of it. Nut gave himself five minutes in the apartment to see if he could find any of the money Peter had stolen from him. He looked high and low, trashing the place before turning to leave. Had he looked a moment longer, he would have found two hundred fifteen thousand dollars hidden in the top of the hallway closet.

Nut drove back north replaying his actions. He had intended on torturing his cousin for hours. He was going to sit in the kitchen, sipping on a Corona beer while Peter remained duct-taped to a chair. He would have asked Peter why he started snitching. He wanted to cut off his fingers and stab him numerous times with an ice pick before finally burning him alive.

But as he stood over his cousin's body he thought about when they were kids and spent the night over each other's houses. And had Nut never chose the crack game and pulled him in, then perhaps Peter wouldn't have had to cross him and would still be alive. At the end of the day he was still his blood, and for that Nut chose to send him off peacefully. Peter didn't even know what hit him.

♋

Nut got back to New York just after seven in the morning, and Head was out there selling hand to hand. He also had a wealth of information.

"Yo, dog, where you been? I've been looking for you."

"Oh, yeah? Why the fuck you looking for me?"

"Did you hear what happened to them Harlem cats that be making all that bread?"

"What Harlem cats?"

"I heard that the feds bagged up Remy, Shue, Dominican Luis, and a few of their soldiers. They didn't get Alonzo, though. I heard he's on the run."

"What?" Fear spread through Nut's veins. "Get the fuck out of here."

"Yeah, man. True story! Shit's fucked up."

After those people arrested most of Harlem, it wasn't long before Nut had his own problems. His mother's door was kicked open three days later and he was dragged down to One Police Plaza for questioning regarding the murder of government informant Peter "Piper" Brown. Nut was held overnight but he wasn't worried at all. They didn't have shit on him, and he had a host of witnesses who would say they were with him on the night in question.

Once released, it was business as usual. Nut was still on a paper chase and nothing nor no one was going to stop him. Ever.

10

"A strong word called consignment, strictly for live men, not for freshmen. If you ain't got the clientele, say hell no, 'cause they gon want they money rain sleet hail snow."

—"Ten Crack Commandments," Notorious B.I.G.

1993

Butter did the right thing and copped out to twenty years. Tamia immediately left him, but that was to be expected. He was a true soldier and didn't snitch. Melissa, on the other hand, wasn't as lucky. She took her case to trial and blew. Her mandatory sentence was life. The news crushed Nut when he heard it. His mother said that Melissa screamed, "Mommy!" when the jury came back with the guilty verdict. Melissa's mother wasn't anywhere around. In fact, she hadn't seen her mother in close to ten years.

Nut felt fucked up. He wondered why life had dealt Melissa that foul hand. On the day of the verdict he sat down and wrote her a letter, hoping she would write him back. He needed her to know that he had her back and would take care of her while she was doing her bid. He'd already told the lawyer that he would pay for her appeal. Nut wasn't going to give up on Melissa, not after she'd traded her freedom for his.

"Listen, whatever it's gonna cost to get her out, I need you to make that happen."

Nut was speaking to Sheinberg, Melissa's attorney, over the

telephone.

"Nelson, I'll do what I can, but you know I can't make any promises. There are a few appealable issues that I could argue, but that's going to cost you."

"I didn't think you were going to do it for a Coke and a smile."

Sheinberg didn't really care for Nelson's smart mouth. He regarded him as a street thug who in no time would need to hire him for his own defense. He knew for a fact that the feds had Nelson on tape going in and out of Luis's, his other client's, apartment to buy drugs. It was only a matter of time before his luck ran out one way or another.

"Well now that we've got that squared away, I have a message for you," Sheinberg said. "Luis said that you owed him some money and that I could expect to receive my retainer fee from you."

Nut couldn't believe his ears. What the fuck were they trying to pull, some extortion shit?

"Fuck you mean Luis said I owe him some paper? That paper expired the moment he got jammed up. Tell that fat motherfucker I said suck my dick!"

Nut slammed down the phone, annoyed. He decided against allowing that incompetent motherfucker to handle Melissa's appeal. And since he knew that he was know fucking with his enemy, he was no longer to be trusted.

Other than Melissa and Butter going down, things were looking up for him. Head was now his lieutenant and they were making mad paper. Nut was making money hand over fist. He went out and bought the new 850i BMW, took a picture in his ride, and sent the flick to Butter. Butter was always calling him and asking him to send him a lot of flicks. Nut could see that he was maturing. He was a man who handled his business and wasn't afraid to let that thing go if he had beef.

The feds had motherfuckers in the game shook. Nut convinced

himself that he had an angel on his back, undoubtedly his pops. There wasn't any other way to explain away how on the day he could have gotten jammed up, he took a walk—a fucking walk to a kiddie park at that. And how about the whole Harlem being taken down, and although he did business with some of those niggas, he wasn't even arrested. And last but not least was how Melissa and Butter held him down. If heaven wasn't looking out for him, he didn't know who was.

Now that half of the hustlers were either locked down doing fed time, or buried six feet under, Nut's operation expanded. He now serviced uptown, Brooklyn, Bronx, and Queens. He wasn't fucking with any out-of-town niggas, though. I-95 South was hotter than fish grease. Too many dudes were getting hemmed up by those state troopers, and Nut didn't want to risk his livelihood. The moment a state trooper cruised by any vehicle with New York plates, it was over. They were pulling your ass over and checking your trunk.

Triple fours was the code he gave all of his customers. That code meant that they needed work. The person would enter his number, and then put triple fours behind it. Nut would then page the person back with triple fours and add the number he was selling the weight for. An example would be 444*18. That meant he was selling a kilo for eighteen thousand dollars. When his freedom depended on staying one step above the law, he had to think of ways to outsmart 5-0.

On this day Bert was the person calling for work. He was hustling down in Charlotte, North Carolina, but was originally from Oakland, California. He needed two pies, but Nut wasn't taking any chances. He needed Bert to come up north.

"Nah, man, you gotta come through," he told Bert.

"You know I would if I could. But I gotta watch my spots."

"Come on now, man. You know better than that!" Nut was annoyed that he was talking drug lingo over the phones. He was supposed to talk in code. "How many cakes you want my sister to bake for your party?"

"I need four cakes and one donut." That meant he needed four and a half keys.

"I got you, but you gotta come through."

"Nut, don't do me like that, man. I need you," Bert whined. Of course he needed Nut. He didn't want to take the risk himself.

"Yo, let me get back to you."

"A'ight. Call me on this same number."

Nut hung up and ignored the next stream of calls coming from his out-of-town customers. He needed time to think.

The thought came to him in his sleep. The next morning he took the Honda they used to transport drugs to his mechanic.

"Listen, I need you to make a secret compartment in the trunk, something high tech like in those James Bond movies."

"For what?"

"For this green paper you're gonna charge me. That's all you need to concern yourself with. Fuck you mean for what?"

"OK, I understand. I will do it perfect. Leave it here and it'll be ready in three days."

Now many people would try to take credit for inventing the stash car, but Lil Nut from Brooklyn swore he was the first man to put the stash car out there. One week later he was putting his drivers on the road to go out of town to service his customers. Each week he stacked steady paper while also schooling Head to the ten crack commandments.

ഗ

"Yo, man, I got the flicks," Butter said from Fort Dix Federal Prison. "What's up with those colorful clothes you got on? Let me find out you going homo."

Laughing, Nut replied, "See, that's how much you know. That's some new shit. It just came out. That shirt I was wearing is Versace. Gianni Versace is a new brand, and that shit cost an arm and leg. Only a baller can afford this shit here."

"Word? That's the new shit?"

"Hell, yeah. I already got my outfit because I'm flying out to the Soul Train Music Awards."

"Soul Train like the TV show? They got an awards show now?"

"Yeah, man. I wish you were out here to go with me." Nut meant those words. He hated that Butter wasn't out on the streets with him after all they'd been through. Butter deserved to enjoy the fruits of their labor.

"So you go and have enough fun for the both of us. And send me some flicks too. Where that joint at?"

"I gotta take a plane out to California. This will be my first time flying, but a nigga can't wait. I got this fly purple and yellow Versace silk shirt. It cost me eleven hundred. And I got a pair of purple linen slacks and purple gators! Motherfuckers gonna be on my dick!"

Butter chuckled. Nut had certainly evolved from wearing Lee jeans and Puma sneakers.

"Yo, before I let you go, I want to thank you for looking out for my moms," Butter said. "She said you be coming through all the time blessing her. Good looking out, kid."

"That's what I'm supposed to do. You my man. And as far as I'm concerned, that's your money."

ᔕᕋ

The March air was unseasonably warm. Nut had on a velour Karl Kani sweat suit and Nike sneakers. He was headed to meet Head in front of Howard projects. As soon as he pulled up, he saw Head up in a female's face. After closer inspection, Nut realized that was his latest broad, Tawana.

Nut had only been fucking with her for a few weeks, but it was definitely official. Tawana wasn't like any other girl he wifed. She was a street chick who was nice with her hands. She also got busy on the boosting tip. In fact, she'd gotten him the sweat suit he was wearing now. The only thing Nut didn't like about her was that she knew too many niggas. She claimed she had to because of her occupation. She sold women's clothes hot from the stores, and most of her customers consisted of dudes who had a little paper and wanted to splurge on wifey.

Head nor Tawana realized he was sitting there watching their exchange. Head was just coming of age at eighteen, and he really reminded Nut of himself at that age. He was fearless and didn't take to authority. Yet he respected Nut. Head kept telling Nut that he wanted to be like him. As Nut watched him flirt with his girl, he wondered if Head wanted to *be* him. Nut beeped his horn and got both of their attentions.

Tawana sauntered over and Head followed closely behind. Nut rolled down the window, and Tawana leaned in and gave him a kiss.

"I didn't know you were coming through," she said.

"I came to scoop up Head. We got shit to do."

Head got into the passenger's seat and gave Nut a pound.

"You got any money on you?" Tawana asked. "I need a few dollars."

Nut began reaching into his pockets. Tawana was always hitting him up for money, but he knew that was part of the game. "How much you need?"

Tawana took her thumb and index finger and spread them about an inch apart, and said, "That much."

Nut smiled. He liked her style. She was the female version of himself. He knew that she could be heartless—she'd sliced up more than a few of her friends' faces. And trifling—she'd already left her baby's daddy the moment he got sentenced to life on a murder wrap. And a hustler—she didn't wait for her mother to give her shit. She took hers. But Nut knew exactly who she was. There would be no surprises with Tawana. Nut peeled off fifteen hundred dollars and gave it to her. "I'll get up with you later."

"Be careful," she replied and gave him a quick peck on the lips. "Later, Head."

"A'ight, later, T."

Nut always took Head with him when he went to collect his money from the spots. Stickup kids were always lurking, and Head was a little, agile dude who was always on point. As they drove from spot to spot, Nut spoke about the award show that was only days away.

"So I talked to the travel agent today and she got us three suites at the Four Seasons Hotel, and we're all riding first class on American Airlines."

"I hope I'm staying in a room with you."

"Nah, man, I'm not sharing a room with y'all niggas. Each night I plan to share my room with a different bitch. The other two rooms are for you, Mike, Slim, and Justice. You choose which one of those niggas you want to room with."

"Damn, Nut. You know those niggas act like little kids."

"As my lieutenant, you gotta school them and set them straight. Because out there in L.A., we're going to be around a different crowd of cats. I don't want them making me look dumb. Nothing but moneymakers will be there, and I'm going to be politicking as well, trying to get new connections and shit. I need you there by my side, because most times you might have to step in and handle some of the business on your own. You think you ready for that?"

"Hell, yeah, I'm ready. I was born ready."

"Your stupid ass was born Henry Jackson. What the fuck you talkin' 'bout?" Nut couldn't help but clown Head, who at times could be a little sensitive.

"You know what I meant. I can handle whatever you throw at me. Haven't I proved that to you already?"

Nut changed the subject. "Did you finish buying your gear?"

"Nah, I didn't even really start. I was waiting for Tawana to come through with some shit so I could get a discount."

Nut was turned off. Head had enough money to go and splurge at the department store as opposed to waiting for the boosters to come through. He was a cheap motherfucker, and that irritated Nut.

"What the fuck you mean you waiting on Tawana? How the fuck that sound? The fucking show is March nineteenth!"

Any other nigga yelling at him like that and Head would have bodied him. His finger itched to pull the trigger on his burner. Head knew that if he killed Nut, he would get instantly upgraded. People from all over would respect and fear him.

"Nut, I'm sitting right here, man, in this small-ass car. You don't gotta be screaming like that all the time to make a point. Today is only the fourteenth. I got five days before we leave. It ain't that serious."

Nut calmed down. They had three more spots to pick up from, and then he was going to drive Head straight to the city to go shopping. Since it was a Saturday, the stores stayed opened late, so Nut had plenty of time.

"Next Saturday I want you to do the pickups on your own," Nut told him. "You think you ready for that?"

"I just told you I am."

"Well I want you to take Mike with you. And from now on y'all do the pickups each Saturday, but only you go to my stash house and leave the bread. You already got the combination to the safe. And if anybody is short, you call me right away, and I'll tell you how to handle the situation."

Head was excited. He loved more responsibility, because that meant that soon he wouldn't be considered a lieutenant. He'd be more of a partner.

"Does this mean I'm getting promoted?" he asked.

"First you gotta prove yourself. Right now you ain't done shit but take direction and orders from me. You gotta learn how to think and make moves on your own. That's why I keep drilling the ten crack commandments in your ear. You see how all these motherfuckers done got either murdered or doing football numbers, and I'm still here. Ask yourself how the fuck I've been able to get money in this game for almost ten straight years. Nigga, that's more than half your life. I was around when this crack epidemic started, and I'm still here!" Nut boasted.

Head had to admit that Nut did accomplish a lot. All these motherfuckers were either murdered or in jail, and Nut had outsmarted the game. On that alone he deserved Head's respect.

ᔕᘓ

Later that night Nut stopped by Tawana's and gave her the Moschino Cheap & Chic dress he'd bought earlier when he took Head shopping. He couldn't believe an item of clothing could make a girl so happy. She squealed, smiled, and thanked him profusely, and then she wanted to fuck. Nut told her to keep it wet, because he wanted to go see his moms first.

When he got to his mom's place, she was in the living room eating a bucket of crab she'd gotten from the fish market. You could smell the beer and seasoning from all the way down the hall. The aroma made Nut's mouth water.

"Ma, you see how you are? You ain't even call me and put me on," he accused. Julie grinned as she broke off a leg and began sucking the juices.

"What you doing here this late?" she asked.

"Don't worry about all that." Nut peered into the pot sitting on the floor on top of an old newspaper. "Let me get some of that."

After they finished eating the crabs, Nut began talking about his plans. He'd never been so hopeful and excited before. Things were really going well for him. He was hitting off Melissa's and Butter's books on a regular basis. He had also paid for Melissa's new attorney to appeal her sentence. And he had a girl that he was checking for and could see himself with her for a long time. But mostly, he wanted to tell his mom about the money he'd saved, and how well his spots were doing.

"Ma, remember I asked you a couple years back to move out of here, and you said no because you didn't know how long of a run I'd have."

"Yeah, I remember."

"Well I've been having a long run, and I'm ready to semi-retire. I got close to a million dollars, give or take a few grand, in my safe at one of my stash houses, and I got six spots that are bringing in ten to fifty grand a week. Here's my plan for my future. I want to buy you a house, so you won't have to worry about a mortgage, and I want to fall back from this drug game for a while. I've been doing this shit since I was fourteen. Now I want to enjoy my money. I've been schooling Head to run my operation, so I'll be taking less risk, but still counting the same paper. All I need is for you to want to get out. Ma, if you stay in the hood, then that's where I'm staying. You know I can't leave you here. And I'm telling you now, I don't want to be here anymore. It's just a matter of time before one of these little motherfuckers tries me and my luck runs out."

Julie heard the sincerity in her son's voice, and frankly she was glad that he'd brought the subject back up. She too was ready to leave the hood. She certainly didn't want to die in the hood.

"Nelson, let's go and buy us a house!"

Nut was elated at his mother's response. He gave her a quick kiss on the cheek and said, "As soon as I come back from the Soul Train Music Awards, we're going house hunting."

ɷ

"Damn, I think we just made a baby," Tawana said the next day as she tried to catch her breath.

"That shit was good, right, ma?"

Tawana languorously stretched and nodded in agreement. She could fuck Nut all day. He had a big dick and certainly knew how to use it. They were at Nut's apartment in Clinton Hills, and her two-year-old son, Hassan, was sleeping peacefully in the next room.

"What are your plans for the day?" she asked.

"You know I got to go check up on my spots. What about you?"

"I wanted to go to the city and see what's up. The stores be sweet on Sundays."

"Well what about little man? Whatchu gonna do with him?"

"My moms is at church, so I know she ain't gonna watch him. I'll just have to take him with me."

Nut was disgusted. "What I tell you about that shit?"

"What?"

"Bringing him on your boosting sprees! What if you get jammed up?"

"It ain't even like that. He'll sit in the car while I'm in the stores."

"You're gonna have him sitting in the car all day? Sometimes you be in them stores for two and three hours. What type of shit is that?" Nut was seriously rethinking having a baby with Tawana. The thought had begun seeping into his head recently, because he wanted a child. Being around Tawana's son had brought out his parenting skills, and since he was playing daddy to another man's baby, he wanted his own seed. But now he realized that Tawana was a horrible mother, and he didn't want any part of that.

"He ain't complaining, so why are you?"

"You know what? Go do you, and I'll take him with me and get him a haircut or something."

"Oh, so he can come with you to pick up drug money, but not with me? How you sound?"

"Bitch, is you stupid? Why the fuck would I take a child on a drug run? I'ma let Head take care of that bullshit and just spend the day with shorty!"

As he promised, Nut took Hassan with him for the day. He decided to take him for a haircut and then to McDonald's. As they cruised the Brooklyn streets, he felt really good about his future. He decided that he was going to cut off Tawana and find a good girl to marry and have his baby. But before he did that he needed to get his key back from her. This was a new year, and he was a new dude.

He looked over at Hassan and realized that he would miss the little guy, but, fuck it, life went on. Just as he pulled up in front of his barbershop, his pager went off. It was Tawana.

He hopped out of his car, took Hassan inside, and got him situated with the barber. "Give him a shape-up and clean up the top. Cut him down lower. His mother still got him rocking a high top fade. That shit is played out."

"I hear you," his barber replied, and began to clean his clippers to cut Hassan's hair. Nut stepped outside to call back Tawana.

"Yo, what's up?" he asked.

"I was thinking about what you said, and you're right. I'm not going to go out today. I'm going to stay at your house and cook Sunday dinner.

Would you like that?"

Nut smiled. She must have known that her time was up. "Yeah, that's cool. I'll be back in an hour—"

The first shot that rang out was forceful enough to spin Nut on his toes. The second shot grazed his left shoulder. Nut reached for his burner, but in a panic it dropped from his hand. He saw the Dominican gunmen as they continued to buck shots at him. He knew their faces well. It was Hector and Juan, two of Luis's men.

Nut took off running down the street, and the gunmen gave chase, continuing to shoot. If he could only make it a few more blocks, he'd be in Langston Hughes projects surrounded by the safety of his soldiers.

The next shot hit Nut in the back and instantly severed his spinal cord. A million things went through Nut's head. He didn't want it to end like this. He was afraid for it to be over.

It ain't over until I say it's over! he thought as he tried to crawl to safety. The pain was excruciating, and he knew he'd taken a hit that could be fatal. *Where the fuck are the police?* he wondered.

As he crawled toward a parked car, he could no longer feel his legs. His whole lower body felt like dead weight. Thoughts of his mother hearing the news of his death flooded his mind. What about all the people who counted on him? Then he thought about Peter Piper. His cousin had murdered him from the grave. He was being taken out over consignment.

Nut felt the Dominicans' presence just as they towered over him. They didn't have much time before the police arrived.

"This is from Luis," Hector said. Two shots were fired to the back of his head, and Nut was dead on the scene.

Nut would have had a lot of people at his funeral had it not been the same day as the Soul Train Music Awards. All of his so-called friends couldn't pass up the opportunity to head to California. Julie didn't have an insurance policy on her son, nor did she have any money to bury him. When she went to his apartment after she'd gotten the news of his demise, she saw that Tawana had cleaned it out of all the valuables. Next she called Head and asked him about the stash house her son told her about where he kept his life savings and all of the money from his spots, but Head told her she was talking crazy.

Julie did the best she could for her son with the money her church raised to bury him. He had a cheap wooden casket and his grave didn't have a headstone. It broke her heart to lay him to rest in that manner.

From her window in her project apartment she saw that Head had taken her son's spot. Within a week of her son's funeral, Head bought a brand new Mercedes Benz 500 SL and a Land Cruiser truck. But what was the icing on the cake was that Tawana was now his girl, sitting shotgun in the front seat of Head's car.

Melissa took the news of Nut's murder just as badly as Julie. In her heart of hearts she truly loved him, no matter how many times she'd tried to convince herself otherwise. She wished over and over again that she could turn back the hands of time and just hold his body once again. Or see his round, expressive eyes. Or listen to his distinctive laugh. She knew that she would go to her grave always wondering *what if?* What if they'd met under different circumstances? Their love was the right love at the wrong time.

Although Julie had sent Butter a kite, the news of Nut's murder had hit the prison only hours after he was pronounced dead on the scene. Butter hung his head low and fought back tears. Lil Nut was his man; more like a brother. Butter felt his friend was invincible and surely wouldn't fall victim to the streets. Lil Nut had outlived his father, Lamiek, Lite, Blue Bug, Fuquan, Red, Peter, and a host of other motherfuckers who fell victim to the crack. Butter realized that they were all casualties of the drug game; there were no winners. He told himself that he'd see his man again on the other side.

Head was now in charge of the organization that Nut had built. He'd called a meeting to lay down the ground rules of what not to do in this crack game. The streets were buzzing that Nut got murdered because he took fifteen keys on consignment, and refused to pay his debt. Head now regarded his icon as a stupid motherfucker, and he vowed never to make the same mistakes Nut had.

"Listen to me, little niggas, there's rules to this crack game here. There's enough money out here for all of us to eat off of. If we follow these rules, we can take over the game and shut it down. I'm talking we can all be millionaires. Now, as y'all know, Nut was my man, but he was hardheaded. We're going to avoid all the pitfalls he ran into and treat this like a business. This ain't the eighties when TNT motherfuckers were jumping out of vans and spraying shit in your face, with crackheads running around like zombies. It's 1993! We the future. We got functioning crackheads, the kind that work all week and get high on the weekends. We got niggas going hard in each state. Those country niggas need weight, and we're the crew that's gonna supply it to them. Those Alabama and Kentucky bamma fucks be on our New York dicks! They wanna talk like us, dress like us, and sell dope like us. I'm not biased. I'm ready to welcome them all with open arms. In this business only one color rules, and that's green.

"As y'all know, I came up with the idea for the stash car. That means that we can have steady product on the highways and the state troopers can't do shit to us. We're invincible. And we all better live by our code. And that's to leave no man behind. If you're in our crew, then can't no one go up against us. If one of us got beef, then we all got beef." A few young dudes nodded their heads.

"Now everyone is gonna have a specific job to do, but everyone's goal is the same—protect Head. There's a reason the saying is, 'Head Nigga in Charge.' If y'all motherfuckers let someone get at the head of the organization, everything around will crumble. For y'all slow motherfuckers who can't understand that logic, peep this. If someone shoots you in the head, your body will shut down and not function. I'm telling y'all motherfuckers, if y'all want to continue to eat, then y'all better watch my back by any means necessary."

Head knew that stepping up to take Nut's place would put him in a vulnerable position, and he didn't want none of the little niggas to get heart and try to take his slot. They could easily see how he got upgraded once Nut got murdered. So to knock down anyone's bright ideas, he had to put fear in their hearts. Head was going to run his organization differently. It was only 1993, and he knew that ten years from now he was going to take over the world.

Head hopped in his ride and headed toward the Tunnel nightclub. He popped in a new cassette by this kid from Brooklyn that he'd been hearing a lot about lately. He was supposed to be performing there tonight. Head wanted to kick it with him. The Brooklyn rapper called himself Biggie Smalls. The song "Party and Bullshit" blasted throughout the luxury jeep.

Yeah, Head knew that he could only go up from here, as long as he adhered to the ten crack commandments.

MELODRAMA PUBLISHING ORDER FORM
WWW.MELODRAMAPUBLISHING.COM

Title	ISBN	QTY	PRICE	TOTAL
Myra	1-934157-20-1		$15.00	$
Menace	1-934157-16-3		$15.00	$
Cartier Cartel	1-934157-18-X		$15.00	$
10 Crack Commandments	1-934157-21-X		$15.00	$
Jealousy: The Complete Saga	1-934157-13-9		$15.00	$
Wifey	0-971702-18-7		$15.00	$
I'm Still Wifey	0-971702-15-2		$15.00	$
Life After Wifey	1-934157-04-X		$15.00	$
Still Wifey Material	1-934157-10-4		$15.00	$
Eva: First Lady of Sin	1-934157-01-5		$15.00	$
Eva 2: First Lady of Sin	1-934157-11-2		$15.00	$
Den of Sin	1-934157-08-2		$15.00	$
Shot Glass Diva	1-934157-14-7		$15.00	$
Dirty Little Angel	1-934157-19-8		$15.00	$
Histress	1-934157-03-1		$15.00	$
In My Hood	0-971702-19-5		$15.00	$
In My Hood 2	1-934157-06-6		$15.00	$
A Deal With Death	1-934157-12-0		$15.00	$
Tale of a Train Wreck Lifestyle	1-934157-15-5		$15.00	$
A Sticky Situation	1-934157-09-0		$15.00	$
Jealousy	1-934157-07-4		$15.00	$
Life, Love & Loneliness	0-971702-10-1		$15.00	$
The Criss Cross	0-971702-12-8		$15.00	$

(GO TO THE NEXT PAGE)

MELODRAMA PUBLISHING ORDER FORM
(CONTINUED)

Title/Author	ISBN	QTY	PRICE	TOTAL
Stripped	1-934157-00-7		$15.00	$
The Candy Shop	1-934157-02-3		$15.00	$
Sex, Sin & Brooklyn	0-971702-16-0		$15.00	$
Up, Close & Personal	0-971702-11-X		$9.95	$
				$
			Subtotal	
			Shipping**	
			Tax*	
	Total			

Instructions:

*NY residents please add $1.79 Tax per book.

**Shipping costs: $3.00 first book, any additional books please add $1.00 per book.

Incarcerated readers receive a 25% discount. Please pay $11.25 per book and apply the same shipping terms as stated above.

Mail to:

MELODRAMA PUBLISHING

P.O. BOX 522

BELLPORT, NY 11713